THE INN AT WALKER BEACH

THE BAREFOOT SISTERHOOD

LINDSAY HARREL

Blue Aster
PRESS

For my brother, Cameron.
Thank you for the gift of your humor.
It made our childhood all the brighter,
and it got us through some hard days too.
Never forget how much you are loved.

PROLOGUE

JULES

*S*he could feel it in her bones—this place was built for something more.

Shielding her eyes from the midday July sun, Jules Baker gazed up at the Barefoot B&B. Once a glorious blend of posh modernity and small-town charm that had enticed tourists to visit from all over the country, the inn now only showcased its age.

Its utter despair.

From missing roof tiles to disintegrating paint, weeds growing as tall as her waist, and broken railings on the private balconies that overlooked the Pacific Ocean, the Barefoot had become lost to the community of Walker Beach, California.

But she was here to restore it to a new glory. To bring it back to life. To give it purpose again.

Or maybe, just maybe, the inn would do that for her.

Eyes burning with tears she refused to shed, Jules left the soft sand of the inn's private beach and trudged around the building to its teal front door, which hung slightly askew. She inserted the key into the rusty lock and turned. The door creaked as she pushed it open and stepped inside the dank space that begged for a fresh breath of air.

She approached the large white registration desk, her jeweled sandals flopping against the wood floors behind her. Dual staircases flanked the desk on either side, curving around the lobby and up to the second story. They had always seemed rich and inviting, but now the banister was cracked in places—whether from age or the devastation of last year's earthquake, who could say.

As she moved past the desk and into the lobby, Jules's heart fluttered with hope that hadn't been her companion for the entire last year. Because despite the cobwebs growing along the crown molding, the dust coating the muted colors of the painted walls, and the holes in the couch left there by who knew what kind of critter, the place fairly sang with light thanks to the far wall of windows facing the ocean. In addition, the vaulted thirty-foot ceilings featured a skylight that gave her a full view of the clouds and radiance above.

There was no denying it—she'd chosen well, just as Chrissy had said she would. The place had good bones. Broken ones, sure, but those could be healed.

As for broken hearts ... she could only pray that was also true.

Blowing out a breath, she shook away the morbid thought and walked through the lobby and out onto a rickety deck that looked over the sand and sea. The breeze blew her hair across her eyes and her bangle bracelets jangled as she pulled a rubber band from her wrist and tugged long red strands back.

Closing her eyes for a moment, she relished the sun on her skin, almost like a hug from beyond.

And maybe it was.

She opened her eyes, and with shaking fingers, took the note from the back pocket of her jeans. It had been folded and unfolded so many times in the last year that she was surprised the paper's soft middle hadn't yet torn. Her eyes scanned the contents of the note, written last July but not delivered until mid-August—after her best friend had taken her final breath on this earth.

Then she got to the part that still gave her pause, that still squeezed her lungs.

Just because I won't be here anymore doesn't mean you shouldn't pursue this without me. It's a brilliant idea and I know you have everything you need to make it happen.

Everything except money—the thing that's stopped us so far.

So I've put aside a little nest egg for you to use when the time is right.

And when is that? You'll know it, Jules. You always do. Use this money to do good, to make our corner of the world a better place—just like we dreamed of doing together. I'm only sorry I won't be there to see it. Maybe God will allow me a little window from heaven so I can look down on you and smile.

Now go and do what you do best. Love on people and remind them that they aren't alone. Take hold of all the bad things that have happened to you and use them to create art—something beautiful.

I love you, and I believe in you. You've got this, my friend.

Jules closed Chrissy's letter and stared out over the ocean her friend had loved—at its constancy and its grace-filled movement. "I found the place, Chris. And I'm going to make our dream a reality."

A tear leaked from her eye before she could stop it, and she breathed out a heavy sigh. There was a lot of work ahead to get this place into shape, and she'd never anticipated doing it all alone.

But ... maybe she wouldn't be alone. Not if the women she'd invited into the Sisterhood came tonight.

Not if they supported each other—which was the whole point, after all.

CHAPTER ONE

JENNA

To Jenna Wakefield, there was nothing better than a blank canvas and free rein.

Her sister Gabrielle had given her both a month ago when she'd asked Jenna to decorate her soon-to-arrive niece's nursery. And now, it was finally ready. All it needed was a baby.

Jenna added a stuffed giraffe that was soft as silk to the white shelves over the dresser and changing table combo, then took a step back to critique her work. Last week, she'd taken a paintbrush to the room, applying lavender just above the white chair rail and wainscoting that traveled all four walls.

Once that was dry, Jenna had hung the wooden letters PDB on the wall. Gabrielle and Tyler weren't sharing Baby Girl's name just yet, but had told her the initials for decoration purposes. Of course, she'd tried to trick Gabrielle into revealing the name, but Gabrielle had just rolled her eyes at her baby sister and smiled.

A gasp sounded behind her. "Oh, Jen." Gabrielle moved into the room to stand next to Jenna, a hand in that familiar spot on her rounded stomach. With only eight and a half weeks till her due date the last day of September, she looked like most pregnant women in the summer with her blonde hair in a perpetual ponytail, face a bit puffy, and ankles a bit swollen—not that Jenna would ever say she was anything but beautiful. "It's absolutely breathtaking."

Jenna's cheeks warmed as she followed Gabrielle's gaze through the nursery. Oh but yes, she could imagine Baby Girl Baker sleeping in the coral-colored crib, staring up at the assorted paper lanterns in various bright shades and patterns that hung like a mobile over the gray chevron sheets. And there, in the stuffed pink rocking chair, Gabrielle would nurse her daughter and sing her to sleep, just like Jenna imagined their own mother had done for them.

How Mom would have loved to be here for this.

Jenna allowed herself the tear that slid down her cheek, then pushed it away and moved on. "I'm glad you like it."

"Like it? I love it." Gabrielle put her arm through Jenna's and squeezed. "Sis, you've got a gift."

"It's a great room." In fact, it was Jenna's old room. When they'd lost their childhood home after Mom had died twelve years ago—when Jenna was just fifteen and Gabrielle was eighteen—they'd moved into the tiny apartment where Jenna now lived with her son, Liam. But a little over a year ago, Jenna's brother-in-law had bought the house back for Gabrielle.

Looking around the room once more, Jenna nodded, satisfied. No one deserved love and happiness more than Gabrielle —especially after all the ways Jenna had nearly wrecked her life.

Her sister let go of Jenna's arm and ran her fingers along the row of children's books Jenna had snuck onto the bookshelf from Liam's old baby collection. "And now, the room is even better because of you."

Yes, a blank canvas was the perfect thing to mollify her artist's itch. It gave Jenna space to create, to transform, to make something new from the old. The tired.

The broken.

If only life would give her such an opportunity. Sometimes, she ached for a do-over.

Then again, if she hadn't been such a screwup, Jenna wouldn't have Liam—and she'd never regretted *that*, even if she had only been seventeen when he was born.

Gabrielle crossed the room and lowered herself into the rocking chair, groaning and wincing at the effort. "I don't know why you don't go into business for yourself. People would be calling you right and left to decorate their homes."

Oh man, wouldn't that be amazing? Jenna walked to the window and adjusted one of the curtain ties, allowing a tiny bit more of the day's afternoon light into the room. "People like to hire interior decorators with experience and, you know, actual credentials."

And neither of those was in the cards for Jenna, especially the latter. Getting into college required good grades, and universities probably didn't favor single moms with a GED. Not that she'd ever tested that theory herself.

"Maybe in the big city, but here in Walker Beach?" Gabrielle huffed out a breath. "People have known you your whole life, Jen."

"Exactly." Ironic how the same thing that got her the occasional free dinner at the Frosted Cake was the very reason Carlotta Jenkins and her fan club of busybodies stared down their noses at the former teen mom every time Jenna passed them on Main Street.

But Gabrielle couldn't understand that. Not only did she and her sister look nothing alike—Jenna with her dark brown hair, small chest, and too-thin frame, Gabrielle with her curves and healthy glow—but they were total opposites in personality as well. While the typical bossy older sister, Gabrielle was also known around town as the responsible one.

And rightly so. It hadn't been until this last year that Jenna had finally gotten her life together enough to make it to work consistently on her own. To live on her own. Support Liam on her own.

Kind of lame for a twenty-seven-year-old woman, even if that woman had been fending off the fangs of depression for the last decade—had only recently been able to find some enthusiasm for life again with the help of medication and counseling.

Still, if she hadn't made such dumb choices as a teenager, maybe she'd never have had to deal with mental health issues at all.

"You know what I mean." Gabrielle fanned herself, even though the high outside was a lovely seventy-something degrees —the blessing of living along the California coast halfway between Los Angeles and San Fran. "You're talented and people know it."

"Businesses take money to start up. And when would I have time? I already work a lot of overtime right now." The summer season was always crazy at the beach equipment rental shop. "And then there's Liam to think about. I have to squeeze every spare minute of time in with him that I can before he leaves me in eight years for college."

"I get that." A frown stretched across Gabrielle's pale face. "As for the money, we could loan you some, you know."

Jenna didn't doubt they could. Tyler was a former pro-football player, and even though he put a lot of money into his Amazing Kids Foundation—where he and Gabrielle both worked—they still had plenty to spare.

"Thanks, but I couldn't accept it." Not after Gabrielle had taken care of her and Liam for her son's entire life right up until she and Tyler got married last fall. "I have to stand on my own two feet. You know how important my counselor said that is."

"But—"

"But nothing." Waving her hand through the air, Jenna signaled an end to the conversation. "So is there anything you'd like me to change in here?"

Her sister was quiet for a moment before speaking. "No. It's perfect."

"Good. Because I have that meeting to get to." The most mysterious meeting ever, considering she didn't even know who'd done the inviting. All she'd been told was the where and the why—well, kind of the why. The fancy invitation had arrived in her mailbox without a return address. She'd read it over enough times in the last week to memorize the whole thing:

You are cordially invited to the inaugural meeting of the Barefoot Sisterhood.
July 31st at seven p.m.
Barefoot B&B
Walker Beach, California
Dress is casual.
Bring yourself, your dreams ... and your discretion.

Naturally, she'd told her sister the details, but no one else.

Gabrielle's blue eyes widened. "It's not seven yet, is it?"

"Only four, but I need to run home and shower. And Cam asked me to stop in to do some quick paperwork at the shop."

"Did he now?" Gabrielle's eyebrows waggled as she rocked gently in the chair, fingers absently stroking her stomach. "Maybe he just wants to see you."

"And that's my cue to leave." One would think after seven years of teasing, her sister would get the hint. Nothing was going to happen between Jenna and her boss-slash-friend.

"Wait, come on. Help me up."

Jenna crossed her arms and stuck out her tongue. "It would serve you right if I just left you there."

"All right, I'm sorry. It's just ... I know we've beat around the bush about this, but are you sure there's nothing going on between the two of you?"

"I'm leaving now," Jenna said in a singsong voice. Turning on her heel, she took a step toward the door.

"Fine, I'll change the subject. But one of these days, we are going to talk about your love life whether you like it or not." Gabrielle sighed. "So back to the invitation … you still have no idea who sent it?"

Finally, a conversation piece she could work with. "Nope." Jenna pushed her bangs out of her eyes. "It might be the person who bought the Barefoot B&B, but since no one knows who that is …"

"I've heard it's driving Carlotta crazy not knowing who owns it now. She's driven by every day for weeks trying to catch a glimpse of someone coming or going, but nothing yet. And the public records just state some company."

"That's just Carlotta being Carlotta." Didn't the forty-something gossip maven have anything better to do? Jenna extended her hand to Gabrielle. "Come on."

Her sister laughed and took the offered help. "It'll be nice when standing isn't so hard." She winced and sucked in a sharp breath as she got to her feet. "Stupid Braxton Hicks."

"I don't remember those hurting so much. Or beginning so early in my pregnancy." They left the room and started down the hallway toward the front door.

"Maybe it's true what they say—you forget all the pain once you have your child in your arms. I sure hope so, anyway, because right now, I never wanna do this again."

"And you haven't even experienced labor yet." Jenna winked and laughed as they rounded the corner and entered the living room, where Tyler and Liam sat playing video games.

Just like the sisters, they were a lesson in opposites—the muscular former football player with his high and tight, the scrawny kid with longish black hair—but the joy on both of their faces as they raced Mario across the screen matched perfectly.

9

"Hey, you two." Gabrielle placed her hand on Tyler's shoulder. "Jenna is leaving."

"Bye, Jen." Tyler's eyes didn't leave the screen.

No response from Liam.

Jenna smirked, shaking her head at Gabrielle. "Boys."

A glint flashed in her sister's eyes. "Should I walk in front of the TV and block them with my belly? They'd have to stop then to properly acknowledge their goodbyes."

"Ooo, you're bad." Chuckling, Jenna moved to the couch and sat beside her son, who leaned forward, his features completely zeroed in on the cars whizzing by on the TV. "But I've got this."

She put her arm around Liam and snuggled her forehead against his neck. "Bye, baby." Jenna attempted her most annoying voice to get his attention. "I'll miss you."

But instead of rolling his eyes like most tweens would, Liam kept right on playing, fingers flying across the controller. "Bye, Mom."

Jenna nudged his foot with her own. "I'll pick you up after my meeting. Be good for Uncle T and Auntie G."

"K."

Well, at least he'd acknowledged her presence. It was more than most moms got from kids his age, right? She'd gotten so lucky with Liam, especially considering his dad was not a nice man. But Liam also seemed much more like Gabrielle—not a troublemaker like Jenna had been.

Thank goodness for that.

Jenna waved one last time and left the Berry Street house, driving the short distance to Main Street, which she most definitely took for granted with its blue, yellow, and pink buildings all in a row and edged just off the boardwalk and Baker Beach—named after Tyler's ginormous founding family. Directly on the other side of the road, similar buildings were backed by tall California oaks and a variety of plant life.

After parking in front of Rise Beach Rentals, she headed for the shop, ignoring the flutterings in her stomach that she couldn't seem to control whenever she set foot inside. Not because this was her dream job—far from it—but because of the man who was almost always here.

The man she loved.

Jenna pushed open the front door and the small but familiar lobby greeted her, resplendent with its newly painted yellow wall displaying ten of their most popular surfboards, a few bicycle cruisers propped against the opposite wall, and a thick three-ring binder sitting on a display table near the front desk.

But she halted at a very unfamiliar sight.

Who was the willowy blonde leaning forward against the counter-height desk and sticking out a booty Destiny's Child would be proud of while typing something into her phone?

The woman swiveled and placed a hand on a generous chest accentuated by the V-neck leopard-print romper she was rocking. "Hi there. I'm Monique. I don't work here, but I can get my boyfriend for you if you'd like."

Monique, huh? Of course that would be her name. Probably meant something like "goddess divine"—and she was exactly the kind of woman Cameron Griffin always went for.

"Oh, that's okay. I'll be leaving in two seconds." Jenna whizzed past Monique and woke up the computer with its mouse.

The woman pointed her finger at the screen. "Are you supposed to be doing that?"

"Yep." With a few clicks, Jenna had entered the missing information on her paperwork—why *couldn't* Cameron have done that himself?—conscious the entire time of Monique smacking her gum as she leaned across the desk to look at the screen.

Jenna ground her teeth, finished up, printed the paperwork, and walked it back to Cameron's office. She heard the low rumble of his voice as he spoke into the phone behind the closed door. Jenna slipped the paper under the door, breezed through the front lobby where Monique was on her phone again, and headed for her car.

After a five-minute drive home, she set her purse on the kitchen table just inside the apartment door, where a stack of bills languished. She'd paid most of them, but had to wait till she got her own paycheck on Monday before she could send in the rent for next month. It'd be cutting it close, but she'd make the deadline—barely. Thank goodness for summer overtime.

Her gaze snagged on Liam's phone next to the bills just as it lit up with a text. He must have forgotten it—unlike some kids, his wasn't yet a permanent extension of his body. Jenna hadn't planned on getting him one in the first place, but Tyler and Gabrielle had insisted on putting both of them on their phone plan. Apparently it was "cheaper that way." Not sure she believed them, but she had to admit it made her feel better to know where he was at all times, since she worked so much during the busy summer months.

The phone screen vibrated again, and Jenna couldn't help but peek. She'd made it clear that Liam couldn't expect privacy on his phone, but that didn't stop the burn of guilt from attacking her stomach.

The text was from Jared Laureano, Liam's best friend: *Come on, man! Just ask her.*

Jenna's heart skipped a beat. Her son wasn't asking girls out already, was he? The kid had to be reminded to shower. No way was he out to impress the ladies. But what else could Jared mean? Ask who what?

Ugh. As much as she wanted to be the cool mom and trust her kid, Jenna slid her finger across the screen to see the rest of the conversation. Relief loosened her lungs as she read the string of messages—it was *not* about girls. Jared had sent Liam a picture of a flyer for space camp during fall break in October. Beneath it, he'd said: *Wanna come?*

Liam had replied: *Looks cool.*

Jared: *Soooo???*

Liam: *Nah, I can't come.*

Jared: *Y not? Cuz it's expensive?*

Jenna enlarged the photo. Whoa. Three thousand dollars? Just last summer, Jared had attended the same sports camp for underserved—aka "poor"—kids that Liam had. But his mom, Stephanie, had just gotten remarried to Abe Tyson, a lawyer in town, and their new situation must have made it possible for Jared's dreams to come true.

A dooming sense of failure crept up and choked Jenna. She locked her son's phone and set it down on the table again. For a moment, she closed her eyes. Oh, how she wished that she could create more for Liam. Transform their lives somehow. Make him prouder than he could be now, to have a mom who'd suffered the effects of depression for too long and still worked a dead-end job teaching surf lessons and renting out equipment to Walker Beach tourists.

Her too-serious son had spent so much of his life worrying about Jenna—and that wasn't his job. Only in the last year had he finally started to relax and be a kid. Or so she'd thought. But Liam was still losing out on the things he really wanted, like space camp. She could just see her *Star Wars*-loving son there, learning about science and having fun with his friends.

He should have that.

Instead, he was suffering the effects of *her* bad choices. Of being *her* son.

Just like Mom had suffered having her as a daughter, and Gabrielle, having her as a sister.

"You're changing your life one day at a time." The mantra of her counselor, Danielle, echoed through her mind. Sometimes, it didn't feel like enough.

But it was all she could do.

Exhaling, Jenna shook out her hands and reopened her eyes,

snagging a glance at the clock on the microwave. Oops. She needed to get moving if she wanted to make it to her meeting on time. Heading to her bedroom only took about five steps down the minuscule hallway.

Jenna took a quick shower, then threw on the white boho maxi dress with short lace sleeves she'd found at the thrift store last week for two dollars and paired it with her brown peep-toe buckled sandals. She pinned her shoulder-length hair back with her favorite artsy clip and swiped some blush on her cheeks.

Did she need anything else?

Oh! The invitation. Was this one of those events where you needed the invite to get in? Might as well grab it just to be safe.

She ran the short distance to her bedroom and plunged her hand deep into her underwear drawer—the only place to keep things private in this tiny apartment. Her fingers met paper, but what Jenna pulled out was no invitation.

Only the very epitome of dead dreams.

The pamphlet was yellowed and smudged with old finger-prints, as anything would be after eleven years of being alternately handled and stuffed away, but the image of a smiling student painting on canvas remained exactly as she remembered it.

When her art teacher had handed the Borden Art Institute pamphlet to Jenna her junior year of high school, neither of them knew yet that Liam grew inside her. How was it that Jenna could recall Mrs. Lancaster's words exactly all these years later? *"You have more artistic instinct in your pinky than most of us do in our whole bodies, Jenna. I see a wonderful future for you in some artistic pursuit—maybe interior design."*

And, for a moment, Jenna had seen it too. Her grades were decent, and she didn't hate the idea of leaving behind Walker Beach with its terrible memories. More than that, she'd longed to find her place in the world, to do something that would make

Gabrielle proud, that would prove to her sister she wasn't the royal screwup everyone thought she was.

But then, a few weeks later, she'd seen the plus sign on the pregnancy test—and all of those dreams had gone up in smoke.

The paper crinkled beneath her fingers. Why had she even kept this thing?

A disgusted grunt found its way out through her lips, and she tossed the old pamphlet into the trash can.

Right where it belonged.

CHAPTER TWO

ELISE

*W*hoever said diamonds were a girl's best friend must have never experienced the heavenly silkiness of a Ghirardelli chocolate square filled with caramel.

Elise Griffin strode down the center aisle of Hardings Market, intent on her mission. She took another quick peek at her watch. Good. Still plenty of time to run this errand and maybe visit a few of her six children before she was due to babysit the twins at Nate's this evening.

The market was crowded even for a Saturday afternoon, with several folks she knew and many she didn't, but that was par for the course during the tourist season in Walker Beach. Elise slowed at the end of the aisle, wincing at the ever-present pain in her arches as she pivoted toward the back corner and zeroed in on her quarry.

Rows and rows of various candies met her gaze, and her stomach quivered at the sight of the blue and gold package filled with celestial bites of chocolate hanging right in front of her. Elise tossed one into the small shopping basket hooked over her elbow.

There. Mission complete.

She turned to leave, but bit her lip. Maybe ... okay, one more wouldn't hurt. It was always good to be prepared if the urge hit in the middle of the night for a chocolate fix. And let's face it—at age sixty-three, it was more likely than not that Elise would find herself awake when she should be sleeping.

Tossing the extra package into the basket, she squared her shoulders and headed toward the front, only momentarily distracted by the boxes of movie theater popcorn. If Charles wasn't going to be home all week, she might as well spend her evenings watching rom-coms. Maybe her daughters would like to come over and join her. Last she'd heard—and much to her chagrin—they still weren't dating anyone and possibly would be available.

She snatched a value-sized box, paused, then grabbed one more. The basket's handle dug into the meaty flesh of her arm as she finished her walk to the front of the store.

And promptly held back a groan.

Only one register out of three was open and of course it had to be Liz Harding—the store's owner—checking out patrons. Her coiffed auburn hair showed not a hint of the gray that had overtaken Elise's head a full decade ago, and she wore a pressed white blouse and an honest-to-goodness strand of pearls at her throat.

Bet the woman had no idea what it was like to shove herself into Spanx only to discover she'd already outgrown the shapewear she'd just purchased six months before.

Or what it was like to discover that her husband had cheated on her with a skinny hospital CEO in Boston—to have lived with that knowledge for a whole year without telling a single soul.

And *Liz's* husband probably hadn't told her just an hour ago that he was leaving for Boston to do a "short consulting job" despite promising he'd never set foot in the city again—thus the need for reinforcements, aka chocolate.

Elise squeezed the candy before shoving it onto the conveyor belt.

Liz handed a receipt to the customer in front of Elise and waved goodbye, then turned to Elise with a smile. "Hi, Elise. How are you doing?"

The question mocked her. What if she actually told someone the truth for once—that life, her marriage, looked nothing like she'd hoped when she'd said her vows nearly forty years ago?

But of course, Liz was just making friendly conversation. She didn't want to actually know how Elise was doing. So Elise did her part and forced a breathy laugh. "I get to babysit Lauren and Aaron tonight, so I'm wonderful." At least that part was true.

"Ah, so that's why you have all of this chocolate." Liz pulled the first bag of chocolate across the scanner, which beeped.

Someone must have turned up the heat inside the market, because her armpits began to sweat. A nervous chuckle spilled from her lips. "It's a grandma's job to spoil the grandkids." Now she'd *have* to share the chocolates with the kids, and Nate wouldn't be happy if he found out.

Liz finished bagging up the treats as they exchanged more pleasantries—all the while, a growing need gnawing at Elise's gut—and Elise paid, snatched her bags, and raced across Main Street to the parking lot as quickly as her squat legs and aching knees could carry her.

As soon as she located her Lexus RX, she slid inside, tossed the two grocery bags into her passenger seat, ripped open one of the Ghirardelli packages, and dug out a candy.

The moment the chocolate hit her tongue, she laid her head against the headrest and groaned. She polished off that caramel plus four more—then sat there as the sugar raced through her veins, her heart beating at first quickly, then steadying out.

Her arms felt heavy. Her whole body, really.

Elise glanced at the clock. Shoot. Not enough time to stop in and see Samantha at her store, Charmed I'm Sure Books, or Cameron at the surf shop or Brittany at the fire station or Spencer at the church he pastored. She could have dropped off some treats to one of her children in town, seen if they needed anything. Made herself useful.

Instead, she'd stuffed her face with something her body most definitely didn't need, judging by the scale reading this morning.

Again.

She fisted the empty chocolate wrappers, opened the car's tiny trash bin, and tried to shove them in—but no luck. The M&M's wrapper from Thursday still took up residence there. Changing direction, she opened the glove box, only for a half-eaten bag of Cheetos to fall out.

Something raw and primal socked her in the gut, and Elise bit the inside of her cheek so hard she tasted blood. She didn't even like Cheetos! But last week, she'd seen them on the shelf as she'd done her weekly grocery shopping trip, and they had triggered the memory of the sextuplets' third birthday party. Chloe, the oldest of the six, had been obsessed with Cheetos and had begged to have them for the party.

Despite how messy they were—and how much time it took to constantly pick up after six children all the same age—Elise had acquiesced, but only if the kids would stay outside while eating them. In seconds, all three boys and all three girls had their fingers coated in Cheetos dust and Cameron had started chasing everyone in circles. Charles and Elise had come outside only to find them running around, squealing, laughing.

Charles had turned to Elise and shrugged. Then into the bag went his own hand, and he'd approached Elise with an orange hand and a mischievous grin. She'd backed away, warning him, but the irritatingly handsome man wouldn't listen. He'd snatched her around the waist, run his fingers down her cheeks, and kissed her breathless.

Elise popped the bag of Cheetos back into the glove box and slammed it closed. How silly of her to think of that now, thirty-three years and one hundred and fifty pounds later. Back then, Charles had worked as an ER doctor at the local hospital. Yes, he'd kept odd hours, but they'd been a team.

A team who loved each other.

But just a year later, he'd started to travel more, leaving her to take care of the kids and their home alone. Which was fine, actually. She'd learned to do it and had loved it. Because she loved their family.

And other than a head of silver hair that made him even more distinguished and handsome, Charles, of course, appeared for all intents and purposes the same.

But slowly, somehow, the years had done something to her.

To them.

Because they no longer were a *them*. Not really.

And Elise didn't know if they ever would be again.

But at least she still had the kids. Not that they really needed her anymore at age thirty-six. So she lived for times like this evening when she got to watch her four-year-old grandkids for her widowed son Nate.

Growling a disgusted sigh, Elise started the car and headed past the buildings of downtown, all pastel and as charming as they'd been since Elise had moved here with Charles as newly-weds full of dreams. She smiled at passersby on the sidewalk in front of Froggies Pizza, Kiki's Antiques on Main, and the newly opened Chrissy Price Public Library where the old hardware store used to be. Now a new hardware store stood just next door.

Between the storefronts, she glimpsed the boardwalk and the public beach beyond that, still crowded at five-thirty in the evening. Then the golf course and marina zipped into view and she turned off of Main Street into one of the older sections of town where some of the largest houses were located, including her own. Just a block away, she pulled into Nate's driveway and cut the ignition.

Before she could even climb from the vehicle, the passenger door opened and two matching pairs of baby blues peered up at her. Her granddaughter Lauren wore a pink princess dress and plastic crown, her hair in a long blonde braid. Meanwhile, Aaron stood in a Spiderman costume minus the mask, his brown hair giving the impression he'd just stuck his finger in an electric outlet. The cowlick was strong with that one.

"Grandma!" Lauren pushed her brother out of the way and climbed inside, shoving the popcorn and chocolate onto the floor and launching herself into Elise's arms.

Elise laughed and squeezed her granddaughter close, inhaling the sweet scent of strawberry yogurt and syrup. "Hi, baby." She peeked around Lauren and found Aaron already unwrapping a chocolate. That boy was a walking sweets hunter. "Hi, Air-bear."

Aaron shoved the chocolate square into his mouth—it was much too big for him—and stared at her wide-eyed. "Hi, Gwandma."

Shaking her head, Elise shifted Lauren to the side and reached out her hand toward her grandson. "Give me some sugar."

The spry little body sailed across the seat and rammed into Elise's gut—and Lauren's back. The girl started screaming at her brother to get off.

"Okay, okay, what's going on out here?" A gruff voice came from the headless body that had materialized next to the passenger door. Her son Nate ducked, sticking his head inside the car. "You guys should really let Grandma out of the vehicle before mauling her. And, Aaron, what in the world is all over your mouth? Get out here, son."

Aaron hung his head and crawled out the door, swiping the back of his hand across his lips.

"Lauren? Join your brother please."

Elise winced as Lauren practically strangled her with a tighter grip. "It's all right, Nate. I'm happy to see them too."

"They shouldn't have been outside alone." He reached in and pulled Lauren off of Elise, set her down, and squatted in front of both of them.

"But we saw Grandma pull up," Lauren said, pouting.

"You guys know better."

"Sorry, Daddy." Their joint chorus speared Elise as she exited the car and gathered the little chicks to her side.

Nate scrubbed his hand across his lightly scruffed jaw and shook his head. It was her habit to arrive a half-hour before his shift at the hospital so he had time to get ready, but he was already in his scrubs, his dark hair combed up into a gelled wave.

Her heart squeezed at the sight of her second oldest—a successful emergency room doctor who worked harder than anyone she knew, who valued order, who strove to save every life he could.

Every loss haunted him—she could always see it in the droop of his shoulders, in the darkness beneath his eyes, in the way he alternately snapped at his children and held them close —but none more than the loss of sweet Mindy four years ago.

He'd been the doctor on call the night that his wife had been run down in the Main Street crosswalk, pregnant with their twins at thirty-five weeks. They'd been able to save the children but she'd lost too much blood to survive. The loss of her just might have killed Nate too except for these precious little ones he now scolded. He'd been strong for them.

And that had given Elise purpose too. Here, at least, she was needed. Never for a moment had she regretted quitting the fourth-grade teaching job she'd returned to after the sextuplets had moved out in order to help Nate raise the twins.

Elise patted Nate's cheek. "You look like you slept better last night."

Shrugging, he offered a small smile. "The miracles of coffee." Nate opened the back door of her car and pulled out her overnight bag.

She laughed as Lauren and Aaron dragged her past the manicured lawn and up the path to the front door, which they all entered together. The whole place smelled of pancakes and bacon. Ah, the old standby—breakfast for dinner. Of course, knowing her son, the pancakes were probably made from almond flour and some other such nonsense, but the kids never complained.

Elise walked into the den, where an ornate oak bookcase displayed every children's book imaginable. A quick sweep of the room confirmed Nate's housekeeper must have come earlier today—there was not a dust mote anywhere, not a toy tucked into a corner where it didn't belong, not a single ring on the coffee table.

"Grandma, come see our new puzzle." Lauren smiled up at her.

Aaron crossed his arms over his little chest. "I wanted to show her!"

"Guys, it'll have to wait." Nate absently stood at the red brick fireplace, where a large photo of him and Mindy on their wedding day hung as the focal point of the room—they'd never had a chance to take one as a whole family. He ran his finger along the edge of the mantel, then rubbed his fingers together, brow furrowed. "I want to talk to Grandma about something first. Why don't you go play quietly in your rooms till we're done?"

"Aw!" Aaron stomped his foot. "Can't we—"

"I won't ask again." Nate lifted an eyebrow and pointed toward the carpeted stairs. "Go, please."

Elise took each child to her voluminous chest and kissed

them on the head. "I think tonight is the perfect night for making cookies. How about you?"

Aaron's and Lauren's eyes lit up and they jumped in short bursts. "Yay!" They continued cheering all the way up the stairs.

Elise turned once more to her son. "Is everything all right?"

"Cookies, Mom? Really? They just had pancakes." Nate sighed. "Come on to the kitchen and I'll get you something to drink. We can talk there."

She didn't like the sound of that. Nate was all efficiency, all directness. If he was going to ply her with a drink, then what he had to say couldn't be good. Leaving her purse on the couch, she followed him into the kitchen. Dishes littered the sink and bacon grease splattered across the granite black countertops.

"Sorry it's such a mess. The kids begged to help make dinner and well …" He shrugged. "I don't expect you to clean it up. I'll do it when I get home in the morning."

"Well, that's just silly. What else will I do once the kids are in bed? Sit around and eat bonbons?" She laughed at the thought— although bonbons *were* quite tasty.

But her whole family knew she wasn't the sit-around type. Even once her kids had started school, she'd been as involved as possible in the PTA, volunteering in their class, baking for their various clubs, carting them to and from sports and other events. For a stay-at-home mom, she sure hadn't stayed home all that much.

Nate grabbed a purple mug from a white cabinet and poured a ribbon of coffee inside. Then he pushed the sugar bowl across the counter and got the heavy cream from the fridge. He knew her well. "I'm just saying. That's not your job."

Settling onto a stool at the large island, she took the lid from the sugar and dipped a spoon inside, sprinkling a few teaspoons into her coffee and swirling while it dissolved. "I really don't mind, sweetie." Didn't he know that asking her to watch the kids during the week and whenever he worked the night shift was a huge blessing to her? What else would she do with herself? At this point, she didn't want to return to teaching. The long days on her feet and hours spent grading had proven rough on her body.

This—mothering, grandmothering—was what she was made for. First, she'd mothered her two younger sisters growing up, and then she'd mothered the sextuplets. Elise Griffin didn't know anything else. And besides, she loved pouring into her family. It gave her purpose. Joy.

She splashed in a tablespoon or so of cream and lifted the mug to her lips.

"I hear Dad is off on another trip tonight."

Her mug tipped at Nate's statement, coffee spilling across the counter. "Oh my." Reaching for a rag near the sink, she dabbed up the mess before Nate could make a move—before he could suspect how much what he'd said had rattled her. "Yes, it's a fast turnaround trip. He'll be back Monday afternoon. I was thinking we could have a family dinner sometime after he gets back. It's been too long since all of you kids were home."

A lawyer in San Francisco, Chloe was the only one who lived outside of Walker Beach. But except holidays, finding time when everyone had an open day in their schedules to get together had proven difficult.

"That sounds good." Nate poured himself a cup of coffee and took a sip of the black brew. That line appeared between his eyebrows again.

Something was bothering him.

"What is it, hon?" Elise popped up from her seat and rounded the counter to the sink, which was on the other side of the island. She flipped on the hot water and grabbed for a sticky plate. "Just say it. You're scaring your old mom."

"I don't mean to scare you. I just ..." Nate took another sip of coffee. "Okay, here it is. Mom, you've been an amazing blessing in our lives, swooping in the way you did when Mindy ..." He cleared his throat. "We couldn't have survived without you. But I also know it's not fair to take up so much of your time."

"You know I love being here for you and spending time with my grandbabies." She worked at a particularly stubborn bit of grease stuck on a frying pan.

"Of course, but it still doesn't change the fact that I basically pulled you out of a career you loved. And you won't accept any sort of money or gift in exchange—"

"Nathaniel Elliott, you know better than that." Why in the world would he think he needed to pay her to spend time in their precious company? Her breathing grew heavy and she slowed down her scrubbing. "But go on."

"I signed them up for preschool, Mom. They start on Monday."

The pan in her hand clattered into the sink and she looked up sharply. "What?" She must not have heard correctly.

"I want you to have the freedom to live your own life."

What was he talking about? Those children *were* her life. "Nate, I appreciate that, but ... preschool?" And starting in just two days?

"Don't worry, it's a great school. Private and really highly rated. I investigated it thoroughly, interviewed other parents, toured it."

Of course he had. "It's not that ..."

He leaned a hip against the counter. "It'll be good for them to be with other kids."

Instead of with you. He hadn't said that of course, but he might as well have.

The steam from the water rose into her eyes, stinging her nose. "If that's what you really want, then of course I support your decision." Give her an Academy Award, because in this moment, she somehow managed to say the words without revealing her true thoughts. But it was what Nate needed, to have his decisions affirmed. He had depended so thoroughly on

Mindy, that the fact he was making decisions like this again was a good thing.

She just wished …

"Mom, look at me." Nate set his coffee mug on the counter. "I knew this would probably be upsetting to you, but it isn't about you not being a good provider for them."

Okay. Apparently she wasn't as good of an actress as she'd hoped. "Then why?"

He shook his head. "I told you. It's not fair to ask you to stay stuck here in town when you're finally retired from your mom duties. Taking care of the kids is *my* job, not yours. So go back to work if you want. Travel with Dad. You should have the space to pursue your dreams. I won't keep you from that anymore."

Her lips trembled at her son's sweet words.

The only problem was, he couldn't have been more wrong in his assessment of what she wanted. And calling her "retired" only made her feel as useless as the pan she'd just cleaned—set aside, scraped of anything that gave it flavor.

Put away.

And as for traveling with Charles, nothing could be more laughable. They didn't even live in the same bedroom anymore, for goodness' sake, or spend their evenings together. She couldn't imagine that he'd be open to bringing his overweight, boring wife with him to wine and dine sleek hospital CEOs and their spouses around the country.

But Nate didn't need to know any of that.

"What about your night shifts? You'll still need me for those, won't you?"

"I switched permanently to days. It pays less, but it'll work best for all of us. The twins need a steady schedule and I'm finally in a place to give it to them."

Elise shut the water off, stacked the last gleaming dish in the drying rack, and toweled off her wet hands. "If this is my last day watching the kids on a regular basis, then we're just going to have to make it the best night ever, won't we?"

Nate cocked his head. "You sure you're okay, Mom?"

"Of course, honey."

At the very least, she'd pretend to be—for his sake and the kids'.

Maybe she should have splurged for a third package of Ghirardelli chocolates after all. It sounded like she was going to need them.

CHAPTER THREE

JENNA

*T*ime to find out what all of the fuss was about.

Jenna came to a stop on the north side of town at the base of Park Road and worked at a knot in her neck. Soon, she'd know who had sent the invitation.

Turning, she drove about a mile north of downtown where three separate inns occupied private beaches overlooking the Pacific.

The first was small and nothing fancy, catering to the budget-friendly crowd like college students and young families on vacation. Next up was the Iridescent Inn, which was owned by Ben Baker—Tyler's cousin—and his new wife, Bella. Together, the two of them had turned the place into a local hotspot, and rumor had it their events calendar was filling up rapidly.

And then, just a little farther down the road, there she was. The Barefoot B&B had always been grander than all the other establishments in town, save the Moonstone Lodge, but now ... well, the poor old girl needed a makeover worse than Josie Grossie in that old rom-com movie that Mom used to love.

What Jenna wouldn't give to get her hands on the interior of the inn. If the outside—with its bland beige paint sun faded, its entire exterior damaged by age and the elements—was any indication of what awaited her inside, she couldn't get a blanker canvas.

But this wasn't her inn. Redesign would fall to the new owner, whoever it was.

Jenna pulled into the empty parking lot. She checked the clock—6:55. Only five minutes early. Was this all a joke, with Jenna as the punchline? Maybe Cameron had cooked up an elaborate prank. She could see him doing that.

Who was she kidding? He was probably too occupied with Monique at the moment to think twice about Jenna.

Her tires spit gravel until she settled into a spot and cut the ignition, then climbed out. She wasn't that far out of town, but the air smelled different here. Sharper and still brackish, but also … sweeter somehow.

Or maybe that was just freedom blowing up from the water. At home and work, Jenna was always surrounded by people, and yet her heart still yearned for a deeper connection.

Here, with the wild wisps of nature and the quiet song of the sea, she felt it—like something calling to her—for the first time in a while.

Which was ridiculous, because she had lots of people in her life that she connected with, that she loved. People like Gabrielle, Liam, Tyler.

Cameron.

Jenna bit the inside of her cheek hard, slamming her car door and striding toward the front door. A purple cruiser bicycle leaned against the chipped porch railing. Where had she seen that before? Maybe it belonged to the mysterious owner. She turned to the teal front door, where a taped paper flapped in the wind. Jenna resecured the bottom piece of tape and read the scrawled words: Come In.

Okay then.

She stepped inside and her breath caught. The scent of lavender hung in the air, vibrating with possibility. Jenna wasn't superstitious, but it felt as if the place was almost … magical. Like it was speaking to her. Like there was more here than met the eye.

Much more.

"Hello?" she called.

No answer.

Hmm.

Immediately, Jenna was drawn into the cavernous lobby. Sunset was still an hour away, but oranges and reds and yellows had already begun to take over the sky, and the room encased in glass windows took on the hues. A row of paintings on the wall caught her attention. They were filled with splashes of color that seemed to have no rhyme or reason.

Seemed to—but they always did.

She had only been studying the paintings for a few minutes when she heard voices outside. The front door opened and in walked two women not much older than her—Heather Campbell and Piper Lansbury. Not exactly a pairing she'd have expected. Though the women were both friendly enough, Jenna had never seen the single mom who worked at her family's vineyard hanging out with the reporter who ran the local paper. And it didn't seem likely that either of them would have invited Jenna here.

Jenna stepped from the shadows. "Hey, guys."

"Jenna?" Heather pushed a brown curl behind her ear as she cocked her head. "Are you the one—"

"Not me. I just got here, as curious as you. Did you come together?"

"We just met up in the parking lot." Piper's brow furrowed and she strode forward, her heels clomping on the wooden floors, her sleek brown ponytail swinging down her back. She made it to the center of the room before crossing her arms and frowning. "I'm assuming you also got an invite?"

Jenna nodded. "And no idea what it's about."

Heather joined them. "Same here. But I don't know ... it's kind of exciting, right?"

"Exciting? It's maddening." Piper paced. "I've been trying to figure out who sent me that invite all week. But I didn't want to break the discretion rule, so I couldn't exactly interview the town members about it."

The woman was wearing a path across the threadbare area rug. Couldn't she just chill for a second? Jenna could picture the magic dissipating like pixie dust blowing in the wind.

Heather laughed, her pretty blue eyes crinkling at the corners. "I don't think it was exactly a rule, Piper."

"You know what I mean." Piper waved her hand in the air and finally stopped moving. "Don't tell me I'm the only one who immediately thought serial killer when I read the invite?"

At that, Jenna and Heather looked at each other and both laughed. "You're *definitely* the only one who thought that," Jenna sputtered.

"Who thought what?"

The three women turned to find Nikki Harding standing at the lobby entrance. The curvy blonde worked at her family's market and sang in a local band on the side—and, as far as Jenna knew, was no more than a mere acquaintance to any of the women here.

Jenna hooked a thumb toward Piper. "She got the invite and had visions of being murdered when she got here."

Nikki's round face brightened. "And you still came?"

"I'm a reporter. I go where the story tells me to go." Piper reached into her purse and pulled out a keychain with pepper spray attached. "And I came prepared."

"Guessing you didn't send the invite, Nikki?" Heather sank

onto the edge of the couch, releasing a puff of dust. She coughed. "Ugh, didn't think that one through."

"Nope." Smiling, Nikki wound her way past the furniture and plopped next to Heather, sending another plume through the air. "It wasn't me."

Then who …?

That's when Jenna heard footsteps above them. All four of the women snapped to attention, their gazes landing first on each other and then moving to the staircase on the right side of the lobby. A pale and petite hand appeared on the banister—a ring adorning each finger—and one by one, the steps creaked with the weight of the person who was descending.

And then, there she was—Jules Baker.

The woman's long feather earrings tangled in her waist-length red hair, and she managed to make her loose-flowing, mocha-colored jumpsuit look both chic and comfortable. In her early forties, the owner of Serene Art—and Tyler's youngest aunt—was the most carefree, independent spirit Jenna knew.

As she faced them all, Jules clapped. "Sisters! Thank you for coming."

Leave it to her to make a dramatic entrance. The woman had always been vivacious, full of life and a little edge of mystery. She was so unlike most of the Bakers. A bit of an oddball, just like Jenna herself.

Okay, so maybe Jenna had always secretly idolized the woman who marched to her own melody. There was something brave and … exciting … about that. And she couldn't help but grin as Jules greeted each of them with a hug—especially when she got to Piper, who put out a hand for Jules to shake instead.

When it was Jenna's turn for an embrace, she knew why the Barefoot had smelled of lavender. The scent emanated off of Jules, as did the peace normally associated with it.

Jules released Jenna and turned to the women. "You're probably wondering what this is about."

Each one nodded.

Jules held up a finger. "I'll be right back. Settle in. Get comfortable, if you can. I know the furnishings leave a lot to be desired. But ..." She stilled, features tightening for a moment before her grin returned. "We'll get to that, I suppose." She turned and whooshed from the room.

"What was that all about?" Piper grimaced as she studied the recliner behind her. She swept her hand across the seat cushion to clear away the dust motes before gingerly lowering herself.

Jenna sat on the couch on the other side of Nikki. "No idea. But I'm intrigued, aren't you?"

"Yeah." Tugging on her curls, Heather chewed her lip thoughtfully. "I mean, why us?"

It was definitely an odd assortment of people. The only thing they really had in common was that they were all women and Walker Beach natives. And even though Jenna knew Jules, it wasn't like they had much of a personal relationship. In fact, none of these women did as far as Jenna knew.

So why had she invited them here?

The only one who could answer that question swung into the room with a silver tray of finger sandwiches, fruit, and a pitcher of lemonade. Jules set the tray onto the small coffee table in front of the couch and lowered herself to the ground. "I have more food in the kitchen but thought these could tide us over while I tell you what I'm envisioning for this group—and this place."

Jenna's stomach gurgled. After living so much of her life depressed and without an appetite, hunger pangs of any sort were a miracle—ones she had learned to indulge. She snatched up a small plate and loaded it with a few sandwiches and some fruit salad.

The other women quietly gathered their own food as Jules started to explain. "As you all know, Chrissy Price and I were best friends." Somehow, the woman's voice didn't tremble.

Jenna wouldn't have blamed her if it had. Chrissy had been the owner of the local hardware store whose aggressive cancer had taken her about a year ago. "We both grew up here, but she was a bit older than me so we didn't really become friends until I came back to town after college and a short stint living in Los Angeles—trying to make it as a struggling artist." She smiled. "I was ... well, I wasn't in a good place when I moved back."

Jenna bit into a sandwich, the taste of creamy mayo blending with chicken and grapes to create the perfect chicken salad.

Twisting one of the rings on her right hand, Jules continued. "Despite being in the throes of raising her niece Madison at the time, Chrissy found the time to befriend me—even when I wasn't very friendly back. And her patience, her kindness ... they changed my life." She stared at the floor for a moment before lifting her head again, clearing her throat. "Chrissy had a gift for mentorship and support. She always knew when someone was hurting, even when others couldn't see it."

How very true. Even though she hadn't known her well, Chrissy had gifted Jenna with a bucket of bright orange paint during one of her particularly brutal battles with depression. Liam had been about three, hadn't he? And one day, Jenna had come home to find the paint on her doorstep, along with a note: *"This color made me think of you, sweet Jenna. I pray this brightens your day—and your walls—just a little bit, a reminder that even in the darkness, there can be light."*

Surprised by the sudden burn assaulting her eyes, Jenna shoved the rest of the sandwich into her mouth and focused on Jules again.

"She told me about this wish she had—to develop a Sisterhood, a place where a group of women in this town could get support for their dreams."

Jenna's heartbeat quickened. The image of the Borden Art Institute pamphlet that now languished in her trash can floated to the forefront of her mind. What if ...?

No.

"We would talk about the Sisterhood, this dream—and it went so well with the dream I'd been developing too. Don't worry, I'll tell you more about that later." Jules winked. "All of that to say, the idea for this Sisterhood started with Chrissy, but it's now one of my dearest desires to see it to fruition. After almost a year of grieving her, I feel certain that this is what's meant to happen." Her eyes scanned the group, slow, lingering on each woman for a few seconds. "That each of you is meant to be here."

Silence hovered for several moments before Nikki spoke up. "That sounds lovely, but what does it mean exactly?"

"I'm glad you asked, Nikki. The truth is … I don't fully know." Jules's shoulders lifted. "I pictured us meeting every week or every other week, sharing a meal and our hearts. And of course, keeping our meetings discreet. What's shared here should be sacred."

"But why us?" Piper set down her sandwich, which she had yet to taste. "And why would any of us want to share our dreams with near strangers? No offense."

Jules's laughter tittered through the entire place. "It's a perfectly valid question, Piper. The truth is, I want each one of you to decide if this is something you want—maybe even need —in your life. And if so, you should have input. You should feel like it's your group as much as it is mine." She paused. "And as for why I invited you all in particular, I prayed about who should be in the Sisterhood and each one of you came to mind. You and one other who isn't here yet."

Each woman stilled, blinking rapidly. And there it was again —that magical something in the air. The one that pulled and tugged and told Jenna that she might actually belong somewhere.

Here.

Even though they all seemed strong and confident on the

outside, maybe some of these women felt just as lost as she sometimes did. And wouldn't it be incredible if Jules's vision actually happened? What if this group of women could band together to do something none of them could do alone?

What if Jenna could actually pursue something she hadn't given herself room to dream of doing since before Liam was born?

Jenna swallowed. "I can't speak for anyone else, but I'm here for it." Lacking a drink to toast the occasion, she lifted half a sandwich in the air. "Where do we start?"

One by one, the other women whispered their agreement. Maybe they felt it too. Maybe they had dreams inside them that were begging for resurrection. Maybe Jenna would get to find out someday.

With a gentle smile, Jules looked up at the skylight in the ceiling—at the stars now sparkling above them. "I think a good place to start is by sharing my own dream. And it has everything to do with the reason I bought the Barefoot B&B."

Was she really going to do this?

As Jenna's finger hovered over the computer mouse, an emptiness gnawed at her stomach. She looked up, her gaze sweeping the Rise Beach Rentals' front lobby, praying for a customer to enter. Unfortunately, the place was empty.

Time to make her decision then. It shouldn't be this difficult. After the meeting at the Barefoot two nights ago, she'd gone straight home, invigorated by everything Jules had said about dreaming. The woman was determined to make the world a better place for herself and others, and had invited Jenna and the other women into that dream.

Jules wasn't wasting a minute of life wondering "what if." Now it was up to Jenna to do the same.

Just submit the application already, you chicken.

The bell over the front door rang and hallelujah! She was saved from making a decision, because in breezed her favorite distraction.

Cameron propped his orange surfboard against the desk and pushed his dripping blond curls out of his eyes. "Hey, Jenna."

"Hey." Jenna allowed herself one eye roam of the blue shorty wetsuit clinging to his muscled body, then flicked her gaze back to the computer—but the view there gave her just as many butterflies. "How was the surf lesson?"

"Two fourteen-year-old boys with a couple of overprotective moms."

"Hmm. So, the usual then." She tried to infuse humor into her voice, to find some way to tease him, but her brainpower zeroed in on the words at the top of the screen—Application for Admission to the Borden Art Institute Online Program.

What if she didn't get in?

What if she did?

Jenna chewed on her thumbnail.

"You okay?"

She jumped at the poke in her lower back. Apparently Cameron had snuck up behind her. "I'm fine. Why?"

"Seems you could use a laugh." He hovered over her, grinning. "So this is for your own good." Then Cameron shook his wet hair, pelting her with seawater.

She pushed against his chest. "It's called a towel." Jenna tried her best not to laugh, but wasn't successful. "When are you ever going to grow up?"

"Come on. You love it."

Oh, how she wished she didn't. Why couldn't they have a normal boss-employee relationship? It would all be easier if she clocked in, worked her hours, and clocked out again without giving him a second thought. But no, he had to go and be all adorable and charming and ... ugh.

Especially in moments like this, their age difference wasn't all that noticeable to her. But if anyone teased her about having feelings for her "much older boss," the nine-year age gap was a convenient excuse.

The real reason was a lot more obvious. He simply viewed her as a kid sister he liked to pester. Case in point—a guy didn't shake water like a dog all over a woman he wanted to date. And with the poor choices she'd made all her life, who could blame him for seeing her that way? Not that his relationships lasted all that long, but of course he preferred the sophisticated thirty-somethings he always seemed to end up with.

The thought sobered Jenna. She turned back toward the computer, where water dotted the screen. "You got the computer wet. Sonia and Steve aren't going to be happy if they have to replace this one."

The owners of the shop lived out of state and only came to visit once a year, if that. They left Cameron to make most of the decisions about the best way to run the shop. One such decision? Not firing Jenna, no matter how many times she'd called in "sick" to work during the lowest valleys of her depression.

For that, Jenna owed him big time. And it was only one of the reasons she loved him.

He grinned. "Eh, they'll get over it."

She felt his presence hovering over her shoulder, and before she could click out of the browser window, Cameron leaned closer, bringing with him the leftover scent of salty waves and his favorite pineapple surf wax. "Wait. What's that?"

Jenna finally clicked the mouse and minimized the window. "It's nothing." She maneuvered around him and rounded the desk to the front door. It was five minutes past closing, so she flipped the sign and locked the door then turned back to face Cameron, whose arms were crossed over his body as he leaned against the desk.

"You're going back to school?"

"No. I don't know. Maybe."

An eyebrow lifted and lips twitched. "Which is it?"

She shrugged and worked on straightening the three-ring binder, working a smudge off the corner of one of the laminated pages showcasing their array of beach umbrellas.

"Well, hey. I think it's great. How about we grab dinner at the Frosted Cake tonight before the town meeting? I could really go for a meatball sub, and we can celebrate you taking this huge step."

Liam was at Jared's tonight, so she *could* go. The real question, though ... was it the best thing for her? Probably not. Torture rarely was. "I'm not sure I'm submitting yet. And I figured you'd have plans with Monique. What would *she* think about us going to dinner together?"

Oops. In aiming for a tease, her tone had held a bit more accusation than she'd intended. Hopefully he wouldn't notice.

Cam snagged a squeeze ball off the cluttered desk. "How do you know Monique?"

"I don't *know* her." She waved her hand as if what Cameron had said held no consequence whatsoever. "She was here when I stopped in to do that paperwork on Saturday afternoon."

"Oh, yeah. Thanks for doing that before your big mysterious meeting." He tossed the ball between his hands, squeezed it, tossed it back. "You still won't tell me what that was all about?"

"Nope." She stole the ball mid-air and tucked it back into its spot, then breezed past him to work on tidying up the rest of the desk. A jar of Hershey's Kisses caught her eye and her stomach rumbled. Oh yeah. She'd worked on that application through her lunch break today and had forgotten to eat. Reaching inside, she dug one out.

"Kiss me."

What? Her hand knocked the jar over, spilling the kisses across the desk. She jerked her eyes toward Cam, who now leaned across the desk from the opposite side, hand outheld, a look of complete innocence on his face.

Oh, that man. If he only knew what a heart attack he'd just given her ...

"I meant give me a kiss."

"Oh, that's much better." Rolling her eyes, Jenna picked up a piece of chocolate and tossed it at his nose.

He reared back and caught it, laughing. "You should have seen the look of terror on your face."

Sure, terror. Let him think that.

"It's not like I would ask you to kiss me for real." He unwrapped the candy and popped it inside his cheek. "We're just friends. And don't worry, Monique knows that."

One by one, Jenna shoved the spilled chocolates back into the jar, ignoring the knife-like pain his words had sliced through her. "How would she know anything about me? She didn't seem to know who I was when I stopped in the other night and had the absolute *privilege* of meeting her."

This time, she allowed the sarcasm to drip like honey from her lips. But she smiled so he'd know she was kidding. So he'd *think* she was kidding, anyway.

"You didn't like her?"

"I was in her presence for like, two seconds. The only thing that matters is if you like her."

"No, really. What did you think?" Cam snuck out a kiss she'd just dropped inside the jar and ate it before she could protest. "I'm kind of fifty-fifty about whether I want to ask her out again."

"Wow." If he was fifty-fifty about a woman like Monique, then Jenna never stood a chance. "Sounds like you had some incredible chemistry there."

"I mean, she *is* a good kisser—"

Jenna coughed as she choked down a bite of chocolate. "TMI! Don't want to know!"

"Don't be jealous." Cam winked. "Green isn't your color."

"Why would I be jealous?" Nose in the air, she allowed her hands to travel the length of her upper body, which was currently sporting a lime-colored tank top. "And I happen to look fabulous in green, thank you very much."

Cameron's eyes followed her hands. "All right, I'll concede the point." He whistled. "You *do* look fabulous."

Darn if she didn't love their banter. Shaking her head with a smile she hoped came off as amused, she did a quick sweep of the desktop and cleared anything that didn't need to be there into the drawer below—spare paperclips, a few pens, and some flyers requesting donations for the Christmas festival. "So long as you recognize it."

"I do."

If only he meant it. But he never did. Cameron Griffin was one big flirt—a good friend and boss, but nothing more—and Jenna would do well to remember that. "Uh huh. Okay."

Cameron was quiet for a moment and she peeked up to find him studying her. When their eyes met, he grinned again. "We both need to eat before the town hall. You sure I can't get you to come with me to dinner? My treat. Then you can tell me all about your no-I-don't-know-maybe school application."

His brown eyes crinkled at the corners and *great*—now he was trying out his stupid pouty-lip thing that should have looked ridiculous but only left her wanting to for-real kiss his dumb face. "I ..." *Stay strong, girl.* "Sure." Ugh. Bad Jenna. "But first, I need to finish cleaning up in here and you need to shower because you stink of seaweed and moldy wetsuit."

"Your charm knows no ends, Wakefield."

Rounding the desk, she popped him on the arm like the good old buddy he was. "Don't forget it, Griffin."

"I wouldn't dream of it." Cameron angled his head toward her, eyes suddenly ... what, serious? No. He was never serious.

And wow, she was standing, like, really close to him.

She needed some space. Some air. An excuse to leave. Now.

Jenna spotted Cam's surfboard behind him and grabbed it. "I'll meet you at the Frosted Cake in fifteen." Then she headed through the wide door behind the desk, which led to their large equipment room in the back.

The shop was more stagnant back here, like a layer of ocean salt particles permanently hung in the air, but it made sense given that the equipment was constantly being exposed to the ocean and beach just outside the back door. Still, Jenna hardly noticed it anymore, especially at the end of a long shift like today.

A rainbow of paddles hung on one wall, and underneath sat a vertical metal rack where their fifteen kayaks were stored. To the right of that was the horizontal rack for the surfboards. Jenna squatted and settled Cam's board on the lowest rungs.

Brrr, it was cold back here. Jenna popped up and wandered to the door, cracking it open. The back patio of the shop faced Baker Beach, where the boardwalk was clogged with inline skaters, dog walkers, and runners with earbuds in—people heading wherever life might be taking them at the moment. Maybe some were going to dinner along Main Street. Others, home.

And what about her? Where was she headed?

If she couldn't submit that application, wasn't it the equivalent of walking in circles around her life? Or worse … sitting still?

She couldn't keep doing the same thing and expect anything to change. And even though she was grateful for this job, for the way it had provided for her and Liam, it didn't fuel her passion the way those hours spent decorating Baby Girl's nursery had.

But the lingering *what-ifs* continued to hover just like the thick, salted air did in the room where she still stood.

Something Jules had said on Saturday came back to Jenna in that moment. *"If your dreams don't scare you as much as they thrill you, then you aren't human. I'm terrified to take this step forward— terrified of failing Chrissy, of failing you all, of failing all of those women out there that I want to help with this project—but I also can see the tiny pinpricks of light ahead. And they tell me that every fear is worth fighting to get there."*

Jenna pushed her way through the doorway and onto the rickety wooden porch that led down to the beach, breathing in the fresh air, relishing the heat of the lowering sun on her skin. She closed her eyes to the rushing of people in front of her, and despite the darkness that suddenly enveloped her, the shadow of lingering light danced in the periphery.

Opening her eyes, Jenna strode back inside, back to the computer, and shook the mouse to wake up the screen. Then, mouth dry, she found the Submit button and clicked.

No hesitation this time around.

The moments ticked away as she waited to see the confirmation screen, and when she finally did, Jenna slumped against the counter, head in her hands, eyes closed once more.

Who knew what came next? But just like Jules, Jenna had seen the pinpricks of light.

CHAPTER FOUR

ELISE

*H*ow was it possible for a three-minute car ride to feel like an eternity?

Elise smoothed a wrinkle from her black blouse as she tried to get comfortable, but the front seat of a Miata was not designed for women like her in mind. The overwhelming lemony scent of whatever cleaner the car detailers had used on Charles's vehicle invaded Elise's nostrils. A country song grated against her ears as it played through the car speakers. She much preferred classical or jazz herself, or even the "oldies," but this was Charles's favorite, so she left the dial untouched.

"You're awfully quiet." Dressed in a white golf shirt and khaki slacks, with a Cartier gold watch on his wrist, not a lock of his full head of hair out of place, and his blue-gray eyes focused on the road, her husband honest-to-goodness looked like he'd stepped off the cover of *Leisure Man* magazine. "Is everything okay?" He tapped his fingers on the steering wheel in time to the beat of the music as he waited for her answer.

But how could he even ask her that? Today had been the twins' first day of preschool, which meant Elise had spent hours in her kitchen baking an array of treats that now sat in the trunk of the car. And when Charles had arrived home from his trip this afternoon, he'd raised an eyebrow. *"Is this all for us?"*

She'd known what he was thinking—Elise certainly didn't need all of those cookies, brownies, cupcakes, and apple turnovers lying around their house. No way was she admitting that there used to be three additional cookies and two more brownies before she'd consumed them.

But instead of offering a smart remark, she'd forced a smile. *"Of course not. They're for the city council meeting tonight."*

Then they'd eaten the pot roast she'd prepared in near silence, Charles answering emails on his phone and Elise attempting to read the latest Danielle Steel novel. How long had it been since they couldn't get enough of each other's company? When she'd begged for details of his workday, and he'd asked for news about the kids' latest accomplishments?

Now? Elise couldn't bear to ask the real question that had been ping-ponging through her mind since he'd sprung the Boston trip on her two days ago—had he seen *her* while he was in Boston?

Had he done *more* than see her?

Elise shivered. "I'm fine."

Charles glanced over at her as he pulled into City Hall's nearly full parking lot. "Good, good." He adjusted the air-conditioning knob down a notch. "I may have to go on the road again soon."

Already? "Oh."

"Nothing's final yet. You know how it is."

Yes. Yes, she did. When Charles had first taken on small consulting jobs teaching hospitals how to run more efficiently from a physician's point of view, he'd relished the challenge. Of course, he'd always be a doctor first, and still worked mostly part-time at the Walker Beach ER, but he'd built his consulting business into a multi-employee operation on the side.

He probably could send one of the younger employees on

this trip. Maybe he would have, if he'd had more of a reason to stay home.

The car glided into a spot at the far end of the lot and came to a stop. Elise unfolded herself from the tiny vehicle, then waited at the trunk. When Charles opened it, she lifted out the two platters that had been stacked on top of each other. The cookies in the bottom tray were a bit squished. She should have insisted on taking her SUV. But Charles had thought the treats would survive the short ride in his favorite vehicle.

Her husband took a platter from her. "That was nice of you to bake for everyone."

"It gave me something to do."

They started walking toward the building, where the council meeting would begin in about ten minutes.

"So it was a rough day then, huh?"

Rough didn't begin to cover it. "It was okay." She couldn't get into it or she'd start crying here in front of everyone.

Groups of locals stood around chatting outside, enjoying the last vestiges of light and the cool nightly breeze that made Walker Beach one of the most pleasant places to live in the summertime.

Elise waved to Lisa and Genevieve Baker, the wives of Charles's cousins Frank and Thomas, along with their mother-in-law Luellen. And there was Dottie Wildman, poor thing—her husband Bill had just passed from a heart attack a few weeks ago. As they walked inside, Elise made a mental note to make another casserole for Dottie and stop by for a visit.

Elise and Charles maneuvered through the crowd, which graciously parted for them as they made their way toward the City Council chambers. A few six-foot tables half filled with refreshments stood in the lobby, and Josephine and Arnie Radcliffe were busy transferring a drink dispenser from a moving cart to one of the tables.

Josephine looked up at their approach, a shock of her white

hair swinging with the movement. "Hi, doll. Thanks again for making those treats." She turned to Arnie and waggled her eyebrows. "Elise made her famous brownies."

The man patted his round stomach and licked his lips in a dramatic fashion. "I call dibs."

Elise chuckled as she placed her platter in an open spot on the table. "You're sweet, but I'm pretty sure nothing tops your desserts, Jo." The woman owned and operated one of the most beloved restaurants in town. The Frosted Cake had started as a bakery twenty-odd years ago and Josephine had expanded it into a full restaurant with takeout and sit-down service for lunch and dinner.

"Pish." Josephine's large arms lifted the last drink dispenser onto the table, and she shook her head. "You go on now and find those kiddos of yours. I saw them walk past a few minutes ago."

"You sure you don't need any more help?" While Elise couldn't wait to find Nate and ask how the twins' first day went —who knew, maybe he regretted sending them?—she didn't want to leave the woman in a rut.

"We're all good here."

"All right." She turned to ask Charles if he was coming, but he'd already left her for a group of new hospital residents who'd pulled him into a discussion. A quick look at her watch told her the meeting would begin in three minutes. Even if he was a terrible mayor, Jim Walsh was at least punctual, which meant she didn't have much time to find her children.

Elise pushed through the growing crowd—"Excuse me, excuse me, I'm so sorry, pardon me"—and finally found most of her kids chatting in a circle down the hallway. Her lungs expanded at the familiar sight.

Nate stood in his scrubs and Brittany in her typical Walker Beach Fire Department T-shirt and jeans, her dirty blonde hair pulled back in a ponytail, and together they rolled their eyes as

Cameron—whose one arm was slung around the waist of an unknown blonde—told some story, gesturing wildly with his free hand.

And there was Spencer, clapping Cameron on the shoulder and laughing along, his muscular frame and tattooed arms giving him the look of a bouncer rather than a pastor. He towered over petite Samantha, who giggled quietly into her hand at her brother's antics.

They may have all been in the womb together, but her children were as varied in looks and personality as any siblings might be.

Samantha caught sight of Elise. "Mom! Hey!"

All five of them—plus Cameron's mysterious female friend—turned and greeted her with smiles. She approached, giving each one a hug. Cameron was just introducing her to Monique when Josephine yelled out that the meeting was about to start.

Guess she'd have to ask about the twins' first day later.

The group moved toward the City Hall chambers like this was a New York subway instead of Walker Beach, waiting for the other people to head inside. Town meetings weren't always this well attended, but there were supposed to be updates regarding the mayoral race and the reveal of a top-secret project led by Jules Baker.

Once they were inside the room, Nate guided them to a row of open seats.

Cameron groaned. "Really, man? The front row?"

"Do you see anything else that's open?" Nate motioned to Elise. "Here, Mom. I know you like the aisle seat."

"Thanks, sweetie. Who has the kids tonight?" Since they were born, she'd watched the children for any city council meetings Nate had wanted to attend.

"I hired the teenager who lives across the street to babysit."

"Tari Johnson?"

"Yeah."

49

Elise sucked the inside of her bottom lip. "Did you remember to tell her that Lauren needs exactly three stories—not two, not four—in order to sleep soundly? Oh, and that Aaron can't have water at bedtime or he has an accident in his sleep?" She paused, thinking. "And what about—"

"Mom." Nate frowned. "They'll be fine. It's just for a few hours."

"Right. But—"

"There you all are." Charles chose that moment to join them. "Good to see you, kids." He shook hands with his sons and gave his daughters quick hugs.

Before anyone could tell him differently, Charles took the aisle seat, so Elise squeezed past and settled between him and Samantha. My, they really were close to the action tonight. It felt a little strange, since she normally sat in the back with the kiddos. Most of the time, she ended up missing half of the meeting because they needed to run around in the foyer.

Just to the right and up a little stood a podium where speakers faced the five city council members, who currently sat at a half-moon-shaped table situated on a dais. The mayor sat in the middle seat. Many women in town thought he was handsome. And oh sure, he was certainly fit and still had all of his hair, but to Elise, the fifty-something had always rather resembled a greasy rat with his pinched nose and beady eyes. Or maybe it was his personality that made him so wholly unattractive.

Jim Walsh knocked his gavel against the table. "I'd like to call this meeting to order."

The crowd quieted down. The mayor welcomed everyone and started off by reviewing the meeting notes from the last gathering. Then his son, Evan—the city's head development officer—and local events planner Ashley Baker Campbell gave an update on the first annual Christmas on the Beach Festival, which was a town-wide effort to help business owners recover from the economic downturn resulting from last year's earthquake.

When Evan and Ashley were done with their update, the mayor got back on the mic to announce an upcoming BBQ, where townspeople could get some free food and bring any of their concerns directly to the mayor.

Then councilman Bud Travis—Jim Walsh's opponent in the mayoral race, who was also the owner of the Walker Beach Bar & Grill along with his wife, Velma—scratched his white beard and let people know about his shrimp boil the same night.

Samantha leaned closer to Elise. "I heard the mayor planned his event after Bud had set a date for his." Her daughter's whisper hissed between them.

Elise sighed and shook her head. It was time for this town to elect a real leader, one who served out of the true kindness of his heart—not because he benefitted from the job.

At last, Jim Walsh called Jules Baker to the front. The youngest of Charles's first cousins, Jules fairly floated to the podium. But instead of facing the council as was tradition, she snagged the mic off the stand and turned to face the crowd. "Hi, friends. It's so good to be with you tonight."

The spotlight softened her milky skin and made her red hair appear almost as if it was on fire. "I wanted to tell you about a project that's near and dear to my heart—something that's been there for a while now—that Chrissy Price and I dreamed up together."

No doubt about it, the woman knew how to command a room. Not even the kids in the audience spoke. The palpable intrigue beat a steady rhythm and grew in intensity.

"The project is going to take a lot of time and energy. Frankly, it'll take a lot of money too, but I'm not as worried about that part. I'm not really worried at all, actually, because I know the people of Walker Beach. And the people of Walker

Beach—you, my family, my friends—come through. So I am confident I can count on each one of you."

Jules paced the front space, stopping in front of Elise. Her gaze was like a warm hug, and something buzzed in Elise as the passion in Jules's words connected with Elise's heart.

Goodness. She didn't even know what this project *was*. She just knew she had to be part of it.

"So here it is. I recently bought the Barefoot B&B, and I intend to remodel and reopen it."

The hush of the crowd broke like a wave as the latest Walker Beach mystery was finally solved. Elise heard an "I knew it!" rise from somewhere in the back and recognized the high-pitched voice of Carlotta Jenkins, the local clothing boutique owner who had made it her personal mission to figure out the B&B's purchaser.

Elise frowned, then berated herself for the reaction. If the local art gallery owner wanted to run a bed and breakfast, then that was fine with her. But then why such a buildup? Why did Jules need the town's help?

The reveal just didn't seem to jibe with the zeal Elise had thought she'd sensed in Jules—the zeal Jules had inspired in Elise.

But wishful thinking was always that way, wasn't it?

Jules smiled at Elise, as if sensing her very thoughts.

Well, that was unnerving.

The woman started pacing again, and the crowd quieted down once more. "But it's not going to be the same bed and breakfast it was. I want to rename it—or rather, add to its name. Instead of the Barefoot B&B, it will now be the Barefoot Refuge."

Interesting. But a name change also didn't seem to warrant all of these dramatics.

Jules paused, the side of her mouth hitching up like she knew a secret. "A refuge is not only a place where people can retreat from their daily lives to relax—a haven—but it's also a safe place. And I want to create that for women, specifically those who have chosen to leave abusive relationships and desire to start over."

Oh. Wow.

Jules continued. "So many of these women stay trapped in marriages and relationships because they don't have a way to provide for themselves, but I want to use the Barefoot Refuge to create a program of sorts. With this program, women would apply to live and work at the inn. They'd stay for a year or so and learn hospitality skills they can use to get future jobs— everything from management to cooking, housekeeping, marketing, bookkeeping, and more. The best part is that once the inn is remodeled and taking in guests, the program could become nearly self-sustaining, with the money earned from stays being used to fund the cost of running the inn, as well as provide food, housing, and small stipends for the women in the program."

The hush remained, and Elise's insides vibrated. What a wonderful idea.

"Are there any questions from the council before we open it up to audience inquiries?" Mayor Walsh asked from the dais.

City councilwoman Kiki Baker West—one of Jules's older sisters and owner of Kiki's Antiques on Main—raised her hand. "Exactly what is it that you need from the town, Jules?"

"Thanks for asking, Kiki. It's going to require a lot of hands to make this happen. The first thing I'll need is a lot of help remodeling. My brother Frank's construction company has already offered to donate the tools and other supplies necessary, but we need bodies. Lots of 'em. I'm going to come up with a list of remodeling dates over the next several months. You don't have to have any prior experience to sign up. We'll find some way for everyone to help."

"When do you hope to have this project completed?" Councilman Doug Doyle asked.

"My goal—and I know it's ambitious—is to have the remodel complete and the first guests staying at the inn during the Christmas festival. At that point, the inn will be all volunteer run and we will start selecting women for the program whenever we're approved for charity status."

Down the row, Cameron whistled. At Charles's sharp look, he shrugged. "What? That'll be a lot of work in what—four months?"

Jules nodded. "Yes, it will. Which is why I also need a coordinator—someone who is all in on this project, who believes as strongly in it as I do, who can help me with the details."

An inexplicable rush of energy burst forward, racing through Elise's veins. What in the world?

No. She couldn't be that someone. Nate might still need her help with the twins. She had to stay available during the week, just in case.

But she couldn't get the idea out of her mind as Jules fielded questions from the crowd. A sense of rightness grew inside until it was like a dinosaur sitting on her chest—and, as Aaron liked to remind her, dinosaurs were big.

Really big.

As the meeting ended and the crowd began to disperse, Elise sat there, unable to move.

"Mom."

She glanced up at Nate, who stood in front of her. The other kids had already headed out to the lobby. "I'm sorry, honey. What's that?"

"Are you okay?" He offered her a hand.

Taking it, she struggled to her feet, which had stiffened from sitting so long. "I'm fine, sweetie." Her mind sharpened at the opportunity to finally ask him what she'd been wondering all day. "So." Thumb rubbing against the strap of her purse, she tried for a casual tone. "How was Lauren and Aaron's first day of school?"

The wrinkles in his forehead disappeared and a rare grin swept across her son's face. "They loved every minute. Didn't even cry when I dropped them off. Their teacher said they did ..." Nate droned on, telling Elise about each of her grandchildren's accomplishments.

And while she loved hearing that they'd done well, that they'd had fun, that mammoth dinosaur settled in and cracked her heart wide open.

Her grandbabies didn't need her anymore. Her children didn't either.

But maybe ... maybe someone else did.

"I'm sorry, hon, but I need to go talk with Jules before she leaves."

"Oh." Nate's eyes widened as if in surprise—and no wonder, since Elise never interrupted stories about her grandkids.

But this was important, and Jules had just stopped talking with her niece Quinn and had turned to gather her things from a nearby seat.

Elise squeezed Nate's arm. "I'll see you in the lobby in a few, okay?"

"Sure." With a backward glance—and worry lines back—her son shoved his hands into his pockets and strode up the aisle toward the back doors.

With a deep breath, Elise approached Jules. "Can I talk with you for a moment?"

Why were her hands shaking?

Jules turned. "Elise, hi." She leaned in for a hug. "How are you?"

"I'm good." Her tongue stuck to the roof of her mouth. *Just spit it out already.*

Cocking her head, Jules smiled softly, her eyes alight with

55

some sort of special knowing. "Is there something you wanted to talk about?"

"Yes." Now or never. "I ... I want to help. Maybe ... to be your coordinator. If you still need someone."

"I do." Jules's nose wrinkled and twitched. "The job is yours."

What? "You don't want me to ... I don't know. Interview or something?"

"There's no need. I can't imagine anyone better suited to seeing others' needs and meeting them in precisely the right way."

A few tears spilled unbidden down Elise's cheeks. She didn't even bother to wipe them away. "Thank you."

"And ..." Even though the room had cleared of everyone but the two of them, Jules glanced around and leaned close, voice lowered. "I wonder if you'd like to help me in another way too."

Why not? "Of course."

Jules clapped her hands like a toddler who'd seen a cookie. "How would you like to be a mentor of sorts?"

"Me?" Elise's curiosity was piqued. "A mentor to who?"

"To the women in the Barefoot Sisterhood."

At the moment, Elise was in her element. But once the women arrived, that might all change.

She hummed as she bustled through the Barefoot B&B's kitchen. Having arrived two hours before the seven o'clock Saturday meeting, she'd managed to whip up lasagna, salad, and bread. That, along with the brownies she'd baked and brought with her, should make for a nice meal for the women in the Barefoot Sisterhood.

The mixed aromas of basil, garlic, and tomato wafted through the air, and Elise leaned down to check on the lasagna in the industrial oven that had seen one—or ten—too many years. A puff of steam hit her in the face as she opened the door. The cheese was just about perfect, so she grabbed a pair of potholders and hauled the casserole dish out. Then she adjusted the temperature, slipped the garlic bread inside, and leaned against the counter, tuning her ears to the door that led into the Barefoot's lobby.

Were those voices? Some of the women must have arrived.

Elise removed the potholders from her hands and tapped her fingertip against her lip as her chest tightened. She could do this, couldn't she? It wasn't as if she was a town outsider. How many functions had she attended at Spencer's church? How many Walker Beach events had she served at, smiling and chatting up folks she'd known her entire life? That was the whole point of living in a small town. Connection.

But serving behind the scenes and being a mentor were two different things. Didn't mentors have it together all the time? Elise may be organized, but her life was far from perfect. *She* was far from perfect. Just ask her husband. There had to be some reason he'd decided their marriage hadn't been enough for him.

That she hadn't been enough.

Pull up your big girl britches and stop complaining right now. She had a lot to be grateful for. After all, Charles hadn't left her. They hadn't divorced. She'd forgiven him and they'd moved on. Somehow, she'd held it together enough to continue with her life. So maybe she did have something to offer after all. And she really did want to help.

Maybe *that* was enough.

The door opened and Jules walked in. "That smells simply heavenly." Her blue eyes sparkled behind a pair of cat-eye glasses. "The ladies have all arrived—even Quinn. She didn't show up to our first meeting, but I reissued her invitation in person. I can tell she's ready to bolt, so hopefully we'll be able to draw her in with this excellent food and conversation."

"Oh, wonderful." Thomas and Genevieve's oldest daughter—and Tyler's twin sister—had been through a bit of a rough patch lately. According to the rumor mill, she'd quit her fancy job in New York City and brought a fake boyfriend to the large Baker family reunion last month. Then that boy had fallen in love with Quinn's younger sister, Shannon. Quinn had decided to stay in Walker Beach for the time being while she figured out what was next for her life.

Maybe the Sisterhood could be a good thing for her.

Elise checked on the bread. Golden brown and perfect. "Everything is pretty much ready. Are we eating out in the dining room?" It had been ages since she'd been inside the Barefoot, but it was hard to forget the gorgeous room where meals had been served to guests. Surrounded by glass from floor to ceiling on the western wall, it offered a superb prospect of the beach bluffs and water below.

"Yes. There's a bit of a moldy smell in there, so I lit a few candles. How can I help?"

"Just get the women in there. Maybe give me five minutes so I can set the table. I'll take care of the rest."

"You got it." Jules disappeared again.

For the next several minutes, Elise traipsed between the kitchen and the dining room, putting out elegant-looking disposable white plates and silver forks. Jules had placed a sparkling white tablecloth at the large round table closest to the windows, which offered a gorgeous view of the approaching sunset despite some grime and salt buildup around the outside edges of the panes.

A lovely centerpiece in the middle of the table consisted of three short vases with purple candles burning bright and giving off some sort of floral scent. Elise wasn't an expert at making things look pretty, but while flower petals and strands of pearls appeared to be randomly placed, she guessed Jules had been much more strategic about it.

Just as Elise had placed the salad dressing on the table, a woman entered the dining room. Piper Lansbury—her daughter Samantha's best friend—set her wide eyes upon Elise. "Mrs. Griffin. Hi."

Elise batted away the address and moved toward Piper. "I've told you over and over again. Now that you're in your thirties, you should call me Elise."

As she wrapped the woman in a hug, Piper stiffened at the contact as usual, but that didn't dissuade Elise. The girl needed some motherly affection as much now as ever. Growing up, she'd been a fixture in the Griffin household when her own mother "worked late"—which, more often than not, actually meant she had to sleep off her alcohol after a shift at the night-club one town over. Then there was her senior year, when Piper had lived with them while her mom went to prison for drug use and lost custody.

Despite all that Elise had attempted to do for Piper—as much as she'd tried to get her to open up—the girl still remained a mystery to her. She was brilliant and a hard worker and could be writing for some big newspaper in the city, but she'd chosen to come back to Walker Beach after college. When Elise had asked Samantha about it once, her daughter had just shrugged. *"She has her reasons, Mom."*

Behind Piper entered Nikki Harding and Heather Campbell. Since they were younger than her children, Elise hadn't had much contact with them over the years, but they were pleasant enough girls—excuse her, women. "Hi, ladies."

"Hi." Heather looked at the table. "Is that your lasagna? I remember having it at a town potluck once and have been trying to recreate the recipe ever since." She pulled out a chair and slipped in.

"You're so sweet." Elise felt the warmth rise in her cheeks. "It's no big mystery. I'm happy to share the recipe with you."

"Hey, Elise! I didn't know you'd be here."

She turned to find Jenna Wakefield at her elbow. "Yes, Jules asked me to come and be a part of your group."

The younger woman's smile wobbled for a moment. "That's … wonderful."

Oh no. If Jenna—her son Cameron's friend and fellow employee—didn't want her here, maybe no one else did either. What if they felt she was intruding?

Maybe she should pull Jules aside. Offer to cook meals for everyone and then slip away. Yes, that could work. She'd still be helping to facilitate all of this togetherness, but she didn't have to horn in on it.

Before she could say another word, Jules came in with a tight-lipped Quinn at her heels. Jules put her arm around her niece's shoulders and cleared her throat. The other women, who had all taken seats at the table, turned their attention to the group's leader.

"I'm sure it's obvious, but we have two newbies here with us tonight."

Brow furrowed, Piper took a sip of her water. "I don't mean to be rude, but I agreed to be part of this group assuming that we wouldn't be adding new people every week. How can we be expected to share our 'dreams'"—she made finger air quotes as she said the word—"and foster this 'Sisterhood' with a constant influx of strangers?"

Strangers? The word socked Elise in the gut, and she gripped the chair in front of her. "I can leave."

"Me too." Quinn's blue eyes whirled like a stormy sea as she stared down her nose at Piper.

"Neither of you is leaving." Normally filled with melodic calm, Jules's voice was edged with determination. Her gaze swept the small group. "I know this is all new, but let me explain. Quinn here was actually one of the original invitees. She just couldn't make it last time." A squeeze showed Jules's solidarity.

As for Quinn, her gaze had shifted to the floor.

"And since Elise is going to be helping me coordinate the renovation of the inn and the implementation of the program for abused women, I thought it would be wonderful to bring her into the fold here. She has a lot to offer us all, and I hope you'll be welcoming."

Elise grew light-headed at the praise, and finally lowered herself into a chair. Maybe she should set Jules straight about just how little she had to offer. She hated to disappoint anyone.

Finally, Jules released Quinn and both of them took seats. Lifting her fork, Jules tapped it against her plate. A sharp *ting, ting, ting* filled the silence. "Look, ladies. I promise not to bring anyone else into the Sisterhood unless we all vote on it and agree, all right?"

One by one, the women nodded their assent. Then Heather grabbed the salad container and unloaded some spring mix onto her plate, while Jules passed the bread to her right. The women handed their plates to Elise and she dished up the lasagna. When everyone was served, they began to eat.

Other than the sound of forks scraping plates and water tinkling in glasses, the room remained quiet.

Clearly, the women were not yet comfortable with one another.

Heart fluttering, Elise took a bite of lasagna and soaked in the comfort of the pasta, cheese, and her grandma's secret sauce. Her own mother hadn't been much of a cook. Before her parents had divorced and Mom had left their home, she'd worked a lot, leaving Elise to figure out the kitchen herself. But her grandma could have been on one of those cooking shows if she'd wanted. She'd lived in Oregon, but Elise still remembered how she made the most delicious meals, pulling the whole family together and leaving everyone comforted and full of wonder and joy.

One day when Elise was about thirteen, after rooting around

the cabinets, she'd found a box of recipe cards written in her grandma's familiar cursive. Since her grandmother had died just the year before, the cards were like a treasure, a peek inside her world and heart. And the first recipe Elise had tried was this lasagna.

"So." Jules finally broke the silence. "How was everyone's week? What's going on with all of you?"

The candles flickered in the growing dimness. No one answered.

Under the table, Elise couldn't keep her knee from bouncing. Her eyes flipped toward Jules, whose face showed no signs of unease or worry.

Just when Elise was about to blurt out something—anything to get rid of the silence—Jenna cleared her throat and set her fork down. "I ... I have something to share with all of you."

Everyone else stopped eating. Nikki and Heather both smiled at Jenna. Quinn simply stared, and Piper sat back in her chair, holding her water goblet in her hand and taking small sips—ever the observant reporter.

Jules nodded her encouragement. "We are all ears, Jenna. Please. Tell us what's on your heart."

"Oh, um, well." Jenna frowned as she stared at her plate, which was still fairly full.

Maybe she didn't like lasagna. Or maybe she was nervous.

Despite the fact she worked with Cameron, Elise didn't know Jenna all that well—she was just about a whole decade younger than her kids, after all. Whenever Elise visited Cameron at work, Jenna was friendly and clearly loved teasing Elise's son. She appeared comfortable in her own skin too, something that Elise admired. If only *she'd* been like that in her younger years, who knew where she might be now.

Jenna played with the left sleeve of her shirt. "Jules, last week I was really inspired by the idea of moving forward and doing something I never thought I'd get a chance to do." She inhaled a shaky breath. "You know, when I had Liam, I pretty much thought my dreams for a real career were over. With the help of my sister, we survived. But I want more than just survival—I want to thrive. I want *him* to thrive. And I'd like to be an example to him too. Of perseverance, maybe. Of dreaming even when all the odds are stacked against him."

She swallowed hard. Next to her, Nikki squeezed her elbow, a clear show of support.

Jenna flashed a grateful smile her way. "A few days ago, I applied for an online interior design program. I should find out in the next few months if I got admitted, and if so, I'll be attending school in January to finally go after the degree I've dreamed about getting for twelve years."

Here was a young woman whose childhood had been stolen from her in many ways, and she was fighting back. "How wonderful," Elise said.

The other women around the table echoed similar sentiments, and Jenna continued telling them about her fears and what had finally made her just go for it. "It was this group. The hope it offers. So … thank you."

And something about one person opening up made the conversation finally flow. No one else shared their hopes and dreams, but they asked Jenna plenty of questions. The woman answered them all with a mixture of humility and humor that drew Elise in.

She may not know it, but she was wise beyond her twenty-seven years. *This* was a woman of strength, and Elise suddenly found herself grateful Jenna was in Cameron's life. If only the foolish boy would stop dating a host of random women and see the treasure right under his nose.

Elise sat up straighter. Hmm. Maybe, at the same time she was playing mentor, she could play matchmaker as well.

Maybe Elise Griffin wasn't done being useful in her children's lives after all.

CHAPTER FIVE

JENNA

*T*his was really happening.

Jenna's hands shook as she sat in her car outside of Gabrielle's house. She lifted her oversized white sunglasses just to make sure she was seeing things correctly, but the same words stared back at her from her phone's screen.

Ms. Wakefield, it is my pleasure to congratulate you on your acceptance to Borden Art Institute!

Attached you will find your official acceptance letter, but I wanted to add a personal note. We know you applied for the spring semester, but we had a last-minute spot open up and—despite the prestigious students on our waiting list—I feel you are the perfect person to fill it.

That being said, we are thrilled to offer you acceptance into the fall semester of our online interior design program. Classes begin in two weeks, so we need to get your registration and financial aid applications completed.

If you are interested in accepting this spot, please contact me as soon as possible at the number below or by replying to this email address. If you would rather proceed with your plans and accept a spot to begin in the spring, that would be fine as well.

Congratulations again!

Dr. Sydney Westenbridge, Dean of Admissions
Borden Art Institute
San Francisco, CA

Jenna set down her phone on the passenger seat of her fifteen-year-old Jeep and pressed her hands against her lips. She'd gotten in. And not for the spring, as anticipated, but the fall.

Whoa. This was all going so fast.

Could she do this? Should she?

Cameron and Gabrielle earlier last week, then The Sisterhood two nights ago—they'd been all kinds of encouraging when Jenna had told them about applying for the institute.

They'd believed in her. Maybe it was time to believe in herself.

Before she could lose her nerve, she picked the phone back up, hit Reply, and told Dr. Westenbridge that she'd be delighted to accept the open spot. That she'd start looking at financial aid options tonight.

She was really doing this. Going back to school.

Jenna let loose a tiny squeal before climbing from the vehicle, opening the back door, and hauling out the twenty-by-twenty wall art she'd found at the thrift store this afternoon. It would look perfect hanging on the nursery wall.

A breeze blew a few fallen leaves from her sister's large tree across the path as she walked through the gate of the picket fence, toward the red door, and rang the doorbell.

And waited.

Huh. Gabrielle's blue Infiniti SUV sat out front, and Tyler was in New York on a business trip. Jenna set the wall hanging down and checked her phone. Four in the afternoon. Maybe her sister was working in the back bedroom and hadn't heard the doorbell.

Jenna pulled out her spare key and inserted it into the lock.

She could just pop in and, if Gabrielle wasn't able to visit, leave the decor in the nursery to hang at a later time.

Picking up the wall hanging, she entered the darkened house, which smelled like fresh lemonade. The whole place hummed with that lazy afternoon vibe perfect for napping. Jenna made her way down the hallway.

But the sound of retching stopped her in her tracks.

It was coming from Tyler and Gabrielle's room.

Jenna put the decor just inside the nursery and rushed down the hallway to the master suite, the door of which was wide open. "G? You okay?"

The only reply was another round of vomiting, followed by crying.

Jenna skidded into the room, sudden heartburn igniting in her chest. Her gaze swept the modest bedroom, with a king-sized bed covered in a purple comforter. But her sister wasn't there.

She rounded the corner into the bathroom and found Gabrielle on her knees hugging the toilet as she emptied her stomach.

"Oh, Sis." Squatting behind her sister, Jenna rubbed her back.

Gabrielle lifted her head and her bloodshot eyes crinkled in confusion. "Jen? What are you doing here?"

But before Jenna could answer, Gabrielle turned back to the toilet. This time, she dry heaved. Poor thing. Was this normal for a woman in her third trimester? Maybe she had a stomach bug or something.

"It's okay. I'm here. I'm here."

Gabrielle sat back again, this time sinking against the bathroom wall, tears leaking from her eyes. "I'm … this …" Her hands shook as she attempted to wipe her nose.

"How long have you been throwing up, G?"

Her sister mumbled something that sounded like "last night."

"And you didn't call me? I would have come to take care of you."

"I didn't want to bother you."

Jenna blew her bangs out of her eyes and grabbed a tissue to mop up the wet streaks running down her sister's cheeks. "You're never a bother." Frowning, she studied Gabrielle's pale complexion. "Have you had anything to drink today?"

"Couldn't hold it down." Gabrielle's hand sat limply on her stomach, but then she lunged for the toilet again.

"That's it. I'm calling Nate Griffin." Cameron's brother was the only doctor Jenna knew well enough to call—and being cousins to the Bakers, he was Gabrielle's family in a way.

Instead of protesting, a pathetic whimper rumbled from Gabrielle's lips.

Jenna fished her phone out of her purse again and dialed Nate, standing to walk a little ways from Gabrielle. *Please don't be working, please don't be working.*

"Nate's phone, Elise speaking."

Oh, thank goodness. "Elise, hi. This is Jenna Wakefield."

"Jenna? Hi." A pause. "You do know you called Nate, not Cameron, right?"

Great. So even Cameron's mom thought Jenna had a thing for her boss. Jenna pinched the bridge of her nose. "Yes, I know. Is Nate there? It's kind of a medical emergency."

"Oh my. Yes, he's here. I'm just over making them all some dinner. Let me find him for you."

"Thanks."

Jenna peeked in at Gabrielle again, her throat constricting at the sight of her normally take-charge sister surrendering to some sort of food poisoning or illness.

"Hey, Jenna, this is Nate." His strong voice filled Jenna with momentary calm.

"Sorry to bother you at home, but I wasn't sure who else to call." Probably could have found Gabrielle's doctor's info, but this had been faster. Jenna started to pace. "My sister is vomiting a whole lot. She says it's been going on since last night and she hadn't had anything to drink."

"Right, okay. How far along is she now?"

She did the mental calculations in her head. "Thirty-two weeks."

"Has she been experiencing any headaches that you know of? Shortness of breath? Abdominal pain?"

"I mean, the normal Braxton-Hicks type pain." Jenna squinted, trying to remember. "And yeah, some headaches, I think."

"What about any visual impairments? Sensitivity to light, blurred vision?"

"Let me ask her." Jenna squatted on the cold tile again and stroked her sister's head, which was leaned back against the wall once more. "G, are you having any trouble with your vision?"

Her sister started to shake her head, then stopped. "Probably nothing, but I keep seeing flashing dots of light."

"You need to get her to the hospital now, Jenna." Nate's voice rang clear, almost forceful, in Jenna's ear. "She may have preeclampsia and that could be dangerous for both her and the baby. At the very least she probably needs fluids."

Jenna's whole body went cold. Preeclampsia? Didn't that have something to do with high blood pressure? "O-okay. I'll get her there ASAP." Her lungs tightened and she blinked hard. "Tyler isn't here. I should call Tyler. But I guess I can do that when I get her to the hospital. Lifting her and getting her out to the car might be a challenge, but I'll figure this out."

Get a grip, girl. If Gabrielle hadn't been right next to her, Jenna would have slapped herself.

"Hang tight," Nate said. In the background, she heard the clanking of metal that sounded like keys banging together on a ring. "I'm on my way over."

"Oh, thank you, Nate." He only lived a few blocks from

Gabrielle and must have realized just how incompetent Jenna was in an emergency. "We're back in the master bathroom. The front door is unlocked."

Jenna hung up the phone and put her arms around her sister, whose head drooped onto her shoulder. Why couldn't she have inherited her mom's quiet strength like Gabrielle had? Instead, she was a complete spaz who needed to be rescued.

But her sister wasn't well. And other than Liam, Gabrielle was Jenna's whole world. So whatever Jenna's natural bent, she needed to pull it together right now. She had to be reliable, strong, for her sister's sake.

"It's going to be okay. Nate is coming over to help you get to the hospital." Her sister didn't respond. "Gabrielle? Come on, don't go to sleep. I know you're probably exhausted, but you've got to stay awake, all right? At least until we know what's going on with you and Baby Girl."

"Baby Girl?" Gabrielle's chin angled up. "Is she okay?"

"She's fine, Sis." *Please let her be fine.* Jenna placed her hand on her sister's stomach and rubbed. Baby Girl rustled around, and Jenna could breathe again. At least for now. "And so are you."

The cold hand of fear that Jenna knew so well started to creep its silent fingers up her arm, to her shoulder, down her back. Attempting to embrace her, it tugged her toward the ocean of despair—fear's feeding ground—and stroked her hand, a reminder that she'd never be free of it, no matter how hard she worked, no matter how far she ran.

It would always come for her. Jenna was its special pet. There was something inherently wrong with her brain, with the way it worked, the way she gave anxiety and fear more rope than other people did. At the very least, there was something wrong with the way she handled it.

Once it ensnared her, fighting free of the tangles was almost impossible. She'd done it before, but it had nearly killed her.

Biting her lip to keep from screaming, Jenna shoved away

her feelings and refocused on her sister. This was not the time to be giving in to fear. Gabrielle needed her. And while Jenna would never be able to repay what she'd stolen from Mom, at the very least she could take care of her sister, to whom she owed an even larger debt.

Swallowing the bile rising in her throat, Jenna squeezed her sister as they waited for Nate to arrive. "It really is going to be okay, Sis. I'm going to take care of you the way you took care of me all of those years. I promise."

CHAPTER SIX

ELISE

*H*ow had Elise's Friday afternoon gotten away from her so quickly?

She swatted at a gray strand of hair hanging in her eyes as she kneaded the dough, pushing and heaving and resting. Repeat.

This should have been done hours ago, but she'd sat down to read some books about women in abusive relationships—Jules had recommended she immerse herself in "the cause" to gain a more complete understanding—and when she'd looked up, the clock had somehow progressed three hours.

Now, her children would all be arriving in one hour for dinner. Even Chloe would join them, since she was driving down from the city for the weekend.

Early-evening sunlight cut through the kitchen window, bringing extra heat into the space along with the preheating oven. She glanced at the kitchen sink, where the Cornish hens—Charles's favorite—languished. Once they'd fully defrosted, Elise still needed to season and roast them, and that would take at least an hour.

Elise pounded the dough, tears pricking her eyes. Why was she even continuing to bother with the bread? It took two hours to rise before she could shape and bake it.

It was no use. At this rate, they'd have to eat at eight, and the twins' bedtime was seven-thirty, which meant Nate would want to leave by seven.

"Something smells delicious in here." Charles breezed into the kitchen, hair slicked back and fresh from the shower he'd taken after a Friday shift at the hospital. The scent of his sandal-wood cologne drifted past as he approached her, nipping off a piece of a cookie from the platter she'd made this morning.

He bit into the cookie and *mmm*ed. "You have a gift, my dear."

Her cheeks warmed at the compliment. "Thank you." For a moment she looked at him, willing him to ask her what else she'd done with her day.

But he stepped away and sat down at the table across the kitchen, reaching for the newspaper without another word.

Of course he didn't care what she'd done. Or maybe he assumed that today had been just like every other day—that she'd cooked and cleaned and maybe gotten coffee with a friend. And why should he think any differently? It wasn't as if she'd told him about helping Jules with the Barefoot B&B remodel and transformation yet, even though she'd been working on research for it since the city council meeting a week and a half ago.

At first, she'd told herself the reason she hadn't enlightened him was because there hadn't been time. He'd taken another business trip earlier this week. He'd worked late every night. They'd hardly had a moment together.

But then she remembered those early years of marriage when he was a resident working eighty-hour weeks. How she'd met him in the hospital parking lot for fifteen-minute dinners, snatching any spare moments with him that she could.

So it couldn't be a time issue. No, instead it was a heart issue. There was something about the whole project that felt intensely personal, something that made her feel useful and seen, as if she had a purpose again. And revealing that to him, even just in part, would feel like a peeling away of her vulnerability, of her shell.

In the past, she would have had no problem with that.

But that was before he'd betrayed her.

She didn't want to be a bitter kind of woman. And she wasn't —she didn't think so, at least. But though she'd forgiven him, she couldn't make herself forget, not when the very act of looking at him sometimes hurt. It ached like a too-deep, always-present muscle pain that a person began to ignore because she'd grown used to it—because she'd grown convinced that it may never go away.

Elise continued to knead the bread, unable to stop because it wasn't in her nature to leave projects half completed. But maybe it wasn't possible to throw herself into this project with Jules, not if it meant forsaking her duty as mom, wife, and grandma. If today had shown her anything, it's that doing one meant she didn't have as much time for the other. And she wanted to be available to her family if they needed her.

A bit of flour flew from the counter onto her sweat pants and black shirt. Not like her children weren't used to seeing her unkempt, but it would be nice to have time to grab a shower. Her armpits had grown sweaty while standing here.

The dough squeezed through her fingers, the same color as her skin. Same consistency too, from her flabby arms to her tire-for-a-middle.

No wonder her husband never touched her anymore.

Elise sighed, shook her head, and stepped away from the dough. That was enough for now. Hopefully it would rise, just probably not in time to feed anyone tonight.

"Everything okay? You seem ... stressed."

Her eyebrow quirked at her husband's remark. If he could sense her mood so well, then why hadn't he said anything about the lack of warmth between them the entire last year? But it's not as if she'd said anything either, so perhaps it wasn't fair to judge him for it. "I got behind on dinner."

Charles folded the paper and glanced at his watch. "Aren't the kids due to arrive at five-thirty?"

"Yes." After washing the dough from her hands, Elise trudged across the kitchen toward the pantry, where she pulled out a variety of spices. When she turned, hands full, she nearly dropped the jars at the sight of Charles standing behind her, blocking the doorway. "Whoa."

"Sorry." He stepped out of the way so she could maneuver past him and set the spices onto the counter. "I just had a thought. What if we went to the Bar & Grill tonight?"

No, no. Food was the one thing she did well. The one thing her family still allowed her to do for them. Her kids had always loved her cooking—it was what brought them together, even though they were all living their separate lives. "Dinner will be a little late, but I've got it."

"Elise." Charles cupped her elbow, and her world stilled.

How ironic, after years of being intimate, that so tiny a touch would send rockets of adrenaline flooding her body.

Goodness, she was a foolish woman.

"Elise," he repeated. "Go shower and change, and I'll take us all out for a family meal."

"But …" She blinked, staring for a moment at where his fingers held her arm.

Clearing his throat, he dropped his hand and slipped it into the pocket of his slacks. "What do you think?"

"Friday nights are always busy." And she had wanted to have everyone here, in the place where they'd raised their kids.

She'd wanted it to feel like a home again.

But how could she tell Charles that without sounding like a petulant wife who still held his mistakes against him? She didn't want to feel the way she did. How she wished she could forget, move on.

But the coldness that lingered in these walls lately wouldn't allow her to do so.

"I'll make reservations for six o'clock. The kids will love it. When was the last time we went out all together?"

"I suppose that sounds nice." Turning on her heel, she went upstairs and got ready. When she came back down, Charles waited on the couch, phone in hand.

He didn't glance up. "I told everyone to meet us there."

"Okay." She ran her hands down the purple-and-white dress she'd purchased a few years ago. It was rare that she dressed up these days—there wasn't a need for it—but she'd tried to make an effort tonight. She'd even squeezed her feet into three-inch heels that cut against her swollen feet.

Charles had always loved the look of her legs in heels.

He stood and looked at her—and for a second, it seemed like he might say something. But after a moment of silence, he palmed his keys. "Ready?"

Withholding a sigh, Elise stepped forward and grabbed her purse from the buffet. "Yes."

Her quiet whisper hung between them for a moment, suspended. She hated how it sounded—almost a request, a tugging beg to be noticed—but even more, she hated how her heart dipped when he turned and headed for the front door without another word.

They rode the short distance to Main Street serenaded by Vince Gill and some female artist with a syrupy voice. After parking, they stepped into the busyness of a downtown mid-August weekend. The Walker Beach Bar & Grill had always been a favorite spot for them. It's where she'd told him she was expecting the babies, though she hadn't known there was more than one at the time. It was also where they'd celebrated nearly every anniversary from one to twenty-five.

After that, they'd kind of stopped counting. They'd stopped celebrating.

Maybe even back then, she should have seen Charles's affair coming.

Her husband opened the door for her and they went inside, where a few dozen people waited for a table. The hostess greeted them, gathered menus, and led them through the main restaurant, where giant TVs tuned to sports channels decked the walls and big comfy booths speckled the room. They ended up out on the back wooden deck.

The young woman placed menus on the ten-top table. "Your table, sir."

After Elise and Charles sat down, Charles picked up a menu, but Elise looked out across the expanse of ocean just below. The coastline dipped and turned as it made its way northward, where the Barefoot B&B sat currently out of view, waiting for a chance at redemption. Several miles beyond that, the outline of a lighthouse made a blip on the horizon.

She filled her lungs with the salt-tinged air, trying to find the positives in tonight. They'd be able to see the sunset from here. It would be gorgeous. She didn't have to do the cooking or cleaning. And her family would be complete for the first time since Christmas, the last time Chloe was able to make it back to Walker Beach.

"Yo, Mom. Dad. Look what the cat dragged in."

Turning, she caught sight of Cameron with his arm slung around their oldest daughter.

Having come straight from work, Chloe still wore a tailored navy blue suit that matched the fire in her cobalt eyes and complemented her strawberry blonde hair. She'd put on a little weight since Elise had last seen her, but who wouldn't with a high-stress desk job?

"Chloe!" Elise pushed away from the table and stood in time to meet her daughter and tuck her into an embrace.

"Hi, Mom." Chloe's voice was muffled by Elise's body. She pulled back, a tired smile on her face. "Good to see you."

"You too, baby." Elise patted her daughter's cheeks. Oh, it always felt good to be together again. Didn't matter how old her children were or how far away—she would always be their mother. Always worry about them. And things would always feel better when they were close.

Her little chicks.

"And what am I, chopped liver?" Cameron nudged himself between Chloe and Elise.

Chloe elbowed him in the stomach. "I see you haven't changed one bit while I've been away."

Placing his hand on his heart, Cameron closed his eyes and lifted his chin. "I'm hurt, sister dearest." He pointed to his hair. "I have, in fact, cut two inches from my hair since Christmas, and you didn't even notice."

Elise chuckled as her oldest and youngest—though really only born minutes apart thanks to her C section—bantered. Charles joined them and had soon engaged Chloe in a conversation about tax law as it involved his business.

The others would arrive soon, but Elise had a question for Cameron first. She turned to him. "How is Jenna doing?" Earlier this week, the woman had called Nate, clearly worried about Gabrielle. Nate had picked them up and taken them to the emergency department, where it had been confirmed that Gabrielle did indeed have preeclampsia like he'd feared. After they'd kept her for observation and pumped her full of fluids and medicine, they'd sent her home. The doctor had mandated bed rest for the rest of her pregnancy. As long as the condition could be managed, they wouldn't take the baby until thirty-seven weeks.

Elise had been home watching the kids, but when Nate got home the next morning, she'd gone to the hospital to sit with Jenna. The poor girl had been trembling, exhausted, pacing the room and staring at Gabrielle as if she'd seen a ghost. Elise and some of the women from the Sisterhood had sent a few casseroles over to Gabrielle and Tyler's once Gabrielle had been released, but Elise's calls to check on Jenna had gone unanswered.

Cameron scratched his chin. "Jenna? I don't know." He plucked a puka necklace from beneath his linen shirt collar and ran his fingers over a shell. "She's fine, I guess."

"Her sister was in the hospital—the same hospital where her mother died." Much as she loved her son, sometimes he lacked ... observation. "If that were me, I'd be a wreck."

While Charles and Chloe stood at the wooden banister of the deck discussing business, Elise and Cameron settled into their seats.

She reached for her ice water and cleared her throat, considering how to broach the subject she'd been wanting to speak with him about for the last week. But if she knew one thing about her son, it was that directness was the best course of action—or he might miss her meaning completely. "Cameron, you really should pay more attention to that woman."

"Who, Jenna?"

"I think she'd be good for you."

Cameron coughed at the same time an incredulous laugh left his throat. "Wait, like romantically?"

"Yes." She sipped her cool water. "If you haven't noticed, she's beautiful. Funny. Responsible. And she loves hard. Just look at how she treats her son and her sister."

Rubbing the back of his neck, Cameron shook his head. "But

she's a lot younger than me, and I'm her boss. I don't see her that way."

The way her adult son fidgeted—just like he had as a toddler when he'd wanted dessert but had been instructed to sit still—told Elise all she needed to know. Cameron had feelings for Jenna, all right. But perhaps he didn't even realize it himself.

Maybe all he needed was a little ... push. "I've been getting to know her better lately. If you'd like, I could talk to her about you—"

"Absolutely not, Mom." His curls bounced with the adamant shaking of his head. "Besides, I'm kind of with Monique still."

"Kind of with ..." She groaned. "She seems like a perfectly nice girl, but Jenna ... Jenna is something special." Elise pointed at him. "And I think you know it."

Cameron's jaw tightened as he stared at her. "No offense, Mom, but you should really stop meddling."

The last word stopped her heart. "I'm not meddling. I love you, and I can see what's best for you in a way you might not be able to, and—"

"In case you haven't noticed, I'm a thirty-six-year-old man. I don't need my mom telling me who to date. Stop trying to take care of everyone else. It's not your job anymore."

Voices erupted behind them, including Lauren's and Aaron's loud shouts. More of her kids and grandkids must have arrived.

But Elise couldn't move. The chair was fused to her, part of her. Frozen, just like her.

Cameron sighed, ran his hand through his hair, and leaned close. "Sorry, Mom. I didn't mean to get upset. I love you. You know that, right?"

Forcing a smile, she patted his arm. "Of course, dear. I'm sorry for ... meddling."

With a nod, Cameron stood and turned to greet his siblings, niece, and nephew.

"It's not your job anymore."

If ever there was a sign that Elise should throw herself fully into a new project, it had just hurled across the universe and smacked her upside the head. Because right now, Elise was like a tree blown free of all its leaves, all its fruit plucked clean years ago.

But trees cycled through seasons of giving up and producing. So perhaps it was finally time for a new season of growth.

CHAPTER SEVEN

JENNA

*H*ad she ever known the meaning of *tired* before today?

Jenna hid a monster yawn behind her disposable coffee cup from Java's Village Bean as she stood in the lobby of the Barefoot B&B on Monday evening, listening to Jules Baker giving assignments and directions for the first official town-wide renovation effort.

"Thanks for being here, everyone." As always, Jules was effortless in her address of the crowd. Dressed in a pair of overalls that featured paint splatters, her hair pulled back, the woman was ready to work. "I know you have other things you could be doing, but I'm proud to have you here working alongside me."

As she splashed back a sip of coffee, Jenna couldn't deny that it would have been nice to spend the evening at home. Between working fifty hours, sitting with Gabrielle first in the hospital and then for the last five days at home, waiting on her sister hand and foot—at Jenna's insistence, not Gabrielle's—and trying to spend time with Liam, the last week had been more than brutal.

And of course, last night, just before she had drifted off to sleep, she'd remembered the school loans—the ones she had yet to apply for. With school starting in a week, she literally couldn't afford to wait. So Jenna had dragged her sorry bum out of her cozy bed, and her muddled brain tried to make sense of the FAFSA. Hours later, when she'd finished, she'd made it back to bed only to lie awake thinking about her to-do list.

About how this seemed like exactly the wrong time to start school.

Now here she stood, surrounded by townspeople who had come together on a weeknight to renovate the inn, because she'd committed to it and because Jules was counting on the Sisterhood for support.

But Jenna would make the best of it. At least she would get to spend some time with Liam. She slipped her arm around her son's shoulders, and man, when had he gotten so tall? She may have promised him ice cream if he spent one of his last nights of summer vacation helping out, but she had a feeling he would have agreed regardless.

He was just that kind of kid.

The same kind who, when she'd gotten up the nerve to question him about his desire to go to space camp, had merely shrugged and said he'd rather spend fall break in Walker Beach.

Now, her son looked at her, a question in his chocolate eyes —eyes that were exact copies of his father's. But the concern in them proved that he was nothing like Brock, not in the ways that mattered. Thank goodness, since her ex had been the type of guy who would knock up an underage girl, tell her to get an abortion, leave her alone and pregnant, and then get thrown in prison for first-degree robbery.

She sure knew how to pick them, didn't she?

Jenna offered Liam a conciliatory smile, ruffling his hair before dropping her hand. As Jules continued by thanking Elise

Griffin for all of her organizational efforts, Jenna scanned the crowd. There must be at least thirty people here, and more had signed up for future slots.

All of the women from the Sisterhood were in attendance, except Quinn, who had volunteered to sit with Gabrielle so Tyler could come. The woman probably had the bedside manner of a lion. Jenna may have been surprised to see Elise at the Sisterhood meeting—and yeah, a tad embarrassed, since she was positive the woman could sense Jenna's love for her son—but Quinn? Well, the fact *she* had joined the Sisterhood hadn't sat well with Jenna, but there was nothing she could do about it except accept Jules's decision.

Jenna's eyes continued to roam the crowd, and she located Tyler across the room where he stood with Cameron. How did the latter manage to make workout clothes look good? Gym shorts, a tight T-shirt, and sneakers weren't much different than his daily work uniform of board shorts, a white tee, and tan sandals, but there was something about the way he stood there, brooding and almost … serious. With his arms folded across his chest, biceps bulging—

Whew. Today was putting the T in *tired*, that was for sure. She normally had better control over her daydreaming than this.

Jenna wiped her lips just to make sure actual drool hadn't fallen out, and good thing, because just then, Cameron glanced up at her. She offered a tiny wave, but instead of the returning grin she expected, he nodded at her and then looked away. What was that all about? Although really, he'd acted strangely at work all day—not laughing at her stupid joke attempts and heading out extremely early for a kayak lesson, almost like he couldn't stand being in the same room as her for longer than necessary.

Had she done something to offend him? Was it even possible

to offend Cameron Griffin? Whatever. Just in case she had, she'd avoid him for the rest of the night. Things would be back to normal tomorrow—after she'd gotten some sleep. Because when this night was over, she planned to slip herself into a nice bubble bath and take a lovely trip to LaLaLand, where there were no sick sisters, no hot-but-unattainable bosses, and no decisions to be made about whether to start school.

Jenna returned her attention to Jules just as she was reading job assignments from a clipboard that had appeared out of nowhere.

"Bella, Shannon, and Ashley, I need you ladies upstairs cleaning out the guest rooms. Toss, donate, and keep piles. You know the drill." She ran her finger down the clipboard. "Jenna and Liam Wakefield, you'll be stripping wallpaper upstairs with the Tyson-Laureano family and Cameron Griffin."

Great. Her plan to avoid him caught fire in her mind, and yep, there was the smoke.

"And that's all!" Jules said. "Let's get to work, people. Elise and I will be here if you have any questions."

"Yes!" Liam pumped his fist in the air at the prospect of working with his best friend Jared's family. "Race you upstairs, Mom!"

Jenna laughed at his enthusiasm and shook her empty cup. "I'll meet you up there, all right? I need to find a place to toss this."

An *okay* on his lips, Liam ran up the creaking steps. If Jules hadn't had an inspector out last week who'd given the all clear to begin renovations, Jenna might be worried the whole staircase would collapse.

People scattered to their various locations throughout the inn. Most of the guys headed to the kitchen, where they'd be demo-ing the cabinets, flooring, and countertops—basically removing all traces of what had been there before.

She spotted an industrial-sized trash can in the far corner and crossed the room. And that's when she heard something she'd never heard in her life ... Cameron's voice, laced with anger.

"Really, Mom?" The man stood in front of his poor mother, whose pale skin was now splotched red. "Still trying to play matchmaker? I already told you that I didn't want to date Jenna. But you couldn't lay off, could you?"

Jenna's cup landed with a thud in the bottom of the trash can and for a moment she considered climbing in with it. Licking her lips, she blinked and stared into the black abyss—trying to shut out the terrible conversation, but unable to walk away.

What was wrong with her? She kept giving her heart to men who didn't want it. Not that she'd actually thought she ever stood a chance with him. But to hear it confirmed ...

Jenna glanced around. Shoot. It was just her, Elise, and Cameron left in the room. Thankfully, they hadn't seemed to notice her. If she could just inch her way to the staircase, maybe she could avoid awkwardness of galactic proportions.

Channeling all the grace of a prima ballerina, she took a step, heart hammering in her throat.

"Honey, I had nothing to do with the list assignments. That was all Jules." A pause. "After our conversation on Friday night, I wouldn't dare meddle again."

Jenna paused, the air suddenly thin. Again? What had happened Friday night?

Didn't matter. She had to get out of here before—

Her foot kicked a stray nail, which skidded across the floor. She froze, afraid to look up.

But when she heard someone jogging toward her, Jenna went into action mode and flew for the steps.

"Jen."

Nope. She kept moving, her fingers grabbing for the banister as she made a quick one-eighty around the bottom step and started upward.

"Wait. Jen." The pleading in Cam's tone made her finally stop. It wasn't like she could avoid the man forever. He was headed to the same place she was.

She tried to school her features into one of nonchalance and looked down at where he stood at the bottom of the staircase. "Oh hey, Cameron. Didn't see you there. You ready to go strip some wallpaper? Sounds like a blast, am I right?"

But instead of smiling like Cameron always did, he took a step toward her, his tall frame coming level with her shorter one even though she was a few steps above him. "What you heard back there ..." He rubbed the back of his neck. And no, she didn't notice how the motion made his bicep flex. Or how his breath smelled like his favorite minty toothpaste.

Sweet mother of pearl, focus, girl.

She shrugged, laughed. Did it sound as forced and garbled to him as it did to her own ears? "Don't worry about it, man. My sister is always hinting about you and me getting together. People can't accept that an amazingly attractive woman like me and a not-so-bad-looking guy like you could just be friends."

For a moment—one sweet, blessed moment—his eyes searched hers and it seemed like he might be leaning in, just a little ...

But then he waggled his eyebrows. "So what you're saying is, I'm the hottest guy in town."

"If that's what you heard, then sure." She patted him on the head. "Monique thinks so anyway, right?"

He waved his hand in the air. "Nah, that fizzled out. She was too high maintenance."

Her limbs tingled and something like hope fluttered in her belly.

But no. She'd just heard the truth—it didn't matter that he

didn't have a girlfriend anymore. He didn't think of Jenna that way.

And he never would.

"Oh." Was that all she could manage to eke out? Jenna bit the inside of her cheek. She needed to move on. But how could she when she worked with the man day in and day out? Hiding her feelings and pretending they didn't exist at all clearly hadn't worked. She couldn't keep doing this—loving him quietly. According to her counselor, at some point, the things bottled up inside always came out in one way or another.

So something had to change. Either she had to stop loving him or she needed to stop torturing herself with his nearness. And so far, despite all her efforts, choice number one wasn't happening. Choice number two meant quitting her job, and she couldn't do that right now because, hello, there was this little thing called bills she needed to pay.

So why have you never gotten a new job?

In that moment, the truth hit her—something she'd never quite realized. She'd stayed in a going-nowhere job just to be near him. Yes, there had been the bouts with depression that at times had made it difficult to work, but surely she could have found something in town that would have not only paid more, but been a lot more in line with her interests than working at a rental shop.

She'd been waiting for something.

Was it him?

Maybe. But she could see there was more too, now that a deeper longing had been awakened inside of her. She wanted more for Liam—and maybe also for herself. It was time to stop waiting around because she couldn't depend on anyone else to make her life better anymore. It wasn't happening unless *she* made it happen.

Unless she started school.

Somehow, someway, she was going to juggle it all. She was

going to do this thing, even if she had to become a permanent zombie to achieve it.

"Come on, Griffin." Turning to start up the stairs, Jenna took her first sure step in a while. "Last one up buys ice cream for Liam after we work our tails off."

Then she ran, Cameron's laughter and steps in pursuit.

CHAPTER EIGHT

ELISE

"*E*xcuse me." Elise sidestepped a couple taking up the entire sidewalk with their double-wide stroller during a mid-morning walk down Main Street.

August was two-thirds of the way over, which meant soon the summer tourism would dwindle. In the distance, halyards clanged against boat masts at the marina, and the ocean just on the other side of the downtown buildings continued its ever-present lullaby.

For once, she hadn't stopped to look in on each of her kids during her trek down Main Street. No, this time she had a new purpose and headed straight for Serene Art, the gallery that Jules Baker owned. Tucked between Kiki's Antiques on Main and the public library, the gallery was located at the south edge of the main drag.

The buildings may have looked similar on the outside—quaint and pastel, with white trim and large windows that welcomed passersby to peek inside—but inside each one beat a unique heart that invited people in with sincerity. It was one of many things Elise loved about Walker Beach. And now, it was *her* job to help make this town even more special. To make it even more welcoming to outsiders, to women who needed a second chance.

Clutching her book bag, Elise pushed through the front door of Serene Art. The well-lit but empty lobby boasted sparkling white marble floors and walls adorned with local art featuring everything from beach scenes to abstract designs. Soft fluted music trickled over the airwaves.

At the desk in back where incense burned, a rack displayed local-made jewelry, and Jules sat looking at the computer. She glanced up at Elise's entry. "Come in, come in. I'm just wrapping something up and then we can head out to lunch."

"Take your time. I don't have anywhere to be." Charles was out of town for the weekend again, so her evening plans included a large Dove Bar—just one ... she'd been good all week —and more of the riveting reading material that Jules had assigned to her. She'd invited Samantha and Brittany over for a girls' night, but Brittany had to work a twenty-four-hour shift and Samantha had plans with friends.

She ambled over to a painting that caught her eye. A woman was poised on the balcony of a large home, gaze fixed on the ocean. Her soft red hair blew backward, and the woman's arms were open, her eyes closed, welcoming the wind.

Below the balcony stood a man. He appeared much shorter than the woman—maybe half her size—and his hands were clasped together as he stared at the figure above him.

It was as if Juliet was ignoring her Romeo. Although maybe he wasn't her Romeo at all. Maybe he had been, but he wasn't ... anymore.

"Do you like that one?"

At Jules's voice, Elise's hand fluttered to her throat. "Oh yes, it's, um, quite riveting."

She expected Jules to smile, but instead the woman stepped past her and ran her fingers over the paint, thick and gloppy in some parts. "It's the very essence of truth."

What a strange thing to say. Squinting at the corner of the painting, Elise saw the artist's signature. Her eyes widened. "It's one of yours."

"Mmm." Jules breathed out hard, then slapped on the expected smile and clapped her hands, eyes bright once more. "Ready to go?"

Hitching the strap of her bag on her shoulder to better secure it, Elise nodded. "Lead the way."

They crossed the gallery and Jules flipped the sign on the door to Closed, then locked up before they walked the short distance to the Frosted Cake. Downtown was growing more clogged by the moment as the lunchtime rush approached.

"I was impressed with how much we got done on Monday night." Elise hustled to keep up with Jules, who seemed to float in and out and through the crowd.

"Me too. And last night, my brothers and nephews all came over and did more demo-ing. We're redoing the fireplace and several of the bathrooms."

"Oh, that's wonderful." They approached the front door of the Frosted Cake, where a line already wrapped around the building. "I can't wait to see the end result."

Jules walked right past the line and held open the door for Elise. "I have been imagining it for months now, but it's been incredible to see others get in on the vision."

Elise entered the establishment, which was separated into the sit-down section in the back and the front section with the To Go counter. The dividing counter extended out, ending in a large glass display case where Josephine's devil's food cake called Elise's name.

Maybe she'd grab a slice on her way out.

No, better not.

Josephine was busy taking orders so Elise didn't call out to her, but offered her friend a wave as she and Jules passed by, heading for the tables in the back. Jules nodded at the hostess, a teen with a nose ring, and glided straight to a two-seater table by the window with a Reserved sign.

Did the Frosted Cake *do* reservations? Apparently they did for Jules.

When Jules and Elise sat, a server came and took their order, and Jules left to use the restroom. Elise took a moment to breathe in the surroundings. Not only did the place always smell like the best comfort food around—a blend of spaghetti sauce, chocolate, and mashed potatoes dripping with butter— but the eclectic beachy decor with lots of white space just had a way of making her feel at home.

The server returned with their drinks, promising a quick turnaround on their food.

Then Jules came back and pulled a pack of stevia from her purse, emptying it into the iced tea in front of her. "How are you feeling about everything?"

"What in particular?" It had only been two and a half weeks since Elise had approached Jules about helping with the Barefoot Refuge project. She and Jules had spoken several times regarding various tasks that needed to be completed to get the program started, but this was their first official meeting to get the particulars down on paper. Before now, they'd mostly been focused on getting the renovation underway.

"Let's start with the Sisterhood. Are you feeling good about that?"

"The women are lovely." And they were. Elise just didn't know if she was truly one of them. "I can see why you selected them."

"Can you?" Before Elise could respond, Jules waved her hand. "I think it's going as well as can be expected for women who don't know each other except as acquaintances."

"So you aren't concerned that some of the women have yet to open up?" In fact, only Jenna had so far.

"It's early yet." Twisting the turquoise ring on her index finger, Jules nodded. "They will."

"I'm not sure about Piper and Quinn." They would be much tougher nuts to crack than bubbly Nikki and sweet but spunky Heather.

"I have full confidence that they'll come around. But perhaps a little encouragement wouldn't hurt." Jules tilted her head. "I've been sitting back, letting the other women take the lead, but maybe it would help if we shared a bit more about ourselves." A pause. "Yes, good idea. I'll share a bit more of my heart tomorrow. What about you? Would you feel comfortable doing the same?"

Oh goodness. The very thought of any of those women finding out Elise's deepest secrets set her heart drumming. "There's not much to tell about me. I'm just a wife, mom, grandma."

"You are so much more than that." Jules smiled. "How about sharing your own dreams for the future?"

"My own? Oh. Well." Elise tapped the table. "I don't know about dreams, but I *have* found the reading you assigned to be very stimulating."

"Wonderful." Jules took the slight change of subject in stride. "How many of the books have you made it through?"

"Almost all of them."

"And? What did you think?" Jules sipped her tea. "Better yet, what did you feel?"

Just then, the server brought them their salads. Much as Elise had wanted to order her favorite—the chicken club sandwich with French fries and a Coke—the number on the scale yesterday had prompted a different decision.

Her stomach grumbled at her, but after thanking the server, she spread the ranch dressing all over the chicken Cobb salad and considered Jules's question. "I felt ... sad. And naive, I guess." The tines of her fork nudged the lettuce around her plate. "I've been so insulated in my safe world all of my life. I've known nothing of abuse or neglect."

Sure, her single dad had worked all the time, leaving her to watch her two younger sisters—in a way, making her grow up before she was ready. But that wasn't real neglect. It was just ... busyness. Survival. He'd needed Elise's help, and most of the time, he'd been kind about it.

Besides, those years had prepared her well for taking care of her husband and kids later in life.

"It's not just about the abuse, though, is it?"

"It's not?"

A noisy group of women bustled by their table.

"No."

Elise leaned in so she wouldn't miss Jules's reply.

"It's about so much more than a man exerting his power physically, mentally, or emotionally. That's the result, sure. But ultimately, it's about the betrayal of trust. And men who betray the women they claim to love are the worst sorts of people on this planet."

Elise flinched at the edge in Jules's voice—in the harsh truth couched within her words.

Because Charles *had* betrayed her.

But Elise hadn't suffered like the women she'd read about. She certainly couldn't compare the two. Straightening in her seat, she shook off the weight Jules's words had placed squarely on her shoulders. "I can't even imagine the horror of being in a relationship with a vicious man."

Charles wasn't perfect, that was for sure, but he'd never once even raised his voice at her. In fact, they'd rarely fought. Their policy had always been to forgive and forget. Don't let the sun go down on your anger and all of that.

It was only lately that she'd had trouble abiding by said policy.

Jules shoved her fork into a fat cherry tomato. The juice ran clear. "You are very fortunate." Then she stuck a mouthful of her Greek salad between her lips and chewed.

Something skittered up Elise's arms at the woman's reaction. Elise studied her companion, who was twenty years her junior. Everyone considered Jules Baker a strong, independent sort, but what else did Elise really know about her? Perhaps she had experienced a kind of unspeakable horror in her past.

And then something clicked in her brain, twisted her gut. "The painting in your gallery ..." Elise didn't want to pry by any means. Would Jules understand her unspoken question?

The corners of Jules's eyes crinkled and her lips flattened for a moment. "I painted that after a particularly brutal nightmare. That part of my past is long dead, but it sometimes still haunts my sleep. Painting is my way of fighting back, reclaiming my life, I guess. Reminding myself that no man owns me, no matter how hard one tried."

"Oh, I'm so sorry." Her throat dry, Elise took a hurried sip of water. "Is that ... is that why you're so passionate about this project? The Refuge, I mean."

Jules managed a small nod. "I was luckier than most. I had a hometown to escape back to, family and friends who were willing to walk me through recovery. But so many women ... have no one. Nothing. Nowhere to go. I want to give them that. A second chance, like I was given."

Wow. "I think that's amazing." Elise wiped at the corners of her mouth. "So how does the Sisterhood fit into that vision?"

Jules moved her gaze to the window and stared out across the boardwalk filled with a mix of tourists and locals marching along like a line of ants. "The Sisterhood was more Chrissy's heart than mine, but we saw how well our two dreams went hand in hand. We knew we needed one to make the other come true. That's how we always worked best—together."

Beyond the window, the sun glinted off the waves, the water like millions of diamonds moving in tandem.

Jules swiped at her cheek, where a tear had left a wet trail. "We loved this idea of women relying on each other, creating a bridge between each other's lives. And I guess what I want from all of this is for women—both those in the Sisterhood and those we help with the Refuge—to realize that there is hope beyond whatever is weighing them down." Her voice shook with passion. "That they can be independent and fierce. That they're not victims, but victors, because they've survived and they've fought back against what life has thrown at them. They haven't given up. Maybe they did at one point, but not anymore. Every woman's life has a purpose, and every woman has a strength inside of her even if she doesn't know it."

White spots danced in the corners of Elise's vision. Or maybe that was the resonance of Jules's fervor leaping out and vibrating on the air.

Elise wanted that for these women too.

But ... she also wanted it for herself.

She'd been sitting on the sidelines of her own life, allowing herself to be a victim of Charles's affair. She'd pretended it was all fine. She'd shoved anything she felt down deep, accepting her fate—accepting that a man like him wouldn't be satisfied with a wife who looked like her, a wife who was used up and spent at the ripe age of sixty-three ... even if she'd become this way while serving the family they'd created together.

Maybe Cameron was right—she *was* a meddler. Had she become so desperate to be *something* to someone, because she was *nothing* to Charles anymore?

Before she could cry and embarrass herself, Elise took a bite of salad. The spice-covered chicken melted in her mouth and the lettuce crunched between her teeth. She washed it down with a sip of refreshing water.

How was she ever going to help other women conquer their problems if she kept ignoring her own?

All of her planning over the last week had culminated in this.

Elise settled onto the picnic blanket she'd spread on the grass at one end of Walker Beach Park, which was tucked away in the forested upper end of town and surrounded by homes on the ridge that overlooked the downtown area. She popped open the wicker basket she'd stuffed full of Charles's favorite picnic foods—everything from mini chicken phyllo pies to kale Waldorf salad with homemade buttermilk dressing and a fruit salad that featured a colorful variety of produce.

"You've outdone yourself, Elise." Charles sent off a text message and set his phone onto the purple-striped blanket. "Might I ask the occasion?"

She was still trying to figure that one out herself. It had been a week since her discussion with Jules at the Frosted Cake, and Elise had been thinking—and overthinking—what she wanted to say to Charles … and how she wanted to say it.

No, she didn't want a divorce.

But she needed … something. An acknowledgment of her pain, maybe. A way forward.

Because she couldn't keep living like this, strangers under one roof.

Getting on her knees, which creaked with the movement, Elise lifted a few plates from the basket. Her fingernails drummed against the white ceramic surface. "Do we really need a special occasion to go on a date?" The words came out a bit strangled, and the breeze came and twisted them up, up, and away.

"Of course not." Charles frowned. "But usually we just eat at a restaurant. I can't remember the last time we had a picnic."

Adjusting her position, Elise settled onto her rump, her legs extended straight in front of her. "Maybe it's time to shake things up a bit." She fluffed her long skirt so it covered her gnarled ankles.

As she got out a few serving utensils, early Friday evening activity swirled all around them. A handful of teenagers played a game of pickup basketball on the courts, and at least a dozen delighted children wound their way around the playground near the ramadas. Not far away, a man and a young boy flew a remote control helicopter. The distant buzzing vibrated in Elise's ears.

"I get the feeling you're talking about more than just our dating life."

She hadn't intended to dive right into the discussion about their future, but maybe it would be better to simply let it fly and see what happened. "You're right." She unsnapped the lids of each Tupperware container and stuck spoons inside the salads, then handed Charles a plate and nudged the kale mixture toward him. "It seems all we ever talk about is the kids and your work. I thought it would be nice to talk—actually talk—about other things."

Charles arched a brown-gray eyebrow as he plopped fruit and kale salad onto the majority of his plate. "What other things *are* there?" Then he took one of the smallest phyllo pies.

Elise's chest burned with all of the things she'd rehearsed in her mind.

But before she could speak, her husband followed up his question with another. "Like this project you've been working on? The Refuge?" He took a bite of food, chewed, his eyes thoughtful. "I didn't know you were interested in something like that."

Okay, not exactly the direction she'd been wanting to take this discussion. But it was the first time since she'd offhandedly told the family about her involvement in the Refuge that he'd really asked about it. Perhaps opening up about it would help ease them into the deeper discussion they needed to have.

"I didn't know either until I got involved. But there is so much to learn—not only about starting a charity, but about how to help these women."

"Are you sure it's what you want to be doing with your free time?" Charles swiped his lips with a cloth napkin. "It certainly is keeping you busy."

And how would he know? The man was hardly home but to eat dinner, and then he disappeared into his study or lingered on the couch watching television or reading his medical journals.

It was as if someone stood inside Elise's chest pumping up a balloon. Any moment, it might burst, but for now, everything simply got a bit tighter, a bit more difficult to breathe.

She didn't want an explosion—just a nice, clear, non-emotional conversation. After all, she was a sixty-three-year-old woman. A grandmother. She wasn't given to yelling or dramatics.

She could do this.

"I appreciate the concern." Elise selected a pie and nibbled on the edge. The sweet warmth of the flaky crust soothed the churning gut that had plagued her all day, ever since she'd decided that—once and for all—she was going to confront Charles.

Why was it so hard to talk with him? He was her husband, for pity's sake. She'd spent two-thirds of her life talking to him.

Swallowing, Elise wiped a few crumbs from her lap. "But it takes up no more time than your job, and I need *something* to do now that Lauren and Aaron are in school and Nate's schedule has changed."

"You could go back to work if you wanted." Charles held up his phyllo pie. "Not that I'm saying you need to. I'm perfectly content for you to stay home and keep cooking and caring for the house." He took another bite and gave a satisfied groan.

At least there was one way she could still please him.

But she was more than that—and she needed more than feeding *him* to satisfy *her*. Didn't he understand that? "I actually really enjoy it."

"I'm just saying that maybe you could take up some hobbies instead, or in addition to your time volunteering." He paused. "I know you've been wanting to try Pilates with Brittany. That could be fun."

The sweet fruit in her mouth turned bitter, and a sharp inhale left her choking and reaching for her water bottle. Had he really just suggested ...?

But why wouldn't he? Of course he looked at her and saw someone who should use her spare time to exercise.

If she hadn't been sitting, the sudden lightness in Elise's head would demand it. The whole park spun.

"Are you all right?" Her husband reached across the blanket as if to whack Elise on the back, but he left his hand dangling between them.

"No." Shame writhed through her, and Elise released an uncontrollable moan. "No, I'm not all right, Charles."

His eyes snapped to attention at her sharp tone. "Should we head home so you can lie down?"

"This isn't about me choking." The corners of Elise's eyes still watered and her throat burned as she stared at the blanket. "It's about the affair. I'm not all right. You cheated on me, Charles. And then, you just ... you have acted as if it never happened. And so have I. Or, I tried." She gripped her napkin in her hands. If it had been made of paper, it would be in shreds right now. "But I can't do it anymore."

Venturing a peek at Charles, her chin trembled when she saw the flash of emotion in his eyes.

He swallowed hard, lips turned downward.

And even though she was frankly terrified of the answer, she had to ask the question that had been ricocheting around in her head like a pinball in constant search of a home. "Why did you do it, Charles? Why did you … betray me like that?"

What did I do wrong?

Unlike Jules, Elise didn't want to believe that her husband was the worst kind of person in the world. But the fact remained. He'd had an affair with a woman half his age. He'd lied about it for over six months. And then, for some reason, he'd confessed it to Elise.

And she'd been so naive, first in not even realizing it had happened, and then, in believing that by saying "I forgive you," all would magically be healed.

She'd certainly learned her lesson, hadn't she? Because in saying the words, in asking the questions now, she'd been handed the pin she needed to pop the balloon inside of her. It had deflated her air supply, yes, but it also finally … at last … had eased some of the pressure, the ache that she'd been carrying for far too long.

The ache she'd been carrying alone.

And she couldn't do that anymore either.

"Elise." Charles licked his lips as he studied her, blinking. "I thought … I thought we were good. Why are you bringing this up now?"

Her jaw slackened. "Really, Charles?"

"I'm sorry. I'm just … I'm trying to wrap my head around all of this." His hand scrubbed his jaw, and the gold band on his fourth finger flickered in the fading sunlight. It mocked her, reminding her of all the broken promises.

Had she broken them first, or had he? Maybe she'd gotten too busy with the kids. Did he feel ignored? And yes, she'd let herself go physically, but she hadn't exactly had the time or energy to devote to that when chasing six children around, being a PTA mom, volunteering to serve as a church deaconess, and any number of other things she'd been doing for the last four decades.

"I've tried to be a good wife to you, Charles. Be a good mother to our kids. I know I'm not perfect, but that ..." Her chest heaved with the exertion of finally speaking what she'd been thinking for the better part of a year. "That doesn't give you the right to break our vows. To turn to someone else."

"I've already apologized, Elise. I'm sorry I hurt you. I was wrong." A storm cloud brewed in his eyes. "I didn't have to tell you, but I did. I wanted to make things right between us."

"Don't act as if you did me some grand favor in telling me. Is that supposed to make it all okay?"

"No," Charles sputtered, his eyes gawking at her. And no wonder—had she ever used this tone with him? With anyone?

Elise sighed and attempted to soften her voice. "I understand that *you've* been fine the last year tiptoeing around, presenting the picture of a happy couple to our children and the world, but I haven't been. I've tried, but I can't."

"I thought we were doing all right." He shook his head. "Yes, it isn't like it used to be, but we're older now. Nothing will be like it used to be."

And he was just ... okay with that? Okay with sharing a house but not their hearts? Not their bed?

She tried not to shiver. No, she wasn't the woman she used to be, the one with supple curves and a confident smile and the ability to hike a mountain on a whim. The one Charles had nuzzled and taken delight in before she'd gone and gotten pregnant and haggard and busy with children and a life that didn't revolve solely around him.

But she still had something to offer. What was it Jules had said? *"Every woman's life has a purpose, and every woman has a strength inside of her even if she doesn't know it."*

Elise Griffin may no longer be a size six, and she may not have a fancy career like the women Charles met on the job every time he traveled, but she wasn't going to cower in the corner anymore.

She was taking charge of her own life, because it was hers to live.

And hopefully, Charles would still want to be part of it. But if not ... then maybe she had to find the strength to discover what life truly looked like outside of him. Outside of *them*. Maybe her identity as Charles's wife had taken up far too large a space in her heart for too long.

She inhaled the sweet fragrance of the mango and strawberries on her plate. "We don't have to settle for that excuse, Charles. And I don't plan to."

Charles's head reared back, as if she'd struck him. "Are you ... leaving me?"

"No. Not yet." Elise bit her lip, her heart playing taps against her chest. "But I'm not all right with living like I've been living the last year, constantly worried that you're going to find something else lacking about me." She swallowed hard, her throat an inferno. "Or that you'll come home from your next business trip to tell me you've found someone new and are moving on."

"Elise, I swear to you—it was just the one time, just the one woman."

"And I wish I could believe you, but ..." She pushed her plate aside, shaking her head.

"What else do you want from me?" Charles spoke through clenched teeth.

She understood his frustration, but honestly ... "It's not about what I want from you. It's what I *need*—what we need as a couple. Because we're dying, you and I, and if we can't figure it out, I'm afraid ..."

And now the tears came, because she couldn't imagine life without him by her side, without her family surrounding them both on the holidays or just because—in their home, together. A family that was whole, complete, and nothing like the one she'd grown up with.

It had been her dream since she was a child, her mom gone,

her father working all the time to make ends meet. And it remained her dream even now.

What would happen if Charles decided it wasn't a dream he cared about anymore?

"Tell me what to do."

Elise grabbed for the Tupperware lids and snapped them back onto the containers. She'd lost her appetite. "How about … counseling?" With all of the emotions roiling through her, a third party who could mediate seemed a good place to start their healing as a couple. She'd already done the research and found the number of one who came highly recommended. Had even taken a leap of faith and scheduled an appointment for tomorrow.

And if Charles wouldn't go with her, she'd go alone.

"Counseling? Is that really necessary? People in this town … they'll talk."

Was the man's reputation all he cared about? Maybe so.

In one fell swoop, Elise gathered up the napkins and spare utensils and tossed them willy-nilly into the picnic basket. Then she snagged Charles's plate and her own—both still covered in food—and, standing, marched them over to the garbage can.

Releasing a wild grunt that, thankfully, no one could hear but herself, she flung all of it—real plates and all—into the receptacle.

Then, without a glance backward, she headed for the car. Let her husband deal with the rest of the cleanup.

After a brief walk, she finally made it to her SUV. Of course, she'd left her purse and keys back with Charles, so she leaned against the door, closing her eyes and trembling from her show of strength.

Was it strength, or had a sixty-three-year-old woman just thrown a tantrum?

"You're right."

Her eyes opened to find her husband standing on the curb, the picnic basket fisted in one hand, her purse in the other.

Charles stared down at the asphalt. "I wanted to pretend that it was all right because I wanted it to be all right. I didn't want to hear all the ways I'd hurt you." Inhaling sharply, he met her gaze, and a deep intensity burned there. "If you think we need counseling, then I will go to counseling with you. I don't want our marriage to end. I just want you to forgive me."

The words were on her lips to reassure him, but something stopped her.

A hasty forgiveness was not what was needed here.

She needed to process, and the only way to do that was counseling—which meant finally telling another soul about her marriage struggles.

About all of her struggles.

So, with a quick nod, Elise stepped forward, took her purse from Charles, and dug out her keys. "Okay."

Without another word, she unlocked the car and climbed inside.

CHAPTER NINE

JENNA

*L*ife was better with dessert—and friends.

Jenna pushed away her cup, leaving half a scoop of olallieberry ice cream to languish at the bottom. "I don't think I could eat another bite." When she and the other ladies from the Sisterhood had decided to go out for ice cream after their fifth meeting—how crazy that it was the end of August already!—her eyes had been much bigger than her stomach. But now, that stomach ached with how quickly she'd filled it.

"Me either." Heather groaned as she sat back in her orange chair. "But no regrets."

All around their large table, the women giggled. A half-hour ago, Jules and Elise had excused themselves, but the rest of the ladies—even Quinn—had stayed to chat a bit longer. Other than their group, the only other person in the establishment was the single teenage employee sweeping in the corner, earbuds stuck in his ears as he wiggled his gangly limbs and used the broom as a mic to sing a song only he could hear.

An ice cream parlor that doubled as a fancy organic coffee shop, Java's Village Bean was next door to Rise Beach Rentals, so Jenna had found herself here quite often for a coffee pick-

THE INN AT WALKER BEACH

me-up in the last week since she'd started school. It wasn't the smartest financial move, since the coffees cost about three dollars a pop, but it was survival, man.

"I can always find the room, no matter how full I am." Waggling her eyebrows, Nikki scraped the last few drops of her cookie dough ice cream out of her cup. A bit dripped onto her bedazzled Diva T-shirt—ironic, because Nikki was probably the least dramatic of all of them. But she did like to be on stage. A few weeks ago, she'd shared about her dream of going the distance with her singing—getting a record deal, touring. The works. And if anyone could do it, she could. Jenna wasn't all that musical herself, but even she could tell that Nikki's voice was something special.

"Aw, man. There I go again." Nikki snagged a napkin and wiped the melted treat from her clothing. "So Jenna, you were pretty quiet about school today. How's it going?"

She hadn't meant to hold back, but she'd wanted to give the other women space to share, especially since the last meeting had been taken up with Jules and Elise sharing all the exciting details about the Refuge—including a bit more about Jules's heart behind it. Jenna had been moved to tears to hear about Jules's fight to regain her identity after an abusive relationship had derailed her life.

The women had also talked about officially applying for 501(c)(3) status as a charity, connecting with domestic violence organizations and shelters in San Fran and LA, and their joint vision for how the program might work. After that, all of the ladies had gotten in on the discussion, pinging ideas off of one another as they ate a delicious picnic of Elise's fried chicken on the beach.

But if Nikki was asking, Jenna didn't have a problem with sharing about school. "It's good. Really good." More than good, actually. "For the next few years, I'll mostly be taking lower-level courses, like English and algebra or whatever, but I'm in an

Intro to Interior Design course right now and …" She sighed, her insides inflating with pleasure. "I know I'm only one week in, but I love it. Every minute. Even if it does keep me awake until three in the morning."

Quinn stood to throw her cup in the trash and headed to the counter to order something else. The Java employee hurried over, nearly tripping over the large black dust bin he'd been using to sweep.

Piper tossed back a sip of coffee. "I'm a night owl, but my job gives me the flexibility to set my own hours. I can't imagine working full time and doing school and taking care of your sister like you've been doing."

"Plus you've got a son." Heather's mouth swung to the side—not quite a frown, but not a smile either. "How's Liam doing with your newfound busyness? I wouldn't be able to get anything done unless Mia was in bed."

"Yeah, but Mia is four years old. You'll see—there's a big difference between four and ten." Jenna smiled despite the way Heather's question had ripped a little tear in the seam of her joy. "I'm still trying to do the things I did before—like eat dinner together, help him with homework if he needs it—but yeah, it's an adjustment for sure."

Speaking of Liam, she should relieve Gabrielle's mother-in-law of her pseudo-grandma duties. Genevieve had already agreed to be with Gabrielle and Liam tonight, but Jenna and Liam were staying the whole weekend at Gabrielle's house since Tyler was out of town for an emergency meeting in New York. Gabrielle had kind of freaked at the idea of her husband being gone with the threat of preeclampsia hovering over her head, but thankfully, bedrest and medication seemed to be keeping it at bay.

Of course, that didn't stop Jenna from keeping a careful eye on her. Things could change so quickly.

Jenna pushed back from the table and stretched, letting a yawn sneak out. Maybe she should grab a coffee to go ...

"Here." Quinn appeared at her side, a large lidded cup in her hand. "I figured you might be studying some more tonight."

"Uh, thanks. I am." Stick a fork in her, and Jenna would be electrocuted by the shock that ricocheted through her whole body. Quinn hadn't said three words all night except to answer Jules's question about her plans for the future—she was doing some freelance marketing work for now and still figuring it all out. Her answer had been stilted, professional. Not cold exactly, but ... well, she and her sister Shannon, who *was* Jenna's friend, couldn't be more opposite.

Before today, she'd always seemed to barely tolerate Jenna. Had definitely never done anything nice for her. And who could forget Quinn's former status as queen bee of Walker Beach High —the one who had ruled with a less than magnanimous spirit?

Maybe like Shannon had suggested, Quinn really *was* on a path to change.

Quinn shrugged and tucked a curl behind her ear, revealing the scar from a childhood car accident that traveled from her temple to her jawline. "No problem." She resumed her spot at the table.

Well, then. Jenna stood and tossed out a wave to the women, who still looked comfortable and settled. Turning, she headed out the door, clutching the warm coffee in her hand.

When she'd walked to the Sisterhood meeting earlier tonight, the weather had been just about perfect, and because she'd been cooped up all day studying, she'd relished being outdoors—even if it had meant a mile-long jaunt outside of town up to the Barefoot. But now, it had dropped into the fifties and a chilly wind nipped at the hairs on her neck, whipping her long earrings against her skin.

Jenna hurried as quickly as she could down Main Street.

Only a few places remained open this late at night—nearly eleven—but a smattering of younger people still lingered under the black antique-looking lampposts lining the road. After a ten-minute walk to Gabrielle's house, her hands trembled to open the door, but the warmth of the inside helped her begin to thaw.

Genevieve sat on the couch watching reruns of *Fixer Upper*. At Jenna's arrival, she muted the television. "Did you have a nice time, dear?"

Setting her coffee on the side table, Jenna sat, sticking her hands between her legs for warmth. "I did. How were your charges?"

The fifty-something woman laughed. She was as petite as Jenna, but carried herself with much more class, as the stylish blouse and slacks she wore without a single wrinkle could attest. "Liam beat me twice at Battleship. Gabrielle was ..." She smiled, shaking her head. "Well, my daughter-in-law is anxious to get her life back, and I don't blame her one bit. She's restless, but at least Baby Girl is still cooking healthily."

"That's what matters." Jenna peeked down the hallway, but the door to the master suite was closed. "Is she still awake?"

"I believe so, dear. She said she was going to read." Genevieve stood and slipped on a pair of low heels. "I'd better go. Thomas doesn't sleep unless I'm there, and he's got an early shift at Froggies in the morning." Thomas and Genevieve's pizza parlor had the best buffalo wings in town. She'd eaten those puppies almost weekly when she was pregnant with Liam.

"I'm sorry. I wouldn't have stayed out so late if I'd known that."

"Don't worry about it. I'm glad you got to go out with your friends. You deserve it with how hard you've been working."

If she had said that about someone else, Jenna would have agreed wholeheartedly. But the fact was, she didn't deserve a break. It was her own fault she was a struggling single mom without better job prospects. And it hadn't been enough that she'd ruined her own life—because before that, she'd ruined her mom's and then Gabrielle's.

Her own bad decisions had led her here, and only hard work and determination were going to get her anywhere else. And while she didn't deserve the good things, she was going to fight for them anyway.

After Genevieve let herself out, Jenna grabbed her coffee, slipped down the hallway to the room where she was staying, put on a pair of yoga pants, peeked in on Liam—whose unconscious head was at the foot of the bed, silly boy—and then headed to Gabrielle's room. She knocked lightly and popped her head in. Her sister sat up in bed, one hand absently rubbing her large stomach while the other held a book.

"Hey, Sis." Gabrielle set her book down and a tired smile streaked across her face. "Come tell me all about your meeting."

Walking around to the other side of the king-sized bed, Jenna climbed up and tucked her legs beneath the comforter. She took a sip of her coffee, which was nearly gone after that long walk. Despite being lukewarm now, there was just enough of the cream left at the bottom to give her a sugary blast of sweetness. "We are really starting to become friends. Who would have guessed it?"

Not her, after that first meeting. It had seemed like such a random group.

"Tonight, after Jules and Elise had gone, Piper said she'd been thinking about why Jules picked us all. She joked that we were the Lost Souls Club." Jenna rolled her eyes. "I don't know what she's talking about. Me? Maybe Quinn? Sure. But Piper Lansbury? She's the very opposite of a lost soul. She's so put together it's disgusting."

Gabrielle ran a hand through her hair, which was looking a bit on the greasy side. Maybe Jenna should buy her some dry shampoo. "You never know what other people are going through, Jen. They may look all starched and crisp on the outside, but on the inside, they could be just as lost." She nudged Jenna with her elbow. "But for the record, I don't think you're a lost soul."

"Just a damaged one." Jenna chuckled.

"Don't say that."

"I was just kidding." Not really, but why was Gabrielle getting defensive? It's not like Jenna had insulted *her*.

"I hate it when you put yourself down." Gabrielle ran her hand over the amethyst-colored comforter, as if smoothing out a wrinkle that wasn't there. "I wish you could see yourself like I do."

"I thought you saw me as your annoying little sister," Jenna teased. "The one who used to steal your clothes, played her music too loud, and was the reason Mom had to quit nursing school."

Oops. Stupid tired brain, bringing up things that didn't need to be discussed.

"What are you talking about?"

"Nothing. What did you do all night? Go for a run?"

"You're hilarious." Gabrielle narrowed her eyes at Jenna. "But back it on up. Why do you think you're the reason Mom quit nursing school?"

"It doesn't matter." Setting her coffee cup onto the nightstand, Jenna sighed. "I'm tired and don't really want to talk about that, okay?"

Gabrielle remained silent for a while. Her finger traced a gold thread that looped in a random floral sort of pattern on the bedspread. "So what *do* you want to talk about? How about the fact you're barely sleeping?" Her sister peeked up at her. "Jen, I'm worried about you."

"About me? Why?"

"Because. You're a mom, work full time, and have been helping me out a ton—and now you've got school. It's just a lot."

"I'm fine, G."

"You say that ... but it's the same thing you used to say even during your worst bouts with depression."

Oh, Sis. Always worried about her little sister, and for a good reason. Still. "This time is different. I really am okay." She'd wasted her life long enough. Ruined so many chances. And now, she was finally—finally—able to deal with life. So what if it made her a little tired? It was totally worth the prize at the end of the road.

"You have to be stressed, right? But you never really talk about your feelings. You just joke around, and I can't get a feel for how you're honestly doing with it all."

"I talk about my feelings with my counselor."

"You haven't been to your sessions the last few weeks."

Her stomach hardened. "So now you're checking up on me?"

"No. Liam told me." A clock in the hallway chimed midnight. "He's worried about you too."

A groan rattled in Jenna's throat as her hands rubbed her face from top to bottom. "I've been so busy. But I promise I'll go back to counseling next week, all right?"

"All right." Gabrielle reached between them and took Jenna's hand, squeezing. "I just love you, you know? You, Tyler, Liam, and Baby Girl are everything to me. After losing Dad, then Mom ..." Her sister pushed out a breath. "You're more than my baby sister. You're my best friend, Jen. And I just can't stand the thought of something happening to you."

She knew what her sister feared—that Jenna would go back to being the depressed, can't-get-out-of-bed mess she'd been just a year ago. That maybe, next time, it would be worse. No, Jenna had never actually gotten suicidal, but there had been times she'd teetered close to the edge.

Closer than even Gabrielle knew. It was what had finally scared her into getting help.

And yes, her counselor and her doctor had warned her that this pivot out of depression's clutches wasn't necessarily permanent, that there might be setbacks or triggers in the future, but they *did* believe with maintenance and monitoring she could live a "normal life."

Whatever that meant. Jenna was still herself, and she couldn't blame every bad thing in her life on her depression. That hadn't kicked in until after Mom had died. Until after Jenna had thrown away her dreams for the future by sleeping with a man much too old for her—and a criminal at that.

Yeah, she'd made a mess of her life long before depression had come knocking. And maybe the depression had been her punishment, the natural consequence of her own actions. Of course, her counselor, Danielle, had said that wasn't true—that it was a disease as much as heart failure or cancer.

And Jenna believed that, for other people. But something about her just wasn't—

Stop. "Focus on the good." Danielle's words in her head again.

Right. The good. Because Jenna had Liam now. And she was pursuing those dreams she'd once thought dead—albeit a decade later than she'd planned.

"Nothing's going to happen to me. I'm better than I've been in a long time." Jenna snuggled up next to her big sister, their shoulders touching as they leaned back against the soft silky headboard. "And so much of that is because of you. Your belief in me. Don't you know?" She choked on the words as tears burned her throat. "You and Liam—your love—saved me. Everything I do … it's for you guys."

And she wasn't going to let them down. Not this time.

CHAPTER TEN

JENNA

$\mathcal{I}$t wasn't professional in the slightest, but Jenna had the urge to lift her hands in the air and let loose a *whoop-whoop.*

Of course, she didn't. Instead, she kept her back ramrod straight in Cameron's office chair and tried to hold in the crazy grin fighting for control of her lips as she listened to her professor praise her first project.

"I was particularly intrigued with your use of lighting and space in the kitchen. Quite unique." On the other side of the computer screen, Renee Champion lifted a well-formed eyebrow. With a sleek blonde bob, tailored jacket, and silver hoop earrings, the forty-something woman was the height of style and professionalism—which made the fact that she found Jenna's work more than satisfactory even crazier to believe. "Where did you get your inspiration for that?"

The door to Cameron's office squeaked open and her boss stood on the other side. Hadn't he heard her say she needed to use his office for a fifteen-minute video chat and to please not disturb her? Ideally she'd be home, but her professor only had office hours on Friday at four, which was right during Jenna's workday. And considering it was the Friday before Labor Day weekend, they'd been busier than usual.

She slid her hand across the desk—hopefully out of sight from the camera—and tried to wave Cameron away while still looking at the computer screen. "Thanks, Professor. I'm constantly looking through magazines and websites for ideas, but I really just considered what the occupants of a luxury housing development would desire." Jenna shrugged, all too aware that Cameron leaned against the doorjamb listening in. The snoop. "I also interviewed a few folks in that age and income bracket to see what they'd want in a home like that."

"Very good, Jenna. What I see a lot of students doing is designing a space they'd like, based on their own experiences." The woman tapped her red fingernails against a printed page on her desk. "If you show even half as much instinct and talent in future projects and courses as this one, you will have a long and successful career ahead of you."

"Th-thank you, Professor Champion."

From the corner of her eyes, she saw an "I told you so" smirk sweep across Cameron's features. Jenna resisted the urge to stick her tongue out at the man—adorable as he was.

See? All kinds of self-restraint going on today.

"I don't say things I don't mean." The professor pursed her lips a bit. "Is it possible for you to gain some real-world experience? An internship, perhaps?"

"I wish." With Cam's eyes boring into her and no air conditioning in the back office, the sweat glands in Jenna's palms tingled. "But I live in a small town and there aren't any internships to be had here."

"That's too bad. If you would ever consider moving to San Francisco, I could help you get one here—with my firm or another, I'm sure. I don't normally offer that sort of thing, but your age and work lend a certain maturity that other students in the lower levels normally lack."

"I'm honored." She'd never imagined having a mentor or making connections so quickly. "Thank you."

"Keep up the good work." Professor Champion's eyes flitted upward for a moment and returned to the computer screen. "I have another student waiting for a meeting, so unless there's something else …?"

"No, no, you answered my question about the next assignment, so I'm good."

"Wonderful. Chat with you soon."

The screen went dark. For a moment, Jenna just stared at it. Had that really happened? Were her dreams really, actually, maybe coming true?

"What about the Refuge?"

She started at Cameron's voice. How could she have forgotten he was there? Especially since the last few weeks—two and a half, to be exact … but who was counting?—since overhearing his conversation with Elise at the Barefoot B&B had made things awkward between them.

Okay, fine. She was probably the only one who felt it. Cameron acted like nothing was different.

And for him, it probably wasn't.

Jenna popped her computer lid closed and pushed away from Cameron's office chair. "What about the Refuge?"

"Your professor said you should get some real-world experience. What if you asked Jules if you could head up the interior design or decorating or whatever she has planned for the inn?"

A light flashed bright inside Jenna, like those old camera bulbs that went off when a photographer took a photo. But just as quickly, she shook her head and rounded the desk, laptop in hand. "That's way too big of a project."

"What's that? 'It's perfect, Cameron.'" He spoke in a high-pitched voice, obviously in an attempt to mimic hers. "I agree, Jenna. It *is* perfect."

No, it *would be* perfect. But she was too new at this, and the

117

project too important to screw up. Surely Jules had already considered who would be the one leading the design—probably Jules herself, as she was quite artsy. Or maybe her niece Shannon, who also had a knack for decorating.

"Come on, admit it." Cam blocked the door. "I'm right."

She pushed his chest to move him. He didn't budge. "No, you're nosy. You weren't supposed to hear any of that. Ever heard of giving someone privacy?"

"I grew up with five siblings, remember? Shared a room with two of them." He squished himself against the doorway when she finally maneuvered past him into the hallway. Following her, he soon matched her pace for pace as they walked to the empty front lobby of Rise Beach Rentals. "All right, fine. I apologize for butting in."

She arched her eyebrow over her shoulder at him as she came to a stop. "Now was that so hard?"

"You have no idea."

She chuckled, squatted behind the front desk, and stuffed her computer into the laptop bag she'd purchased at the Goodwill a few towns over when she and Liam had gone back-to-school shopping. Inside, she found three of Liam's library books that needed to be returned.

"So, hey."

She popped back up, books in hand. "Hey, what?"

Without asking, he snagged the top book from Jenna's hands and looked at the cover. "*The Lion, the Witch and the Wardrobe,* huh? Can't go wrong with Narnia." Cameron gave a quick laugh.

Was he ... nervous? Why?

"Hey, what?" she repeated. Reaching back for the book, Jenna tugged, but Cam kept hold.

Finally, he released it. "Want to come over for pizza after work? We haven't hung out in a while and I want to hear all about how things are going with you."

If there was one thing her heart couldn't handle, it was even more time with Cameron Griffin. Turned out being super busy was a blessing in disguise. It not only kept her mind off what-could-have-been-but-definitely-wasn't, but also gave her the perfect excuse to avoid being alone with him outside of work hours.

"Sorry, can't. I need to—"

"Study. I know." Cameron pushed a hand through his blond locks. "You sure that's all it is? Sometimes it feels like you're ..."

"I'll be right back, okay? Gotta return these." Jenna tried to swoop past him, but he snagged her elbow. Her breath got stuck in her throat and she tightened her grip on the three Narnia books. "What?"

A glance upward told her he was closer than she'd thought. His breath feathered across her cheek. "You're not avoiding me because of that one night, right?"

This isn't happening. Jenna swallowed and squinted her brow in what she hoped looked like confusion. "What night was that?"

Cam's mouth opened but closed without a word. He shook his head. "Never mind."

"Be right back." Jenna's chipper voice probably wasn't fooling him, and if the raised hairs on the back of her neck were any indication, Cameron's gaze followed her the whole way outside.

Okay, so maybe he *had* noticed her strange behavior.

Chiding herself the whole way, she hurried south down Main Street toward the library. She entered the building and waved to the librarian, Madison Price, who sat behind the semi-circle circulation desk in the middle of the sprawling room.

The woman adjusted her purple glasses and pointed toward the kids' section. "I saw Liam and Jared head that way a while ago."

Oh, yeah. "I forgot Stephanie was bringing them here this afternoon." Jenna held up the books in her hand and set them on the desk in front of Madison. "I was just bringing these back."

"I'll take them." As Madison took the books, Jenna noticed her new engagement ring. Her fiancé was Evan Walsh, the mayor's son.

"How are your wedding plans coming?"

A pretty blush passed over Madison's cheeks. "We're hoping for next spring, but don't have a date set for sure. It's been hard with Evan in school and the Christmas festival and the mayoral race. So much going on."

Jenna had heard the race wasn't going in Jim Walsh's favor, not a fact anyone seemed all that sad about. How the man had managed to get elected the first time was still a mystery to her. As far as she was concerned, Bud Travis had it in the bag.

"I can relate. School and work are keeping me really busy too."

"And you're helping with the Refuge, right?" The librarian scanned each of the books and placed them in a stack on the desk.

"Yeah, I am." Thoughts of the Refuge filled her mind, whirling, churning, transforming. Its gorgeous potential just waited for a skilled hand to make it over.

Not that hers was skilled enough, but ... what if she did what Cam had suggested? Would Jules go for it?

Maybe it didn't hurt to ask.

Madison pushed her wispy brown bangs out of her eyes. "I've been meaning to get over there to help with one of the renovation nights."

"We'd love to see you there anytime."

After saying goodbye, Jenna rounded the corner toward the children's section. There were a variety of spaces—from one designed for preschoolers, a rainbow rug adorning the floor along with bins of puzzles and building blocks, to one created with older kids in mind.

The latter was farther back in the corner and featured an assortment of colorful chairs, tables, and shelves filled with middle grade chapter books. Liam and Jared took up two bean bag chairs, each kid with his nose shoved inside a book.

As Jenna grew closer, she was able to read the title of Liam's thick volume—*All About Space and the Race to the Moon*. Her heart thunked against her chest, and she nearly turned on her heel without saying hi, but at that moment, her son glanced up. "Mom?"

"Hey, dude." She waved at him and Jared too, who gave her the what's-up head nod. "I was just dropping off a few books I found at home this morning."

Lowering herself to the floor beside him, she leaned forward. "How was school? Are you guys doing a unit on space exploration?"

"No, it's just interesting."

Jared jerked his head up again. "Liam's obsessed with space stuff. He knows all the constellations and facts I can't ever remember."

He did? Why hadn't he ever told Jenna that?

Liam shrugged and brought the book closer to his face. "I like it, yeah."

"I wish you could go to space camp with me. My mom said signups weren't full yet."

Her son glared at his best friend. "I said I didn't want to go."

Like he was fooling anyone. "Are you sure, bud? It sounds pretty neat." Maybe she could ask Gabrielle and Tyler for help paying for it … just this once.

But no. Her counselor, Danielle, had been clear—she had to stop using them as a backup plan. It wasn't about pride. It was about developing real strength.

In this moment, though? She'd give anything to ease the crinkles at the corners of her baby boy's eyes.

Who was she kidding? He wasn't a baby anymore.

And he knew—just like she did—that there was no way she could afford to send him to space camp.

Clearing her throat, she tapped the edge of his book. "I'm all for reading for pleasure, but make sure your homework is finished first."

"That's what I told them too." Jared's mom, Stephanie, appeared, her three-year-old daughter Sarah on her hip. "Guys, we'll pack up and leave in about fifteen, okay? I've got to get dinner on."

Jenna stood. "Thanks again for watching Liam today. I'll swing by around six once I'm off."

"Not a problem at all. I remember what it was like being a single mom." Stephanie set her daughter down and adjusted her shirt. "It's the hardest job in the world."

Tears pricked the backs of Jenna's eyes. Even though Stephanie had certainly suffered when her first husband had died and left her with some major debt, she'd never known the shame Jenna had brought on herself. Still, it felt nice to have a bit of solidarity acknowledged. "We do what we can, right?"

"For sure." Stephanie followed her daughter a few feet down the first book aisle. "By the way, since it's Friday, Jared would love for Liam to stay overnight if you don't mind."

"Oh." She'd been hoping for a little extra time with him tonight. But he absolutely loved spending time with Jared and his family. And if she could give him even the smallest pleasures, like sleeping over at a friend's house, she would. "That would be fun for the boys."

"Good." Stephanie took her eagle eyes off of Sarah for a minute and shot Jenna a look full of meaning. Her finger crooked, indicating Jenna should come closer. Clearly she had something to say that she didn't want the boys to overhear.

Jenna stepped into the aisle with Stephanie. "Everything okay?"

"I just ..." Biting her lip, Stephanie stooped to re-shelve a book her daughter had pulled out of place and lost interest in. "I hope I'm not overstepping. But Jared told me that Liam doesn't bring anything to school for snack time. I'm happy to pack something extra for him."

"What? No, that's not necessary. We have food." Things had never gotten *that* bad. Even at their poorest, they'd had food stamps. So why wouldn't Liam bring a snack? Surely he wasn't depriving himself because he thought he was helping ...

She peeked at him. Thankfully, he didn't seem to have heard the conversation.

Jenna shook her head. "I'll talk with him about that. Or maybe I should just start sneaking an extra granola bar into his lunch."

"Okay. Like I said ... I don't mean to overstep at all." Stephanie worried her bottom lip.

Was there more? "You're not."

"So, I noticed Liam's shoes have holes in them and his pants are a bit short. I'm happy to give you some of Jared's hand-me-downs if you need them."

Cold reality slapped Jenna's cheeks as she glanced at her son. The *Star Wars* shirt he wore was a bit old and ratty, but it was his favorite. Still, Stephanie was right on the other counts. His pants rode up to mid-calf while sitting, and the soles of his sneakers were much more worn than the last time she'd looked at them closely—which, if she were honest, was not very recently. She'd just trusted he would tell her when he needed new clothing.

Her chin dipped and her lips wobbled as she attempted a smile. "I guess I've been a little preoccupied." And Liam hadn't said a word.

Of course not. Because he thought he had to be the parent. The one to take care of his mom—just like always. It didn't matter what she did or how hard she tried. She was failing him.

Failing to take the burden of responsibility from his shoulders.

Failing to notice what he needed.

What if all of these attempts to make things better for him were only making things worse, taking her attention from where it should be?

Jenna placed her hands on her cheeks and blew out. "That's really kind of you, but again, not necessary." She glanced at her wrist—which was completely dumb, because she didn't even wear a watch. "I'm sorry, it's late. I need to get back to work. I'll pick Liam up in the morning. Just have him text me with a time."

Before Stephanie could say anything else, Jenna hauled it out the front of the library. Each step of her feet pounded the truth into her skull.

Failure. Failure. Failure.

By the time she reached Rise Beach Rentals, tears streamed down her cheeks. She stepped inside—and right into Cameron's arms.

"Whoa, there." He laughed as she collided with his chest, but his laughter soon died when she didn't move—when, in all her weakness, she slipped her arms around his waist and buried her face in his shirt and let herself cry harder. And when Cam's arms came around her, cocooning her, and he set his chin on the top of her head, she hated herself for how safe and content she felt. "Jen? What's wrong?"

She couldn't answer, just sputtered her misery all down his shirt like the hot mess she was.

"It'll be all right." His hand moved up and down her back. "Tell you what … we're closing early, okay? And we're going to go get that pizza and go back to my place, and you're going to tell me everything."

She pulled back slightly and looked up at him, unable to protest—unable to say anything, really.

His thumb came to her cheek and he traced her trail of tears downward, wiping them away. "Or, if you'd rather not, we're still going to stuff our faces and we can just eat and eat until we explode. Maybe toss a movie in there that we can mock-watch. That sounds good, right?"

Good? No. It sounded amazing. Dangerous to her heart, but amazing.

So all Jenna could do was nod.

Turned out, stuffing her face with pizza really did make her feel better.

"I don't think I can eat another bite." Cameron tossed an unfinished slice of pizza—crust and all—onto his plate.

"Wimp. You only ate, what? Three and a half slices?" Jenna bit into her third piece and chewed, swallowed. "You're losing your touch."

They sat on the back patio of his two-bedroom rented bungalow, which was tucked away in the forested neighborhood behind the high school. It was six-something on Friday evening, nearing sunset. The wind was flirting with the ends of her hair and tickling her shoulders and all of nature played a symphony around her—from the rustling of the leaves in the tall California oaks that created a natural fence around Cam's small yard to the ever-quieting chattering of the birds above and the cicadas strumming along.

Her stomach hurt from laughing at Cam's ridiculous jokes, and she'd tamped down any negativity regarding Liam, school, and everything else that had caused her to rush like a mad fool into her friend's arms a couple of hours before.

Yep. At the moment, there was nowhere she'd rather be—and it had everything to do with her surroundings. And, of course, nothing whatsoever with the man whose slanted grin reminded her of that cat in *Alice's Adventures in Wonderland*.

Yep. She was one hundred percent fine with lying to herself. Mm-hmm.

From his seat across from her at the green metal table, Cameron leaned sideways and scanned her up and down. "I have no idea where you're putting all of that food, Tiny, but I must concede you to be the pizza-eating champ."

"You ate more than I did." Jenna set the rest of her slice down and wiped tomato sauce from the tips of her fingers. The chilly breeze rippled goosebumps across her bare arms. "Therefore, I can't be the champion."

"Yes, but if we consider our relative weights and how much we each ate as a percentage of that weight—"

"Ugh, don't make me do math!" Jenna picked up one of her nibbled-on crusts and flung it at him.

Laughing, he ducked and the crust landed with a thump in the grass. "Sorry, what was I thinking, asking the college student a math question?"

"Ha ha." Jenna stood and gathered the paper plates. "Just because I'm a college student doesn't mean I suddenly got super smart." She started inside with the garbage.

"Where are you going?" He leaped up and grabbed the nearly empty Froggies pizza box. "Don't tell me you're leaving already."

"I told you." With a *whizz*, the sliding back door opened and Jenna stepped inside. "I need to study." The warmth of the little kitchen laid her goosebumps to rest.

Cam slid in behind her and shut the door with his free hand, then popped open the garbage can for her. "But we didn't get to watch a movie."

"You can still watch one by yourself." After dumping the plates into the trash, she moved to the faucet and washed her hands. From the framed Bob Marley poster in the eat-in area to the fraying blue couch in the living room and the dirty blender on the laminate kitchen countertop, this place screamed bachelor pad.

For a minute, she wondered if any of Cameron's girlfriends had ever tried to girl it up. A vision came, unbidden and fast, of cushy gray sofas with a shag rug, clean lines, and a deep blue on the walls along with abstract beach art. Cozy, not exactly feminine or masculine, but a place where both a man and a woman could still feel comfortable.

A place she'd feel comfortable.

Inhaling sharply, Jenna dried her hands and moved toward the couch, where she'd left her purse. But before she got there, she was hauled off her feet. She squealed as Cameron tossed her over the back of the couch, then hopped over to join her.

She sat up, sputtering, mouth hanging open. "What was that all about?"

He shrugged, grinning. "I don't want to watch a movie alone. That defeats the purpose." He picked up the remote and flipped on the television. Without looking at her, he snagged a blanket off the arm of the couch and tossed it at her. "Here. I know you get cold easily."

The man was infuriating. "I'll only fall asleep if I stay."

"That's okay."

"But then you'd still be watching the movie alone. I might as well go home and study."

"I might be watching the movie alone, but I wouldn't *be* alone." His crazy grin made a comeback. "I could threaten to do something mean to you if you fall asleep. That would motivate you to stay awake."

"Sounds super tempting." Standing, she dropped the blanket to the floor.

"Come on, please?" He reached for her hand.

She froze when his thumb danced across her knuckles for the barest of seconds.

It wasn't like it was the first time he'd ever touched her. He was flirty, affectionate—just that kind of guy. And yet something in his eyes pleaded with her to sit.

Why was watching this movie so important to him? Sighing, she sank back onto the couch.

He released her hand and turned back to face the television. But before he'd made a selection, he hit the Power button. The screen went dark again. "Jen, about that night at the Barefoot. What you heard …"

Uh uh, they were *not* having this conversation. She leaned across him, snagged the remote, and punched the button to turn the TV back on. "So what were you thinking of watching? Let me guess—something Marvel related?"

"It wasn't about you. You know that, right?" What was the guy's problem? He kept right on talking, even though Jenna scrolled through the movie options on his screen like her life depended on it.

"Of course. We already talked about it." The icon on the screen stopped moving and she mashed her thumb down. Come on, come on.

Great, it had frozen.

Sighing, she gathered the blanket onto her lap and finally allowed herself to look at Cameron again.

He simply watched her, unchecked concern in his eyes. "Yeah, we sort of talked about it, but you've been acting funny for weeks. At first I thought it was just school and the fact you're way more tired than normal."

"Which is a completely viable explanation." Pulling her legs up to her chest, she draped the blanket over her knees and buried her nose in the soft material. It smelled of lemon and … was that curry?

"But you act normal around everyone else." Cameron turned his whole body so he faced her fully. His bare foot sidled up next to hers, but he didn't seem to notice—not unless he also felt the fire ants racing across his toes. "I know my reaction to my mom was extreme, but there's a reason for it."

Yeah. He didn't like Jenna. She got it. He didn't have to keep beating that dead horse.

"It's just that I never let myself think about my friends as anything other than friends. Not since ..." His nose wrinkled like someone had stuck a smelly gym sock in his face.

Jenna straightened. "Not since what?"

Groaning, Cameron made a fist and leaned his forehead into it. "Not since I fell in love with one of my best friends and she married someone else."

Ouch. "I'm sorry."

"Thanks." He picked up a corner of the blanket and rubbed it between his fingers. "But now you know why I've got a rule about dating friends. It makes things way less sticky to only date women I don't know all that well."

Even though she hated that he'd been hurt, some part of her was happy to know why someone as great as him had dated a carousel of random women—and only casually, as far as she could tell. "Thanks for sharing that with me." She nudged him with her foot. "And don't worry. Things between us are fine. We're good. I promise."

"I'm glad, because I miss this, Jen. We have fun together, but I can always count on you to listen if I really have something to get off my chest."

"That's what friends are for." The words stuck in her throat, salty and dry.

"True." He cocked his head. "Which is why I'm going to bring up what happened this afternoon—because we're friends and I want you to know I'm here if you want someone to talk to."

As tempted as she was to get the television working ASAP and drown out the opportunity for confession with blazing guns and hot demi-gods like Thor and Captain America, Jenna couldn't deny it would be nice to talk with someone other than her counselor—who she'd called up after her chat with Gabrielle last weekend. "What do you want to know?"

He pulled half the blanket onto his lap so they shared. Their commingled body heat filled the space between them and oh, how she wished she could lean into it.

"You kept saying, 'I don't want to fail him.' Who were you talking about?"

Her lips trembled at the memory, and she stared down at the blanket as the awful shame pummeled her once more like a rag doll standing in the surf.

"Liam?" His gentle prompting brought her back.

Glancing at him, Jenna nodded. She shouldn't share any of this with him, the guy she wanted to be so much more than a friend. Could her heart really take any more pounding?

But then he scooted forward just slightly, draping his arm over the back of the couch so he could touch her shoulder. The pad of his thumb rubbed gentle circles there as he waited for her to share.

If she didn't leave or start talking, she was liable to lean forward and kiss the man.

And since there was no way she was leaving—yeah, yeah, she was weak—Jenna took a deep breath and told him what had happened at the library. About the effects of her depression on Liam, how it had changed him. About how, more than anything, she just wanted to give her son a good life, to make his dreams come true, to send him to space camp this fall.

"But I'm not sure I can escape the truth."

"The truth about what?"

Biting her lip, Jenna angled toward his touch, though it took her a moment to realize she'd done it. "That I'm a dream destroyer to everyone I love."

And there came that scrunched-up nose again, this time with a good dose of droopy eyebrows. "What are you talking about?"

"I thought everyone in town knew the story." Jenna couldn't help the snarl in her lip. "When I was twelve, I got suspended for having pot at school. So my mom—who had always dreamed of becoming a nurse—quit school to spend more time with me."

Which, looking back in a selfish sort of way, she was actually grateful for, since Mom had died just three years later. But she still couldn't push past the sick feeling that she'd ruined Mom's chance of happiness.

Jenna kicked off the blanket and stood, moving away from Cameron. She didn't deserve his comfort.

"Jen—"

"Then after she died, because I slept with some loser who was years older than me, my sister couldn't join the love of her life at college in Florida." Moving closer to the television, she paced, hands flying. "She stayed here for ten years, giving up everything to take care of me. I nearly destroyed her dream. If Tyler hadn't moved back ..." Jenna shook her head. "And now, I'm doing the same thing to Liam. He's stuck with a mom who spent all this time being depressed and now is such a loser that—"

"Hey." Cameron stood and approached the mantel. "I'm not going to let you talk about my friend like that."

Oh great. How was it possible for her to have even more tears at the moment? She shoved them from her eyes, furious with herself. "I just love that kid more than life itself, you know?"

"Yeah, and he does too." A pause. "And guess what else I know?"

The sun had completely gone down outside now, leaving them in relative dimness since they had left the light off in anticipation of watching a movie. Cameron stood inches away, and though they weren't touching, she could feel the connection between them. Could feel the warmth of his nearness, the solidness of who he was, all bundled in a handsome six-foot-something exterior.

"What?" The word emerged raw, because in this moment, that's exactly what she was—unrefined, unpolished, chafing.

"You, Jenna Wakefield, are strong and fierce and ... amazing."

She snorted her disbelief, and in an instant, Cameron

stepped forward and his large hand cupped her chin. "I'm serious." He slid his other hand around her waist, tugging her to him and leaving her with little breath in her lungs. "Liam is lucky to have a mom like you. It's not easy to look your past in the eyes and say, 'You don't own me anymore,' but that's exactly what you've done. If it were me, I think I'd have more choice words for my past, but you're much more graceful."

Now he had her laughing. Okay, laugh-crying. "That's me." She rolled her eyes. "Just call me Grace."

The twinkle in his eyes abated, growing more serious. "Jen."

Her hand found his chest, her fingers digging into the fabric of his T-shirt like it was a lifeline. And, maybe, it was. *Oh. My. Goodness.* Just shoot her now, because the rest of life couldn't possibly feel as glorious as this moment.

"First of all, your depression—that wasn't your fault." She opened her mouth to protest, but he plowed on. "And these years when you're trying to work and do school and be all the things to all the people are going to be hard, no question. But Liam is going to look back and see that the whole time you were fighting for him. You're not a dream destroyer, Jenna." Cameron pressed his lips against her forehead. "You're a dream maker. A warrior. And those of us who get to be close to you ..."

Silence hovered between them. Her eyes flicked upward— and then she shivered. Even in the dim light, she could see the desire in Cameron's eyes. The way he licked his lips, leaned closer just a touch ...

And suddenly stepped away, leaving the space between them cold, unfeeling.

Dead.

"Um, hey. I have an idea." Pivoting away from her, Cam walked to the far wall, flipped a switch, and flooded the room with light.

Jenna's eyes—and more than that, really—recoiled at the sudden reality check.

What had just happened? Every nerve in her body felt like a firecracker that had fizzled and plummeted to the ground.

"W-what idea?" She moved back to the couch where he now sat, lowering herself and leaving several feet between them.

He grabbed his computer off the coffee table and opened it. "Scholarships."

Scholarships? They'd almost kissed—hadn't they?—and he wanted to talk scholarships? "I already applied for those. I think most of them were already taken since I started applying just before the semester started."

"Not for you." Clicking around for a minute on the keyboard, Cam studied the screen. Then he sat back, smiled, and turned the laptop in her direction so she could see it. "For Liam."

She squinted at the website on the screen. California Space Camp Scholarships. Why hadn't she thought of that? Still ... "It's probably too late."

"It says they're still accepting applications."

And despite the roller coaster of the last few minutes, her lips twitched with a smile. "Can you imagine how happy he'd be if he actually got to go?"

With a wink, Cameron shoved the computer into her hands. "I don't know who would be happier—Liam or his awesome mom."

CHAPTER ELEVEN

ELISE

She'd thought counseling would be the answer to healing the rift between her and Charles.

But all it had done so far was scrape the tender scabs off Elise's wounds and pour a truckload of salt inside. And they were only at the second session.

Counselor Danielle Fibbs sat in an overstuffed pale pink chair across from the couch that Elise and Charles currently occupied, tapping a pen against a notepad she had yet to write anything in. Not a trace of gray in her brown hair and her face as smooth as glass, the woman didn't seem much older than the sextuplets, but the degrees on her wall declared her more than qualified to help couples with marriage problems.

Elise never would have imagined she and Charles would be one of them, yet here they sat at 10:01 on the Saturday morning of Labor Day weekend.

"Last time we spoke about the basics of what had brought you here." One of Danielle's legs came up and crossed the other at the knee. "And I assigned you homework. Did you both do it?"

Elise glanced at Charles. Unlike her, whose homework

rested on her lap, he didn't appear to have done it. But then he nodded and pulled out his phone. "Yes."

Trying to hold back a sigh, Elise also replied in the affirmative. The last eight days since her husband had agreed to come to counseling had been some of the most tense of their marriage. It was as if Charles was afraid to say the wrong thing, so he just didn't speak to her except for essential information she needed to know, like the fact his dry cleaning was ready for pickup and that he'd be working late—again.

Not that she'd done much better. Anytime he'd been near, she'd had the overwhelming itch to scream. It was as if, once uncorked, the wine of her negative thoughts wanted to flow out and drown him.

Which had made the homework even more difficult.

"Wonderful." Setting her notepad aside, Danielle folded her hands over her knee. "Charles, why don't you go first? Read us your list of what you most appreciate about Elise."

Elise swallowed hard. The air in the room seemed to compress and bend as she shifted in her seat, positioning herself to better look at him.

Charles fiddled with his phone. For a moment, there was silence, and his gaze flicked up at her then back to his screen.

A clock ticked loudly in the corner.

He cleared his throat. "I really appreciate Elise's good cooking. She also keeps a really nice home. She is available to help the kids when they need her. She sacrifices for others." He rattled off a few more items, all along the same vein. "And finally, I can always count on her to do what she says she is going to do."

His cheeks reddened as he clicked off the screen and shoved the phone back onto the holster clipped to his belt.

Elise's fingertips tingled, numb. The things he'd said were … nice. But anyone could have said those nice things about her.

She glanced at her own list. Even though Charles had obviously betrayed her, she'd tried to look past that to his good qualities. Like Item 1: *"When something matters greatly to Charles or those he loves, he will put everything he has into it. For example, when the kids showed an interest in boating, Charles bought a boat, taught them each to drive it, and took the family out on the water every weekend for years."*

"Elise."

Her head shot up as Danielle's voice broke through her thoughts. Had she missed something? "Yes?"

The counselor held no judgment in her soft brown eyes, which reminded Elise of the center of an M&M. "How do you feel after hearing Charles's list?"

The paper in her lap fluttered as the air conditioning kicked on. How *did* she feel? "He seems to value what I do around the house."

Danielle was quiet, giving Elise time to process.

Charles undid the top button of his blue dress shirt, which gave his eyes a piercing edge. The grim pull of his lips didn't reveal much about what he was thinking. He was such a private man. This whole thing had to be torture to him.

Perhaps they didn't really need to be here. Could they sort all of this out on their own? Had she made a mistake in insisting upon this?

No.

Because if the last week of silence had proven anything, it was that, left to their own devices, their marriage might never get better.

And she just wasn't willing to settle for that anymore.

Elise tugged at a stray thread on her pants, then smoothed her hand over it. "Honestly? Okay." Nausea fluttered through her stomach as she looked at Charles. "I'm glad you appreciate all of that. Those are the things I've worked hard to be good at, ever since I was a girl and had to take care of my sisters by myself."

"Good," Danielle said. "Tell us more about that, Elise."

A deep breath shuddered through her as she worked it out from her lungs. "My dad used to praise me for keeping my sisters fed, keeping the house clean. Keeping the peace." A memory came to the surface of her mind, something she hadn't thought about in ages. But now, it pricked her conscious, stabbing in its clarity. "There was this one time when I was sixteen. Oh, never mind, that's not relevant."

"On the contrary." Danielle's eyebrows lifted. "It sounds very relevant. Keep going. It's okay to process out loud."

Nodding, Elise rubbed her upper left arm as a dull ache accompanied the memory. "When I was sixteen, I'd saved babysitting money for about six months so I could buy a dress I'd seen in a shop window. I was so proud when I finally brought it home, and planned to wear it to a school dance."

The dress had been as yellow as the daisies her mother had grown once upon a time—before she'd remarried and moved to another state. It had fit Elise perfectly. For the first time since she'd developed her teenage curves, she'd felt truly beautiful.

"But then my fourteen-year-old sister Hannah saw it, wanted it, and begged me to let her wear it to her school dance instead. Hannah was the baby of the family and knew exactly how to get what she wanted. And my dad was always so exhausted after work. He couldn't stand her tears, and he asked me to please let Hannah wear the dress."

"We won't get any peace around here if you don't."

"But Daddy ..."

"Please, Elise. Be a good girl. Just let your sister have the dress."

A sniffle and a pause. "Okay, Daddy."

"And what happened?"

Elise jumped a bit at Charles's question—at the intensity in it. Had she really never told him the story? "I let her wear it."

Crossing his arms, Charles sat back against the couch, eyebrows furrowed. "Hmm."

"Thank you for sharing that, Elise." Danielle brought the focus back. "So how does all of that relate to how you felt hearing Charles's list?"

"I'm not sure, exactly." The ache in her arm deepened—a reminder that doing this work was going to hurt. The scabs that had formed over her wounds had been flaky at best. They needed to be pried off completely so the lesions didn't fester.

So they could heal properly.

Her eyes drifting closed momentarily, Elise got out her emotional scalpel.

Then she fixed Charles with another look, forcing herself to keep a steady gaze. "I like doing things for other people, because I truly believe that bringing joy into others' lives is my purpose on this earth." Her heart throbbed. She kept going. "But if I'm being completely honest, the fact that you, the person who should know me best, most appreciates what I can *do* for you—"

"Elise." Charles leaned forward, his voice reaching out, almost gentle. "That's not what I meant to communicate to you."

She just stared at him.

"What did you mean to communicate, Charles?"

Danielle had spoken, but Elise only had eyes for her husband. Something in the way he edged closer to her, the crackle of something in the air between them—it felt distantly familiar.

As if maybe, just maybe, he was coming home to her. Not because it was his duty. Not because he was bound by vows that, yes, he'd broken, but still obviously cared something for. But because he *wanted* to.

Maybe even because he loved her still.

Of course, that might be her wishful brain making things up. But for now, she'd hold onto the first bit of hope she'd found in a long time.

Charles absently rubbed his finger and thumb over one of the top buttons on his shirt. "I just wanted to tell you that I see you, Elise. Your sacrifices, the things you've done for me, for our family, haven't gone unnoticed. I know a lot of stay-at-home wives feel unappreciated, and that's never what I wanted for you. But I also don't want you believing that you are only as valuable as the next thing you do for me." He coughed. "That's not why I want to stay with you."

His words should warm her, but the *whys* swirled cold in her brain instead. Why *did* he want to stay with her? And why had he cheated in the first place?

Ouch. She massaged the deeper ache in her arm.

What a fool she'd been. The wounds she'd imagined as a scrape were actually a gunshot, and she'd been trying to place a Band-Aid over the mess instead of stopping the bleeding in the first place.

The paper in her hands suddenly felt so very trite. Not enough.

Today had made one thing quite clear—Charles's affair wasn't the only issue. It might not even be the main issue. Instead, it was an outward result that had sprung from problems they'd had for years.

Maybe for the entirety of their marriage.

And while Charles's decision to cheat was his alone, he very obviously wasn't the only one with issues to work through.

It was going to be a long road ahead.

CHAPTER TWELVE

JENNA

*J*enna wanted nothing more than to kick back, enjoy the gorgeous Saturday evening picnic spread along the beach, and dive back into listening to Nikki tell stories of her crazy experiences as the lead singer in her band.

But even as she sat on a blanket beneath the shadow of the Barefoot B&B, the taste of grilled barbecue chicken still on her tongue, she couldn't keep the worry at bay.

Meeting with Danielle this afternoon had helped some, but between her utter confusion over her near-kiss with Cameron last night and Gabrielle saying she wondered if she might be having contractions this evening, a proverbial fist tightened its hold on Jenna's middle.

"And then, in the middle of our set, my guitarist proposed to my drummer. I hadn't even known they were dating!" Nikki lay on her stomach, kicking her feet up in the air behind her. "Of course, she said yes and they got married and it was a gorgeous wedding. But now they're having a baby and have decided to quit."

Pulling her brown hair from its ponytail holder, Heather

fluffed it out and tugged at the ends. "What are you going to do?"

The mention of a baby put Jenna on autopilot—she picked up her phone again. No new messages from Gabrielle since the last one two hours ago. Jenna reread it for the thousandth time. *False alarm. The contractions stopped. Just Braxton Hicks. Again! Stay at your meeting and don't you dare come to pick up Liam until it's over.*

Holding in a sigh and closing her ears to the rest of Nikki's story—*sorry, girl, love you, but not tonight*—Jenna moved her gaze to the inn. On the outside, it looked so different than it had at the first Sisterhood meeting five weeks ago. Jules's brother Frank and his volunteer construction crew had repaired the roof and replaced the wooden planks along the damaged walls. Because paint had yet to be applied, the new planks stood out— whitish brown and pristine compared with the older ones.

But the weathered wood had withstood the test of time. It brought character to the old inn, a reminder that nothing could be completely made over without bringing along a bit of its past.

And Jenna didn't quite know what to make of that—if it gave her hope or made her want to cry.

Maybe a little of both.

The inside was still in disarray, although they were making progress. Being Labor Day weekend, they still had three months to finish up the remodel before the Christmas festival deadline. In good faith, Jules and Elise had already opened up reservations online for festival goers.

"What about the Refuge?" Cameron's suggestion from yesterday kept pinging in Jenna's mind. She'd intended to get up the nerve tonight to ask Jules about helping with the interior decorating and redesign, but their fearless leader had come down with a cold and wasn't here. Of course, she'd given the women her blessing to meet without her, so Elise and Heather

had cooked up a feast. Now, Elise was readying dessert in the inn's kitchen as the rest of them chatted outside.

"I can understand why they might want to take a break for a while." Heather's voice came back into focus. "Babies change everything, that's for sure."

Again with the babies! Ugh. Jenna hit the button on the front of her phone once more. Still nothing.

"I've been checking mine constantly too," Quinn said, her direct gaze on Jenna.

The conversation stilled. Nikki, Heather, and Piper swung their heads between the two women.

"Checking on what?" Of course it was Piper who was first to speak. In the weeks since getting to know her better, Jenna had learned there wasn't any bone too small for the reporter to gnaw if she thought it might hold some juice.

"Gabrielle." Tonight, instead of heels and an expensive blazer —her normal fare even for casual Sisterhood meetings—Quinn wore ankle-length jeans and a cotton blouse with black ballet flats. The lavender hue of the shirt softened the lines of her face, which were illuminated by the strand of lights overhead that someone had strung between a few wooden poles anchored in the sand. "She's thirty-six weeks along. So far, they've managed to keep her blood pressure in check with bed rest and medication, but Tyler said they could induce at any time if signs of her preeclampsia return."

Wow, Quinn had actually paid attention. And the quirk of Quinn's eyebrow demonstrated that the woman was aware of Jenna's impression of her. But could anyone blame her, really? Other than handing her a coffee a week ago, Quinn hadn't spoken two words to Jenna—or any of them, for that matter.

Still, Jules had invited Quinn into the Sisterhood for a reason, and Quinn had shown up to all of the renovation meetings. Being a former manager at a marketing agency, she did possess a certain knack for taking charge and getting things done.

Plus ... the two of them were going to share a niece.

Jenna attempted a smile at Quinn before passing her gaze to all the other women. "I've been a nervous wreck."

A door closed in the distance, and Elise headed down the path from the inn, holding a large platter. Jenna popped up to help the woman, who looked to be having difficulty balancing everything and walking in the soft sand.

"Here, let me get that." Before Elise could protest, she took the platter where there sat a pitcher, cups, and plates filled with some sort of chocolate dessert. "Is that cheesecake?"

"Thank you, dear." Elise huffed as she followed Jenna to the blanket where everyone else was seated. "And yes, it's one of my specialties. All of my kids love it, especially Cameron."

Jenna nearly fumbled the platter at the mention of him. "I feel like I've heard him mention it." She set down the dessert and the others fawned over it.

"I'll be right back." Though it was rather cool out, Elise fanned herself. "I have to get the secret strawberry sauce."

"I can grab it." Jenna caught up to the woman, who had been so busy serving them all night that she hadn't even eaten dinner herself ... not really. Just a few small bites and then it was back to the kitchen to get dessert ready.

She was the very embodiment of a servant, so much like Jenna's own mother had been.

Her breath hitched at the thought.

Elise waved a hand. "I can grab it myself, dear."

Maybe she could, but Jenna didn't want Elise to feel alone. Even though Cameron's mom was a part of the Sisterhood officially, she rarely talked about herself. Rarely talked unless someone asked her a direct question ... kind of like Quinn, actually. Except Elise had never seemed to think of herself as being above everyone else.

Maybe it was the exact opposite. Perhaps Jenna could help her feel like a valued member of the group by asking her opinion. After all, she feared she hadn't been all that welcoming when Elise had first been instated as a member—but that had been all about her own insecurities. It had nothing to do with Elise as a person, because as far as Jenna could tell, she was pretty much a saint.

Jenna kept pace with Elise despite her protests. "Well, let me come along so I can pick your brain then."

They reached the inn's back porch and went inside. The whole place smelled of a strange mixture of chemicals, solvents, paint, and wood dust. Elise glanced back at Jenna, a blank look on her face. "You want to pick *my* brain? About what?"

"Something I'm thinking about doing."

"I'm intrigued." They walked through the lobby and dining area and entered the kitchen, which now boasted gleaming granite countertops, new cherrywood cabinets, and stainless steel appliances. Elise headed straight for the refrigerator and pulled out a mason jar filled with a bright red substance. She set it on the counter and cocked her head. "Tell me more."

Joining her, Jenna touched the jar. The coldness of the glass shocked her fingertips. "It was Cameron's idea, actually."

"Are you sure I should get involved?" Elise glanced away, out the window that gave a pretty prospect of the ocean. "He is ... very private."

Yikes. Did Elise think she was coming to her for some sort of relationship advice? "No, no, the idea is for me to ask Jules about helping with the interior decorating of this place."

"Oh, silly me." Red tinged Elise's cheeks. "That sounds like a wonderful idea. You are so talented, from what I hear, and you *are* going to school for it." She cleared her throat and nodded. "Yes, I think it's a fabulous idea. The companies I was considering are quite pricey. You would probably be much more affordable and you obviously have a personal connection to the place. What do you charge?"

Whoa, okay. "I would do this for free. My professor mentioned that I should try to gain some real-world experience like an internship or something. Plus, I just … I don't know. This place just kind of speaks to me." Even if that draw scared her a little at the same time.

Elise tapped her chin. "Tell you what. I'm going to run this sauce out to the girls and then you can show me around and tell me your vision for the various spaces throughout the inn."

It almost sounded as if Elise, not Jules, was the one in charge of the details surrounding the renovation. Jenna knew that Elise had taken on a lot, but would she be the one to hire Jenna?

The woman bustled through the kitchen door before Jenna could confirm her suspicions, and Jenna headed to the lobby where she'd stood that first night at the end of July. The artwork had been taken down, the fireplace rebuilt with new bricks, and the stairs had been repaired, sanded, and repainted. But the essence of the old inn remained.

The magic of *what if*, of possibility, still blanketed the air.

And even though her professor had said she should consider what others would want in a space, Jenna could only picture how to enhance what *she* felt when here.

Large wooden beams crisscrossing the lofty ceilings.

Lights—everywhere.

Three, maybe four, antique chandeliers that would glisten and do double duty as a light source and purveyor of beauty.

Walls the color of melted butter to draw on the already existing warmth of the space.

Couches covered in brocade fabric patterned in a variety of colorful swirls. Wine. Burnt orange. Teal.

The sound of the creaking back door interrupted the bursting of Jenna's imagination as Elise reentered the inn. "I can see your mind is already at work." The woman's gentle smile was like a warm hug. She sat on the couch, which had been thoroughly cleaned and dusted since that first meeting. "Tell me what you're thinking."

So, turning and pointing as she spoke, Jenna did her best to describe the picture in her mind. And even though it wasn't the least bit professional, she allowed emotion to soak her words. A few times, much to her horror, she got choked up, but she pushed forward and kept going.

Finally, as she ran her fingertips over the brick face of the fireplace, she inhaled a deep breath. "Of course, if that doesn't work—"

"No, no. It works."

Jenna turned, peeked at Elise.

Shaking her head slowly, the woman played with the gold cross necklace at her throat. "Jenna Wakefield, you may not believe this, but you are already an interior decorator."

Jenna's lungs expanded as she moved to take a seat next to Elise. "What does that …" She squinted. "Does that mean I can have the job?"

"Yes, you can." Elise took her hand, squeezed, let go. "Because you, my dear girl, were meant for this job."

"I know." Oh. Oops. Jenna rushed on. "That sounded arrogant. What I mean is, for so long I've felt like a huge piece of me was missing. But going back to school, working toward a degree so I can finally do what I've dreamed of doing since I was little …" Jenna shrugged. "You're right. It's like it was meant to be."

Elise frowned slightly. "While I am very happy that you're getting a chance to pursue your dreams, that's not quite what I was saying."

"Then what were you saying?"

"I was referring to the fact that *this job*—decorating the Refuge—was meant to be yours."

"Oh. Right."

Silence invaded the sanctity of the space, but a moment later, the other women's distant laughter floated up from the beach.

"Jenna, a degree is a piece of paper. And a job is ... well, it's a calling, and maybe *part* of your purpose, yes, but it won't tell you who you are. Believe me." Elise sighed. "I spent a lot of years defining myself by my job—which in my case, was being a stay-at-home mom. So every medal the kids won, every time they did something right instead of wrong, I took that as affirmation that I was good at my job. That I had cared enough, loved them enough. But in turn, that meant every failure of theirs told me I was bad at my job." Her frown twisted into a type of ironic smile. "I've lived my life with this sort of black-and-white system of evaluation, and only now am I realizing that ... maybe it wasn't an accurate picture of anything."

"I think I understand what you're saying. And I'm aware that a degree is just a degree, but it proves something too, you know?"

"And what's that?"

Jenna tipped her chin to the ceiling skylight. The half-moon had been obscured by the clouds. She knew it was there—could see a patch of its light bleeding through the wisps of white—but it had become hidden. Not doing what it was supposed to do.

"I've made a lot of mistakes and I know that people never thought I'd amount to much. For Liam's sake, though, I'm trying." She swallowed hard. "But there's still a part of me that believes I can never make up for the bad choices I've made early on in life. Even though I really want to get to the end of the journey, I worry that I'll never move past the muck in the middle."

"Oh, my dear. The middle is mucky, yes, but it's also beautiful. Take it from an old woman who wishes she'd done so many things differently. Who is still figuring out what she's meant to do and be." Elise patted Jenna's shoulder. "Don't be like me, Jenna. Don't be so intent on getting somewhere else—or on merely surviving—that you lose yourself along the way."

CHAPTER THIRTEEN

ELISE

*E*lise was the last person who should be giving advice.

But Jenna had looked so sad, so in need of encour-agement—and Elise knew how that felt. It was a gift to be able to unburden oneself to another, and she had only wanted to help.

Yet even now, an hour later, Elise chided herself as she walked up the pathway to Jules's house with a jar full of home-made chicken soup. She'd left the Sisterhood meeting early under the guise of delivering this to their absentee leader. In reality, she'd probably have removed herself anyway. Those women were all so young, so beautiful, so strong, and Elise was wholly underqualified to serve as a mentor.

Now, silent chef and baker for the group? That, she could be. But a mentor? No.

Elise climbed the steps of Jules's porch, where a wooden swing hung to one side of the door. Several potted plants—flowers in various stages of bloom—adorned the deck, and the vibrant yellow of the door was muted in the moonlight. It was only eight-something, so hopefully she wouldn't wake the woman up.

She knocked. If Jules didn't answer, Elise would just leave the soup on the doorstep and text her, or try to bring it by tomorrow after church since Jules lived right down the street.

Just as Elise had given up, the door opened. Jules's hair sat on the top of her head in a bun held together with two pens, and she wore an off-the-shoulder thin sweatshirt and sweatpants. Her nose was a bit red and her eyes puffy behind thick black frames. "Hi, Elise."

Poor woman. Her voice sounded like she'd screamed for a few hours straight. "Sorry to bother you." Elise held up the container of soup. "Just wanted to drop this by and say I hope you feel better."

"You're so thoughtful." Jules leaned against the doorway and offered a sleepy smile. "I'd invite you inside but don't want you to get my germs."

"I'm not afraid of germs. My husband is a doctor, remember?" He'd probably exposed them all to countless illnesses over the years. "But I don't want to keep you up. You should be resting."

Jules took the soup from Elise's hands. "I should be, but I keep almost falling asleep and then thinking of a new idea for the Refuge. The curse of a passion project, I suppose."

A breeze rippled through the trees and Elise pulled her sweater tight across her chest. "The blessing, you mean. I'm finding so much purpose in everything, even the tiniest of details. By the way, I've decided to hire Jenna to do the interior decorating. I hope that's all right. I probably should have run the decision by you first."

Turning to place the soup just inside the house, Jules took a tissue from her pocket and swiped at her nose. "No, no, that's perfect. I had actually thought about it, but didn't know if she'd be too busy or overwhelmed."

Relief twined through Elise's whole body, releasing the tension she didn't know she'd been holding in her shoulders. "I think she might be overwhelmed, but when she told me her vision for the place ... well, it seemed a good fit."

Jules stepped out onto the porch and sat on the edge of the swing, pushing herself backward with her tiptoes. "How was the meeting tonight? I was sorry to miss. It's the highlight of my week."

"It was good. The women seem to be getting along well. Piper and Quinn still haven't shared their stories yet, but Heather shared tonight that she's always wanted to open her own restaurant."

But then she'd shrugged. *"It's only a pipe dream, though."* Elise understood. With her father battling end-stage renal disease, Heather's family needed her help at the vineyard.

The swing creaked with Jules's movement. "Hmm. That's wonderful." She quieted, seemingly lost in thought.

Elise cleared her throat. "Well, you've put together a great group."

"Which includes you." Now Jules studied Elise.

What was it about her? The woman seemed to have a sixth sense about people, to be able to see deeper than the exterior. It was the same quality that had allowed her to see potential in the Barefoot B&B when everyone else in town had only seen a mess.

The same that had allowed her to observe a ragtag group of women with no real ties to one another—except their longtime residency in Walker Beach—and create a Sisterhood.

Elise fiddled with a large waxy leaf on one of the house-plants. "I know."

"And yet ..." As she rocked in the swing, a patient smile slid across Jules's face. She patted the spot next to her.

If Elise hadn't feared her weight would cause the swing to topple, she'd have planted herself beside Jules. There was something soothing about being in the woman's presence. Something that allowed Elise to process.

"Well." Easing herself down onto the top step of the porch, Elise faced Jules and leaned back against the staircase post. "I feel as if perhaps you might have been wrong about my place in the Sisterhood. You asked me to be a mentor, but I've always functioned best behind the scenes. That's where I'm most comfortable."

"Hmm."

So much meaning reverberated in a single hum.

"Elise, wouldn't you say that the work you're doing with the Refuge is out of your comfort zone? I mean, sure, you're serving, but you're largely in charge, making decisions when I'm not there." Despite her puffy eyes, Jules winked. "And you're really good at it."

"I don't know about that." The wooden post dug into Elise's back and she shifted to relieve the pressure. "What I do know is that even though I enjoy my time with the ladies in the Sisterhood, I don't feel that I have much to contribute beyond the food."

"The amazing thing about the Sisterhood—the thing that Chrissy envisioned when she dreamed the whole thing up—is that it's not really about what each person contributes."

"Then what?"

Gripping the chain of the swing affixed to the porch roof, Jules slid her thumb along the link in her fist. "In many ways, it's just about being together. Creating a place to belong. And you're part of that." She tilted her head and her hair toppled from its bun, the pens clattering to the ground. "I probably put too much pressure on you by asking you to be a mentor. It doesn't mean you have to impart any great wisdom like a guru. It's just about being there to listen and encourage the women when they need it. Believe me, Elise, we all look up to you."

"But you shouldn't." The words hurled from her mouth, giving the wind competition with their forceful blow.

But Jules either didn't hear the tension belying Elise's

response or wasn't ruffled by it. "I know you're not perfect—no one is—but you have built such a beautiful life. We can all learn something from you."

"That life is a lie."

And oh goodness, she hadn't meant to ever admit that to anyone but her counselor. But now that it was out, the truth couldn't be stopped. "Charles cheated on me a year ago, Jules. We've been pretending everything is all right, but obviously there are some deeper issues at play, and we're only beginning to scratch the surface of them. I ... I don't even know if we'll end up together when all of this is said and done."

And that thought still shredded her insides. What she'd said to Jenna was true—she'd lost herself. Or maybe, she'd never really known herself to begin with. And somehow, she had to figure out who she was outside of the context of wife and mom. Had to sort out what she wanted, who she wanted to be, before she could be significant to anyone else.

Didn't she?

"Oh, Elise. I'm sorry." Jules stood and came to sit beside Elise. She gave her a side hug before pulling back. "I'm here if you want to talk about it."

Did she?

Yes. So much.

And Jules, with her kindness and non-judgmental spirit, was the perfect person to hear her confessions.

So for the first time outside of a counseling session, Elise lifted the heavy thoughts that had been weighing on her soul and shared them with someone else—someone not paid to mediate between her and Charles, but a friend to listen and encourage.

Which, ironically, were the simple things Jules had asked Elise to do for the women in the Sisterhood—for all the women to do for each other, really. So in the process of spilling her secrets and her truth to Jules, Elise finally accepted her place. She became one of them.

A sister.

And the newfound closeness hadn't come because she'd given of herself. It had come by receiving what someone else had extended to her.

Comfort. Consolation. Friendship. All the things she'd been missing by holding back out of fear of rejection.

She didn't want to hold back anymore. Perhaps honesty and openness, while exposing her to potential hurt, really were the best policies after all.

CHAPTER FOURTEEN

JENNA

*S*he didn't know what she'd done to deserve a day like today, but Jenna would take it.

Stretching out on a lounge chair, she held a virgin margarita in one hand and adjusted her sunglasses with the other. The heat from the sand soaked into her toes, warming her from the outside in.

She glanced over at the chair next to her. Gabrielle was there, in her swimsuit as well—but there was something different about her.

Jenna cocked her head, narrowed her eyes.

Why wasn't her sister pregnant? "Where's your baby?"

Her sister just laughed and pointed to the ocean ... where Cameron surfed with a baby girl in his arms.

What in the—

"Mom."

Jenna squinted. She opened her mouth to yell at Cameron to get back here with that baby, but nothing came out.

"Mom."

Something poked her side. Jenna looked down but nothing was there.

"Wake up, Mom."

Jolting at the words, Jenna opened her eyes and blinked. The room was dark except for light streaming in from the hallway through her open door. Liam stood next to her bed in his Minecraft pajamas, his hair rivaling Einstein's.

"Liam?"

Something pounded from the front of the apartment, and Jenna pushed her comforter aside. Cold air bit into her skin. Her head throbbed, probably from staying up until midnight yesterday—Labor Day—even when she'd completed her math assignment at ten. Thanks a lot, Red Bull.

"What time is it?"

Liam yawned. "Four something."

"Why are you waking me up so early, baby?"

"Someone's at the door."

"What?" Oh yeah. The pounding. There it went again.

"Should we answer it?"

Poor Liam. Kid had been startled awake in the middle of the night and his mom had the mental capacity of sludge and the physical prowess of a sloth. "Yeah, bud. Hang on."

Jenna stood, slipped a robe on over her silky tank top and shorts, and hurried to the door. Who would it be? Maybe the neighbor had locked himself out after a bender again.

She peeked through the peephole and saw Quinn—her hair frizzy, face free of makeup, dressed in yoga pants, a T-shirt, and a tight white hoodie.

Jenna yanked open the door. "Quinn? What are you doing here?"

"Gabrielle is in labor."

It took Jenna's brain a few moments to process Quinn's quick words. "What? But she's not thirty-seven weeks yet." Only thirty-six. Something must be wrong. "Why didn't she text me or call?"

"She did. A bunch." Quinn stepped inside and shut the door

behind her. The sweet smell of coffee and cream wafted from her, like she'd been sitting for hours in a coffee shop. "Sorry to wake you up, but your sister wants you there."

"Is she okay?" Liam piped up behind Jenna.

Jenna glanced back at him. He was chewing on a nail, so she put her arm around his shoulder and squeezed. "I'm sure she's fine, bud." Her eyes flicked back to Quinn, begging her to confirm.

"Yes, she and the baby are fine so far."

"Did her water break or ...?"

"No. She started complaining of a headache last night that wouldn't go away with Tylenol, and Tyler insisted they go to OB triage just in case. When she got there, her blood pressure was high and kept getting worse, so the nurses called the doctor and he decided to induce." Hands flying, Quinn walked the living room, her pace matching that of her words. Had Jenna ever seen Tyler's sister so flustered?

"Once the decision was made, they started texting the family. Gabrielle hadn't wanted to worry anyone until they had definitive news." Quinn started gathering up empty paper plates and trash from the takeout containers that Jenna hadn't yet cleaned up from last night.

The gremlins in Jenna's head drummed on her skull with sticks. "But she's okay."

Marching to the trash can, Quinn dumped the garbage in her hands. "Yes. The labor is slow going, but I guess that's normal for first-time moms and at this point in her pregnancy."

"And they're not doing a C-section right away?"

Quinn shrugged. "I guess not. The doctor gave her an epidural—I guess it can help to lower blood pressure and it's good to have in case they do have to perform a C-section. He also started her on something called magnesium sulfate to keep her from having a seizure."

"A seizure?" Jenna had to sit down. No. She had to get to the hospital. But what about Liam? She didn't want to drag him down there. What if something happened to his aunt and—

"Hey." Quinn grabbed Jenna's upper arms and gave her a little shake. "Breathe. I volunteered to come here so you could go. I'll get Liam to school for you and then I'll come back to the hospital."

"Are you sure? Thank you so much." Jenna kissed the top of Liam's head. "I'm going to go. Quinn is—"

"I heard, Mom. It's okay." Liam frowned. "But Aunt G ..."

"Is going to be just fine. I'll text Jared's mom and ask if you can go home with him after school, all right?" It was a Tuesday, but surely that would be all right, given the circumstances.

"Sure."

Turning grateful eyes to Quinn, Jenna raced to her room and threw on some clothing, then snatched her purse and hopped in her car. Thankfully the hospital—like everything in Walker Beach—was just a short drive away, especially in the early morning hours when traffic was minimal.

As she drove, she told her phone to text Cameron, letting him know she couldn't work today and he'd have to cover for her. Now that Labor Day was over, they'd be working a lot of opposite shifts. Honestly, that was probably a good thing. With everything going on, trying to figure out what had happened between them last Friday just added too much stress to her life.

After pulling into the hospital parking lot, Jenna flung herself from the vehicle and ran toward the maternity ward. The bright fluorescents of the hospital contrasted with the darkness outside and Jenna blinked as she entered. Her tennis shoes squeaked on the white vinyl tile as she made her way to the information desk and then, after inquiring a room number, to Gabrielle's room on the second floor.

Along the way, she had to force memories of other trips to the hospital from her mind.

More than a decade ago, Liam had been born to a seventeen-year-old single mom who had no idea what to do with a baby. A mom who had cried—both from love and despair—when the nurse had placed him in her arms.

And it had been twelve years since Jenna and Gabrielle had visited Mom here for the last time. She'd been so frail by then, cancer having eaten away all her vibrancy, leaving her skin pale and paper-thin, her lips dry, cracked. They'd watched as she'd slowly slipped away, helpless to do anything but sing her favorite song as she went.

When we've been there ten thousand years,
Bright shining as the sun,
We've no less days to sing God's praise
Than when we'd first begun.

Yes, the lemon-and-antiseptic smell of the hospital was the same now as then, and the greetings from the staff just as syrupy and full of pep. But this time, Jenna was here for a happy reason.

Please, please, let it be a happy reason. Let it all end up okay.

Of course it would. Yes. As Jenna careened around the corner and finally found Gabrielle's room, she paused, inhaled, and reminded herself that Gabrielle needed her to be strong.

When she entered, her eyes were drawn first to the monitors then to the IV pole pumping medication into her sister's veins. Tyler stood over Gabrielle, their foreheads together, and he spoke to her in soothing, low tones.

Jenna was most definitely intruding, but the picture they made squeezed her heart and kept her frozen. How different the birth of Baby Girl would be from Liam's.

Tyler pulled back and saw Jenna standing there. "You made it." Despite his bloodshot eyes, he stood straight as a soldier.

Turning her eyes onto Jenna, Gabrielle smiled and held out a hand—the one not taped up with an IV needle. "I'm so happy to see you."

Jenna strode forward. "I'm sorry I didn't see my texts before now. How are you?"

Laughing, Gabrielle waved her hand toward the equipment. "Fine so far. Not really dilated much. I think it's going to be a while. But I got an epidural so I don't feel a thing." Her sister yawned. "Sorry. We didn't sleep last night."

"Don't even worry about it." Jenna was going to need some coffee soon herself. Maybe the caffeine would soothe her headache. "Is there anyone else you want here?"

Tyler stretched, rolling his neck. "I texted my parents and sisters to let them know they don't need to come until the baby is here. It'll just be a lot of sitting around and waiting."

"Speaking of that …" Jenna quirked an eyebrow at him. "Now that I'm here, why don't you go take a break, Tyler?"

He looked at Gabrielle, clearly wary. "I don't—"

"You can go, babe. I'm fine." Her sister yawned again. "I think I might take a nap, actually."

After a few more minutes of hemming and hawing, Tyler finally agreed to go down to the café to fetch some coffees and breakfast for him and Jenna. While he did that, Gabrielle slept. Jenna pulled out her phone—should have remembered to bring her laptop too, but this would have to do—and started reading for her class.

A text from Cameron came through: *Of course I'll work for you. Keep me posted on how she's doing! Congrats, Aunt J! ;)*

Aunt J. She liked it.

Jenna sat there alternately reading and nodding off for who knew how long. When the nurses changed shifts at seven, the new nurse came in to check on Gabrielle, waking her up to check her vitals and take measurements. Tyler came back with food, and Jenna choked down half of the worst breakfast burrito she'd ever had—the potatoes were definitely *not* fully cooked—before setting it aside and picking her phone back up to post discussion questions in her interior design class.

Before she knew it, six hours had passed and Gabrielle was

still only dilated to a four. Tyler ducked out to grab some lunch while Gabrielle napped again, and Jenna rubbed her neck while continuing to work on her phone, which would have been dead at this point if Quinn hadn't brought her a charger an hour ago before heading to the waiting room.

A moan broke Jenna's focus. Her head snapped up. "G? You okay?"

Her sister glanced at her, frowned, and then her whole body stiffened. Gabrielle cried out and Jenna jumped up, rushing to her side. What was happening?

Then Gabrielle started to convulse.

Jenna raced to the door, flung it open, and yelled for help then rushed back to Gabrielle's side. "It's okay, Sis." Her throat swelled and thickened as she watched her beautiful sister's face contort, her body thrash.

A nurse rushed in and pushed Jenna out of the way.

Another joined them. "What's happening?"

"Seizure." The first nurse, who had rather large arms, turned Gabrielle onto her side. "Check the IV catheter."

In the chaos, more nurses filled the room. Jenna pushed herself up against the wall and stared, heart thumping wildly, watching her sister go white as she shook.

The second nurse examined the IV. "The magnesium got disconnected and is dripping on the floor!"

It had? It was? Why hadn't Jenna noticed that? She could have saved her sister all of this heartache if she'd just been paying attention to something other than her school stuff. Something other than herself.

The nurses reconnected the catheter, hung a new bag of magnesium, and started pumping it into her faster than before.

Something clattered to the floor behind her and Jenna turned to find Tyler there, a container of spilled salad at his feet. He rushed forward. "What's going on?"

"I ..." Jenna's chest caved in on itself. "She was f-f-fine one minute and then …" She saw dark spots, and a groan emerged from deep in her throat. "Gabrielle!" Why was she still shaking?

The first nurse turned to them both. "You need to leave right now. We'll come to get you when the patient is stable."

Tyler set his jaw. "I'm not leaving my wife and daughter."

The nurse pointed to Tyler. "Okay, Dad, you can stay." Then she moved her finger to Jenna. "I'm sorry, but you need to go. The room is too crowded and we need space to work."

Everything in her told Jenna to plant her feet there and not move, but there was nothing she could do for Gabrielle right now. Nodding numbly, she grabbed her things and shuffled to the waiting room, fire in her belly.

Quinn was there and glanced up, gaze sharp. "What's wrong?"

Plopping into the seat next to her, Jenna put her head in her hands. Heaviness expanded in the very core of her body. "She's going to be okay. They're going to be okay." Her voice warbled.

"Jenna." Quinn's sharp tone prodded. "What's going on?"

"Seizure." It's all she could say before she completely lost it. No. Not this time. She wasn't going to be weak, the one others had to hold up and worry about.

Sucking in a breath, she put her head between her knees and breathed until the lightheadedness passed. Then she sat up and looked at Quinn, whose mouth was drawn tight. She quickly filled her in on what had happened—what was happening right now. "Can you call your parents and let them know?"

"Of course."

While Quinn did that, Jenna shot off texts to Stephanie, asking if Liam could spend the night—she had to erase the message several times thanks to her shaking hands—and to Cameron, letting him know he'd need to cover for her tomorrow. Maybe all week long. No way could she even think about working. Gabrielle would need her.

Because her sister *would* still be here.

She wasn't going to die. And neither was her baby.

They're not going to die.

Jenna stood, swaying slightly as she paced. Quinn stayed seated, gripping the arms of her chair. Some soap opera flickered from the television hanging in the corner, and a few other families sat waiting for news—one couple read, while another played cards at a table—but Jenna and Quinn remained silent, both lost in their own thoughts.

It took only fifteen minutes for Tyler's parents, Thomas and Genevieve, to arrive. Thomas's hair was peppered with white flecks. He must have been working at the pizza parlor when he got the call. Then Shannon, Tyler and Quinn's younger sister, flew through the door, eyes wide with concern. She must have had to find a last-minute sub for her preschool class. After hugging everyone else, Shannon gave Jenna an extra-long squeeze.

Jenna nearly lost it then, but knew that if she allowed the tears to come, she'd never get them corked.

They waited. And waited. Quinn marched to the nurses' station to inquire, but they said they couldn't tell her anything useful.

Finally, Tyler sent a group text letting them know Gabrielle was stable, but they were prepping her for a Cesarean.

"That's good," Jenna mused out loud. "Gabrielle will be totally out of danger at that point, right?"

"Not necessarily." Quinn waved her phone in the air. "According to this website I've been reading, the effects of eclampsia could last up to six weeks after delivery, but are most common in the forty-eight hours afterward. Depending on how everything goes, they might keep her for a week or two for observation."

How could the woman say it all so matter-of-factly, without feeling? Maybe because it wasn't *her* sister in there.

No, that wasn't fair. Gabrielle was carrying Quinn's niece

too, after all.

Jenna crumpled back into her seat, folding her arm across her stomach, trying to keep her dizziness at bay.

After that, a steady stream of Bakers stopped in. Ben Baker, the cousin Tyler was closest with, and his wife Bella brought everyone food from the Frosted Cake. "Compliments of Ms. Josephine," he said.

Then Ben's sister, Ashley, flew through the door, her blonde hair swaying at her waist. She sat beside Shannon and told everyone stories of her latest bridezilla to try to distract people from the current situation.

But there was no distracting Jenna from what was going on in that back room. Anything could be happening. Her sister could be bleeding out, seizing again.

Dying.

And her niece ...

Was she okay?

Gasping, Jenna stood and briskly walked around the corner to an empty hallway. Her insides quivered like an earthquake registering an eight on the Richter scale. She might be sick.

And then, much as she'd tried not to, Jenna cried. She slid down the wall and into a squat, rocking back and forth on the balls of her feet while tears plopped onto the tile.

She didn't know how long she rocked like that. But one minute, she was alone—cold—and the next, strong arms came around her, sheltering her, warming her. And the scent of pineapple told her exactly whose arms she was in.

Lowering himself to a sitting position, Cameron pulled Jenna onto his lap, cradling her. "I came as soon as I saw your text."

Turning her face into the crook of his neck, she allowed herself to be held for the second time in one week. Seemed like this was becoming a habit—one she didn't hate.

"I'm here, Jen." He stroked her hair as she cried into the soft cotton of his shirt. "You aren't alone."

And oh, how nice it felt.

Finally, the tears stopped and she relished the feel of his arms for one moment longer. "Thank you for coming." Then Jenna pulled back, cringing at the sight of black smudges now staining his white shirt. She must have forgotten to remove her makeup last night before bed—again. "I'm sorry for being so weak."

"Jenna, are you kidding? You're the strongest woman I know." He shook his head, then placed his forehead against hers. The image of Tyler doing the same to Gabrielle earlier today flashed, piercing her heart. "Just let me be here for you, okay?"

Maybe it wasn't a weakness to let someone hold her up. In the past, she'd relied upon it too much, but now? She *could* stand on her own—but did she want to? Maybe sometimes. But now, when she felt weak? When her world was spinning out of control?

Not so much.

"Okay."

They sat that way in silence for another few minutes. Then Jenna stood, wiping the salty residue from her cheeks as best as she could.

Snagging her hand, Cameron led the way back to the crowded waiting room. They managed to sneak in without anyone seeming to notice them.

After what felt like forever, the head labor and delivery nurse came out, asking for the family of Gabrielle Baker. "She and Baby Girl Baker made it through surgery beautifully. Mom is in the recovery room and the baby has been taken to the NICU for observation."

Cameron squeezed Jenna's hand as she slumped against him in relief.

Some of the family members left, but the core group of them —plus Cameron—stayed for several hours, waiting for a chance to see Gabrielle and the baby. Finally, Tyler emerged from the back hallway, a huge grin on his face.

"Penelope Donna Baker is here, you guys." Donna—after Mom. Jenna's heart squeezed as Tyler batted away a tear from his cheek. "And she's beautiful. Mom, Dad, you want to come to meet her?"

"Of course." Genevieve leaped out of her chair and gave her son a hug. "Congrats, Daddy."

Standing, Jenna twisted her hands together. "Can I see my sister?"

"Yeah, sorry." Her brother-in-law ran a hand through his hair. "I'm a bit tired after all that. Gabrielle is in her room sleeping, but she said she wants you with her as soon as you've seen the baby."

"I'll go see her now, if that's okay. Then when Penelope"— beautiful name!—"can have more visitors, please come and get me so I can meet my niece."

But first, she had to make sure her sister was really okay.

Before she left the room, she turned to Cameron. "Thank you for being here today."

"Always."

And she was waaay too tired to allow herself to think too much on *that* one.

Turning on her heel, Jenna followed Tyler and his folks down the hallway and veered off toward Gabrielle's room while they headed to the NICU. She pushed open the door and tiptoed into the space where her sister rested.

Skin that had been pale now glowed with health, and a smile curved on the new mama's lips. Gabrielle's chest rose and fell in steady respiration—which meant that Jenna herself could finally breathe.

As quietly as she could, she pulled a chair up to the bed beside Gabrielle, kissed her sleeping sister's forehead, and thanked God for keeping her alive.

CHAPTER FIFTEEN

ELISE

*T*he Refuge project was taking over her life—and she couldn't be happier about that.

Elise tapped her pen against the clipboard she held propped against her ample hip. "We're planning a soft opening of sorts the first weekend in December." She scanned the small group, which included Jules, several city council members—Mayor Jim Walsh, his rival Bud Travis, and Rosa Diaz—and Evan Walsh, the one heading up the Christmas on the Beach Festival the second weekend in December. "Of course, you are all invited to stay free of charge."

Leaning against the newly installed railing of the Barefoot B&B's upper balcony, Evan crinkled his brow. "Do you really think you can be finished with everything by then?"

There certainly was a lot to do to get the inn fully operational, but Elise and Jules were working around the clock. Since it was now the third week in September, that left them a little over ten weeks to make it happen.

Jules jumped into the conversation. "We've submitted an application for charity status, and that should come in around the same time, which means we won't have the actual program in place before then."

The mayor folded his arms across his chest and widened his stance. As hardened with gel as his hair was, not even the cool evening breeze could ruffle it. "Isn't that the whole point of this project? The community hasn't spent countless hours coming together on this—splitting their efforts between this and the festival itself, which is set to bring in actual profit to our city coffers, mind you—just so *you* can make money, Ms. Baker."

Despite the flash of something dark in her eyes, Jules laughed, her armful of purple bracelets banging against one another as she waved her hand nonchalantly in the air. "Mayor Walsh, I can assure you that even if I made money off of this, I would put it all back into the Refuge."

Elise believed it. Last week, she'd gone to Jules with her budget, concerned that some of the supplies and fees to start up the charity had been more expensive than they'd anticipated. But as if she owned a magic wand, Jules had said she'd take care of it. The next day, ten thousand extra dollars had appeared in their account.

Elise suspected the woman had put some of her own money into the project. And it was only right that she do the same, so she'd asked Charles if they could contribute a bit. At first he'd asked if all her free work wasn't enough, but then paused, nodded, and wrote a check for five thousand.

It was the first time in the few weeks since their break-through counseling session that she'd felt he supported her work here. For some reason, he just didn't seem to understand her desire to do this job.

To be honest, she didn't always understand it herself.

But she was eternally grateful for it all the same.

As the mayor hmm-ed in reply to Jules's statement, Elise butted back in. "All of that to say, the program is still in the works and will not be completely ready by December. But the renovation of the inn is on track to be finished by the end of November, if not sooner."

"Really?" Nose wrinkled, Rosa peered back through the balcony doors to the inside of the inn.

All of the old baseboards had been torn out and the wooden floors had yet to be restored. Most of the guest rooms had been cleared of old linens and furniture that was severely outdated, and Elise was still in the process of creating an inventory of what they needed to buy. She also had to hire and train employees who would oversee the running of the inn and eventually work with the women entering the program.

And of course, nothing in the place had been painted or decorated, given Jenna's absence in all things Sisterhood and Refuge since Gabrielle had given birth nearly two weeks ago. She was supposed to be here during tonight's renovation efforts to give Elise an update on her vision and to talk budget items, but Elise wouldn't be surprised if the younger woman canceled. She had to be simply exhausted.

The last rays of daylight pinked Jules's cheeks. "Not to worry. Elise has everything in hand." She winked at Elise. Ever since Elise had spilled her woes to Charles's cousin, she had felt lighter, more connected, and more committed to the Sisterhood and to Jules in particular. "If she says the inn will be ready, it will."

"Great." Evan tapped his chin. "I'm assuming the soft opening will be a chance to practice before you receive actual guests the weekend of the festival?"

"That's right," Elise said. "And on that note, we plan to put pamphlets in all of the rooms about our mission, why we were created, and our need for donors. It'll be a wonderful chance to recruit people who will hopefully invest in the Refuge not just by coming back year after year, but who also could contribute to a charity that will help so many."

"What if ..." As he stroked his beard, Bud's eyes sparked with excitement. "What if we could ask local business owners to offer discounts to those staying at the Refuge or those who donate? Say, twenty-five percent off their meal at the Bar & Grill? People like to help charities, especially if they feel they're getting a nice little perk for themselves."

"Maybe some people." Mayor Walsh adjusted his tie, his nose slightly turned upward. "But not all of us are so greedy, Bud."

As if the mayor was one to talk! But he was probably just sore because Bud was leading in the popularity polls seventy percent to thirty. Elise wouldn't be surprised if Jim dropped out of the race soon under some guise of having a better opportunity elsewhere—all so he didn't have to lose.

Bud cleared his throat. "I think—"

"All right, then." Jules clapped her hands together like a preschool teacher trying to distract three-year-olds. "Elise, I know you've got a lot to accomplish tonight, so I'm happy to answer the rest of the team's questions here if you want to go."

"Thank you." Elise waved to them all then ducked back inside, where the whir of wood saws hummed from the upstairs hallway and Latino music with a spicy beat flowed from somewhere downstairs. Townspeople had already arrived to start working on their various assigned tasks, and Elise breathed in the happy chatter of worker bees buzzing in the hive. She headed for the top of the staircase so she could descend and check out the progress in the lobby.

"Elise, hi. Just the woman we were looking for."

She stopped short of the first step and turned to find Carlotta Jenkins and a few of her friends whose names escaped Elise at the moment. Huh. Didn't remember seeing them on the list of volunteers for tonight, but she and Jules had told people they could stop in even if they hadn't signed up ahead of time.

Carlotta's red hair was piled up on her head, her bangs pulled back in a retro-style headscarf with a large bow. All three of the women wore tight workout clothes, their makeup smooth and thick—as if they didn't realize they'd probably end the night dripping with sweat that would leave dirty streaks down their cheeks.

But they were here to help, and that was the important thing.

"Thank you for coming, ladies." Elise peeked at her clipboard, doing some mental calisthenics. "We could use you in the upstairs bathrooms tonight. The walls all need a good scrubbing."

Carlotta's eyebrow quirked and she glanced at each of her friends. Then she held up her hands and smiled. "Afraid I just got a manicure. Is there any way we could do something less … grungy?"

"Of course." Holding back a sigh, Elise scanned the list again. She'd just ask Samantha and Brittany to switch out. "How about helping to clear out the attic?" She pointed down the northern hallway. "Just go that way and you'll see the pull-down stairs. You can tell my daughters to see me about a different job."

"Thanks, Elise. You're a peach." But instead of leaving, Carlotta inclined her head toward Elise and lowered her voice. "Where is Charles these days? I haven't seen much of him. Heard he hasn't been able to help with the renovation at all."

Oh, that woman. Did she really have nothing better to do than pry into others' lives? Elise tightened her grip on her pen as she scratched through her daughters' names and wrote in Carlotta's and company's. "Unfortunately, he's been out of town a lot lately."

Not really in the last few weeks, since they'd started attending counseling. But Carlotta didn't need to know that.

Truth was, she'd never actually asked Charles to help with the Refuge renovation. She'd hoped he would come on his own as a way to support her.

But he hadn't. She couldn't be upset about him not being able to read her mind though.

Still, after forty years …

"Oh?" Carlotta leaned close, lowering her voice. "But I saw you both coming out of Danielle Fibbs's office just two days ago." Pausing, she schooled her features into something that looked like sympathy—but Elise knew better. "I hope everything is all right between you."

And there it was, the shark sniffing for blood, out on a hunt.

Well, Elise may be bleeding, but she'd rather lose a limb than acknowledge it in front of the town's gossip queen.

"Of course it is." Sweat broke out along the nape of Elise's neck. She fanned herself with the clipboard. "Now, if you'll excuse me."

Carlotta kept that fake smile plastered to her face, as did her accomplices. Reaching out, she patted Elise's arm. "If you ever need to talk, I'm here." Then she and her posse walked down the hallway. When they were out of sight, laughter tittered in their wake.

Unbelievable. It wasn't enough that people were hurting …

Elise inhaled a sharp breath and turned to go to the lobby as planned. But before she could, a precarious stack of lumber leaning vertically against the far wall shifted and one long plank clattered to the floor.

Her hand flew to her heart. Thank goodness it had fallen when no one was next to it, or it might have done some serious damage. Who had stacked these so dangerously? She'd need to get someone to lay them horizontally right away.

Or … well, why not? She could do it herself, couldn't she? It would be nice to do some physical labor on the old place instead of merely advising others to do it. And besides, it might help her work out some of the aggression currently roiling through her veins. Carlotta seemed to have that effect on people.

Elise set her clipboard on the dusty floor and shook out her hands as she cautiously approached the stack of wood. But the moment she lifted the first plank of wood, Elise regretted the action. It was heavy—too heavy—and she nearly fell backward with the added weight.

"Mom!" Brittany's voice reached Elise before she did, but thankfully it was only a few seconds before her daughter's strong hands arrived on the wood. "What were you thinking?" She tossed the wood to the ground on top of the other horizontal plank as if it weighed nothing more than a piece of paper.

Elise gripped her left shoulder. What *had* she been thinking? She couldn't lift that load on her own. It had been foolish to try.

But she'd been alone …

Samantha came jogging up behind Brittany and placed her hand on Elise's back. "Are you okay?"

"Fine, fine." Elise held her waist with both hands, steadying her breath. "Just bit off more than I could chew, I guess."

"You're working too hard, Mom." Brittany glanced at Samantha. "We're worried about you."

"What?" Had they been talking with Charles? This sounded exactly like the concerns he'd been expressing lately. "No, I'm really not. This is the first time I've attempted any manual labor with the renovation, I promise."

"But Dad said you're working late into the night, every night." Samantha bit her bottom lip. "And Nate said you were too busy to watch the twins during fall break next month."

"That's not true. I merely said I couldn't commit to it." Which had been difficult for her. But she had looked at her to-do list and wasn't sure she could give up an entire week—even though her heart ached with missing the grandkids. "I'm still assessing my schedule so I can try to make it happen."

"But come on." Brittany tugged at the sleeve of her ratty Fire Department T-shirt. "That's not like you. You haven't even hosted a family dinner since Chloe was in town, and that was like, over a month ago."

Elise's heart hitched. She hadn't meant to step back from her family responsibilities in such a drastic way. But it wasn't forever. And she'd found a passion project, as Jules had called it. Weren't they happy for her?

Or maybe they couldn't imagine her in any other role than wife and mom. Not that she could blame them. Caring for her family had been her whole life for so long.

Over the years, she'd heard women talk about practicing "self-care" and she hadn't been able to keep from laughing, maybe even scoffing a bit. What mother had time for that? But perhaps she'd done her children a disservice by making them the absolute center of her world.

Thankfully, whatever her failings, her children had turned into wonderful people. And, as Elise was discovering, it was never too late to change. To grow.

But she did miss spending time with her family—of course she did. "Tell you what. Let's have a girls' night sometime soon. You pick the date. Maybe Chloe can even come."

"That sounds really great, Mom." Samantha smiled softly. "How about Sunday night? Do you work, Britt?"

"Nope, I'm off. Works for me." Brittany cracked her knuckles. "Now, where did you want us? Should we go ahead and move these planks for you?"

"No need, ladies."

Elise jolted at the masculine voice behind her—one she hadn't expected to hear. She turned to find Charles standing at the top of the stairs wearing jeans and a silky-looking exercise shirt. His muscled arms looked good for a sixty-four-year-old man.

Really, they looked good for any man.

He strode forward. "I'll help your mother with these."

"H-hi." Goodness. Could she sound any more like an awkward teenager having a first phone conversation with a boy she really liked?

Thankfully, her daughters didn't seem to notice. They just

gave their dad hugs and turned back to Elise. "Where are we working now?" Brittany asked again.

"Oh." Elise blinked, then frowned. "Scrubbing the bathroom walls upstairs. I'm sorry in advance."

"No problem." Samantha shrugged. "Happy to help."

She and Brittany headed down the stairs, presumably to get the necessary supplies for their task.

Charles took another step, his gaze tentative. "So." He indicated the wood. "Shall we get started?"

"Okay. Um, yes." Despite her cold muscles, she managed to move toward the stack of wood once more and placed her fingers against the smooth plane of the topmost piece.

Before she could lift the burden fully onto herself, Charles joined her, filling the space between them with the scent of his cologne.

But wait.

It wasn't his typical sandalwood mixture of amber and patchouli, an earthy blend of elegance she admittedly had come to love when he'd started wearing it years ago—after receiving his first paycheck as a full-fledged attending physician.

The aroma of *this* cologne was much lighter—citrus and sea breeze. It tantalized her nose, and she instinctively leaned closer. Why did it smell somewhat familiar?

Oh my goodness. Could it be? Had he rummaged underneath their sink and located the bottle of his old cologne—the one he'd worn when she'd fallen in love with him as a poor med school student?

The one she'd commented more than once on loving?

Her eyes found Charles's, and he smiled as if he *could* read her mind after all. For a moment, their gazes held, something unspoken hovering between them.

Then, wordless but together, they moved the planks of wood one by one until the task was complete.

CHAPTER SIXTEEN

JENNA

*A*side from being a mom, being an aunt was the most amazing feeling in the world.

Jenna pressed her lips against the feather-soft skin of her niece, who was currently curled up on her chest as she sat in the nursery rocker. Despite coming several weeks early, Penny was perfect, all the way from the tuft of black hair on her head to her ten little toes with exquisitely tiny nails. She hadn't had a bit of trouble breathing on her own from the beginning, and now that Gabrielle was home after a week of postpartum observation in the hospital, they'd all developed a new routine.

"You're one lucky little lady, you know that?" Jenna pushed her heels into the ground as she inhaled the powder-fresh scent that was Penny. The baby stirred, mewling with one cheek pressed against Jenna's chest, her bow-shaped lips parted as she slept. "To be loved so much."

Their baby was only two and a half weeks old, and already Tyler and Gabrielle were amazing parents—sacrificing sleep, working together to make sure Gabrielle recovered from her surgery and still got adequate skin to skin time with Penny. Jenna was so thankful to be able to help, to repay just a little of what Gabrielle had done when Liam was born. She and Liam had been over here as much as possible to help cook, clean, and hold the baby while her parents snagged naps.

Cam had been super understanding of her need to cut back on her work hours. He'd even hired one of his youngest Baker cousins—Rachelle, a high school student—to fill in for Jenna and help out as needed.

"What are we going to do about him, hmm, Miss Penny?" Stroking her niece's arm, Jenna allowed her thoughts to drift once more—for like, maybe the thousandth time … okay, millionth—to that day in the hospital when he'd held her, calmed her, been by her side. And in the days after, all the texts he'd sent checking in on her, offering to pick up Liam and keep him so Jenna could be at the hospital.

The few times he'd stopped by while she'd been sitting by Gabrielle's bedside, eyes bloodshot from worry and lack of sleep, and dropped off a coffee and a gift card for the hospital cafeteria.

He'd become much more than just a boss. Much more than even a friend—he was becoming one of her best friends.

So much for her resolution to stop loving him.

Because his actions lately had only made her heart cling even more firmly to the idea that he could be the love of her life—if only he'd see it too.

Her phone vibrated where it was shoved between her thigh and the rocking chair. Jenna picked it up and thumbed past the security screen to find a new email notification. Humming to Penny, she swiped to open the email—and all sound ceased coming from her throat.

Liam had received the scholarship for space camp, which would start in two weeks, during fall break.

But … they'd already announced the winners and Liam hadn't been one of them. She'd been relieved she hadn't told Liam about applying. So how had this happened? Jenna kept reading the email, a smile blooming on her lips. Apparently, another student who'd received the scholarship couldn't take it, and Liam was next on the list.

Her son was going to flip his lid.

Penny stirred and her hand found her mouth. She began to suck and gnaw, and her little face scrunched up. Her eyes opened and she whimpered, sucking harder on her fist.

"Time to get you to your mama, huh, Baby Girl?" Jenna stood, padding across the carpeted room and down the hall to where her sister lay in her room. She hated to wake her up, but Penny wasn't yet taking bottles so there wasn't much else to be done.

The baby started to cry full force, and Gabrielle woke up without Jenna having to say a word. For a minute, she looked confused until she saw Jenna. "You're still here?" Working her way to a seated position, she reached for Penny.

Jenna settled the baby into her sister's arms. "Yep."

Unsnapping the front of her nursing tank, Gabrielle positioned Penny and started to feed her. The baby latched, sucking as if she'd never get another meal. Gabrielle breathed a sigh of relief and leaned her head back against the headboard. "You're here so much that I don't know how you're managing school."

"You'd be surprised how much work you can get done while holding a baby." Jenna winked. "When you're not the mom, that is."

"Yeah, I don't remember being this tired when Liam was born. Then again, I was ten years younger, and you were the one who had to carry, birth, and nurse him."

Near the front of the house, a door opened and closed. Jenna peeked out into the hallway and saw Tyler walk from the living room into the kitchen holding a pizza box. "Your hubby is back with dinner. I think I might sneak out. I got some exciting news and I need to share it with someone."

"Someone, huh?" Gabrielle's eyebrow lifted and an amused

smile took over her face. "Don't suppose his name rhymes with Bameron?"

"Really, Sis?"

"Hey, I'm tired, okay? It's hard to think up any zingers when you're going on two hours of sleep."

"I'll be back to help you with the late shift tonight. Liam's spending the night with Jared again, so I've got nowhere to be."

"It's Friday night. Go do something fun with friends. Or … someone." Gabrielle waggled her eyebrows, which looked ridiculous since her eyelids were so droopy.

"Technically it's still Friday afternoon." Four forty-five, but who was counting? "And partying with my niece at midnight when she's actually awake *is* fun." Jenna blew a kiss. "See you later. Love you."

"Love you too."

After saying goodbye to Tyler, Jenna hopped in her car and headed to Rise. Since it was almost the last week of September and the big summer season was over, parking was easier to come by, though spots were filling up with locals heading to dinner at Mimosa's Steak and Seafood, the Bar & Grill, the Frosted Cake, and other restaurants along Main Street.

The late-afternoon air off the ocean had a fresh autumn nip to it, and Jenna zipped up her hoodie before entering the rental shop. Cameron looked up from behind the desk and grinned. "Didn't expect to see you today." He wore a long wetsuit, and his hair had been freshly cut since the last time she'd seen him a few days ago.

"I had something I wanted to tell you." Jenna glanced around, expecting to see Rachelle. But it seemed they were alone. Maybe he'd sent her home early, given the shop closed at five in the off-season. Or maybe she hadn't worked today. "Liam got the space camp scholarship."

"What? No way!" Cam held up a hand across the desk for a high five.

"I know." Jenna slapped his palm. "I couldn't believe it."

"What did he say when you told him?"

"I haven't yet. I'll tell him tomorrow when I pick him up from Jared's." She couldn't imagine giving him the news over the phone. She wanted to see his face. "I literally just got the email and came here to tell you." Aaand she sounded really pathetic admitting that, didn't she? She totally should have told Liam first. But ... "I mean, you were the one who encouraged me to apply, so." Jenna shrugged, biting the inside of her cheek.

"He's going to be so happy, Jen." Cam walked around the desk and leaned against it right next to where Jenna stood. "And you did that."

"*We* did that." And yep, that sounded waaay too ... something. She rushed on. "I just wanted to let you know. So. Yeah. Now you know." Turning on her heel, she took a step toward the door like the coward she was.

"Hang on there just a sec." Cam snagged her elbow and spun her to face him again. "Where are you off to now? Let me guess. I know you're not working. But studying? Taking care of Penny and Gabrielle?"

"And your point is?" Jenna nudged her chin up just a smidge, eyes challenging him.

"My point is, you've been working yourself to the bone. I think you deserve a break."

It sounded nice—more than nice, really—but ... "I have a paper due tomorrow, and I'd like to stay in my professor's good favor."

Somehow, she'd managed to do so, meeting one-on-one with Professor Champion during her office hours every week to discuss the future of interior design and decorating, where she saw herself in five years, and what she could do to make herself stand out among other job candidates for future positions.

To think that Jenna potentially could be like the woman she'd come to respect so much in such a short time, that she—

high school dropout and teen mom—could ever amount to anything ... well, it was pretty incredible.

"That's tomorrow. Today is today."

Ugh. Staring up into his warm chocolate eyes, Jenna felt her insides melting into pudding. "What did you have in mind?"

"I was about to take my WaveRunner out. Come with me."

No way. Sobbing in his arms on a tragic day was one thing, but wrapping her arms around him, her cheek pressed to his back as they rode as closely as life jackets would allow? Her heart would never survive that.

"Okay." Ugh. Apparently her mouth had a mind of its own.

"Great. Put on your wetsuit, though."

Rolling her eyes, she gave him a push. "You think I'm an amateur or something?" Jenna strode into the back room where she kept her work wetsuit, then ducked into the bathroom to change.

Before she knew it, Cameron was locking up and they were walking down the boardwalk toward the marina at the south end of town. "How's your sister doing?"

"Oh, you know Gabrielle." Jenna side-stepped to avoid a family with small children. "She's as amazing as ever. You'd never know she had emergency surgery just two and a half weeks ago."

"Gotta love those older siblings, don't you?"

Something simmered beneath the surface of his tone. "What do you mean?"

"They're just so ..."

"Perfect?"

"Yep, that's the word for it." He laughed, but the edges were rough, grating—not at all a normal Cameron laugh.

Hmm. "You've never really talked much about being the youngest." Pushing her sunglasses up onto the top of her head, she studied him. "I guess I figured since you were all born within minutes of each other, birth order didn't quite play a role in your identity." Not like it had for Jenna.

"Uh, when you have a lawyer, doctor, bookstore owner, fire-fighter paramedic, and pastor for older siblings, and you merely manage a shop in town? Yeah. It comes into play." He ran a hand through his hair. "I mean, no one has ever come right out and said I'm the black sheep of the family, but ..."

"Believe me, I totally get it." Although in her case, people *had* said as much when they thought she wasn't listening. "But what about growing up? Did you always feel like the underachiever?"

Sand skittered across the boardwalk as a cyclist passed them. They walked for a few long moments before he answered. "No. I guess I just felt ... unremarkable. Unnoticed. I mean, I know I'm the 'baby' of the family technically, and the baby normally gets a lot more attention—"

"Hey."

Cameron shoulder bumped her, smiling. "It's just a fact." Then he sobered. "Not really in my case, though. My parents were just so overwhelmed with six kids, which is totally under-standable, but that meant we all had to perform in some way to get attention. Since I wasn't brilliant like Chloe and Nate or fierce like Brittany or charming and sweet like Samantha or dedicated and faithful like Spencer, well ..."

They reached the marina and walked to the dock, where Cameron's Yamaha WaveRunner was parked.

"But you're ... you." Jenna swallowed. "And I think that's much better than being any of your siblings."

Cam jumped onto the dock and lifted the seat of his Wave-Runner to check for gas vapors and vent the engine compart-ment. Waves lapped against the dock several feet below. "Mindy didn't agree with you."

"Mindy?" She paused. Wait ... "When you said you fell in love with your best friend and someone else married her, you were talking about Mindy?"

As in, Nate's wife, who had died after a terrible accident?

He grimaced. "Yeah."

Jenna blinked. She'd been in the throes of early motherhood when Nate and Mindy had gotten together, and the Griffin siblings were nearly a decade older than her, so she didn't exactly know all the details.

But she did remember how Mindy and Nate had been attached at the hip for a few years before they'd gotten married. She also remembered being jealous of the seemingly perfect couple and their Hallmark-like love story, especially after Brock had broken her heart.

But it seemed their romance had also left a broken heart in its wake.

"So you fell in love with Mindy." She stepped onto the tiny personal watercraft dock as Cameron checked that the drain plugs were securely installed. "How did that happen?"

"The usual way, I guess." His hands stayed busy with his launch pre-check, but his voice grew husky. "We'd known Mindy our whole lives in school, and at different points, she was closer with some of us more than others. But it wasn't until senior year that she and I got really close. We even went to prom together, but just as friends. She and Nate didn't start dating till after college, and at that point, she and I were hanging out all the time."

"That must have been terrible when she chose Nate instead." Jenna knew a little something about that kind of pain. "How did she react when you told her you loved her?"

"I never did."

"What? Why?" Jenna plopped onto the seat of the watercraft next to Cameron's.

"I tried to kiss her once, but she freaked out. Then I had to play it off like I'd been kidding."

"Yikes."

"Yeah." He slammed the seat of his WaveRunner back on.

"Apparently she preferred the serious doctor type over the chucklehead who didn't even go to college. Can't say I blame her."

Wow. She'd never heard Cam talk like this, as if he actually questioned his own self-worth. He'd always seemed so confident, so full of life and humor. "Being serious is overrated."

"I like my life. I do." Grabbing a container of fuel, he gassed up the craft. "But sometimes I wish I could do something with my life that actually helps people, you know? Something that makes an impact."

"Are you kidding? In the seven years since I've worked at Rise, do you have any idea how many times you bolstered my spirits when I was depressed and in serious need of a laugh?" Jenna stood, placing her hand on his arm, waiting until he looked down at her. She wanted him to really hear her on this. "Sometimes, seeing you was the only good part of my day. You never treated me like I was a depressed mess, even though I was. And you did everything possible to make me feel better. Laughter is some of the best medicine, which makes you a doctor of another kind."

His Adam's apple bobbed. "I liked to make it my mission to make you smile. If I did that, my day was a success."

"And you were—you are—so good at it." Jenna squeezed his bicep, the rubber of his wetsuit smooth beneath her fingertips. She wanted so badly to soothe his hurt, but would saying what was really in her heart cross the line he'd clearly established for their friendship?

His eyes flicked down to her lips momentarily and he leaned in, as if waiting for her to say more.

Oh, forget it. "I would choose you any day, Cameron Griffin."

Her whispered words seemed to knock him back a bit. His brow furrowed and he stared at her, studying her like he'd never seen her before in his life. Clearing his throat, he motioned toward the WaveRunner. "Ready to ride?"

She sighed, the spell broken. Well, she might as well get a fun time out of this. "Yep, and I'm driving."

His surprised laugh followed her as she shrugged into a life jacket, climbed on, and started the engine. It rumbled to life, purring beneath her legs. Cameron climbed on behind her, and she had to suck in a breath when he hugged her waist with his strong arms.

Oh, how she wanted to lean back and nestle against him. Instead, she pulled off the dock and throttled the gas a bit more until they were out in the waves. The fresh spray of salt mist cooled her warm cheeks, and soon she was whooping and laughing at the constant up and down. She even did a few tricks, spinning and enjoying Cam's laughs against her ear.

"Look!" He pointed to the right, where a pod of dolphins exited and entered the water with a grace that had always amazed Jenna. Theirs was a beautiful dance, leaps combined with forward motion, and soon the WaveRunner was surrounded by them. It was as if they were inviting Jenna and Cameron to participate in their ballet—and Jenna couldn't say anything but yes.

After a few minutes, she slowed and came to a bobbing stop so they could watch the creatures more closely. Peace filled the air. Back on land, there were a thousand things constantly threatening to take Jenna down a notch, to tumble her back into the abyss she'd clawed her way out of more than once.

But out here, there was only sea and sun, light and calm and joy bursting from all around her.

She sighed. "It's beautiful, isn't it?"

Cameron didn't answer her, only tightened his hold on her waist. What was he thinking?

Curious, she glanced over her shoulder at him—and found his lips so close they nearly brushed her cheek.

"Hi."

"Um, hi." Jenna's heart knocked against her ribcage and it had nothing to do with the adrenaline left over from the ride. What was happening?

"Jenna?"

"Yeah?"

"Did you really mean what you said?" A pause. "About choosing me?"

She swallowed. "Yeah."

"I think …" His breath fanned warm against her skin. "I think I've broken my own rule."

He wasn't saying what she thought he was … was he?

She licked her lips, and something in his eyes lit, a slow flame that burned through her. "Your rule?"

"About not falling for my friends."

"Oh."

Oh.

And slowly, like thick syrup being poured from a bottle, he moved his lips toward hers. A thousand suns burst in her fingers, her toes, and he tasted like chocolate-covered nuts. His kiss was slow and sweet—and it was more intimate than any romantic contact she'd ever experienced. Never had she felt so cherished, so in tune with someone else.

It was only a kiss, but it was so much more.

As the WaveRunner rocked beneath them, he trailed his lips from hers across her cheekbone, to her ear, down to the hollow of her neck.

After landing one more kiss on her lips, he exhaled. "What have you done to me, Jenna Wakefield?"

She laughed, still not believing this was real. "Whatever it is, I hope to repeat it."

"From your lips …" Growling, he nipped her earlobe again. "What are you waiting for? Let's get this puppy back to dock so I can kiss you even more thoroughly."

Jenna shivered at the thought. "That wasn't thorough?"

"Not even close."

Whoa, buddy. She needed solid ground. Pronto. "Hang on tight, Romeo."

"With pleasure."

CHAPTER SEVENTEEN

ELISE

*H*er offerings for the Sunday girls' night were meager —but with five minutes to spare, what could she do?

Hands on her hips, Elise harrumphed as she surveyed the single bag of tortilla chips, the half-eaten jar of salsa, and the tiny bag of M&M's she'd scrounged up from the pantry.

If she wasn't so distraught, it would be comical, because honestly ... when was the last time Elise Griffin hadn't had a mountain of chocolate and junk food in her possession waiting in the wings for a rotten day or a happy moment or basically any occasion?

Though now that she thought about it, she hadn't eaten dessert all week long.

Was it busyness ... or just a lack of need for it?

Either way, she'd been far too buried in her to-do list to go shopping lately, so Charles had either picked up dinner on his way home or they'd eaten whatever she could toss together from the ingredients in the pantry and deep freezer in the garage.

"What's wrong? You look like you ate a lemon." Charles

strode into the kitchen, shoulders relaxed. And why shouldn't they be? He'd spent his entire Sunday afternoon golfing with a few work buddies.

It didn't bother Elise like it once had, that he'd spend one of his only days off doing something with friends instead of her or the kids. Perhaps part of that was because after their morning session with Danielle yesterday, he'd suggested they go out to lunch.

They'd talked about surface-level things—work, the kids and grandkids, the list of things they still wanted to remodel in their home. It was nothing world shifting, but it was a start. In that moment, he'd shown her that he was trying.

Elise motioned to the snacks taking up a pathetically small amount of counter space. "I got so wrapped up in work again that I forgot I needed to shop for our girls' night."

"It's not like you all eat bucketloads of food. This looks fine."

Shaking her head, she barked out a laugh, which released some tension from her chest. "Clearly you have never been to a girls' night." She sighed. "I fear they're going to be disappointed. I always bake several treats." Maybe she *was* being derelict in her duty as a mom ...

"They'll understand." Charles snapped up his car keys from where they hung next to the garage door. "But since I know that you'll be worried about a lack of snacks, I'll pick up whatever you need at Hardings."

"Really?"

"Really." He stepped closer, and his hand suspended between them for a few achingly long moments before he finally placed it at her elbow. His thumb stroked her skin. "You've been working really hard, and I'd like to do my part in helping you have a relaxing night off."

How long had it been since someone else had taken care of Elise? The fact she couldn't remember probably told her something.

But was it because Charles hadn't offered—or because Elise hadn't let him?

She shook away the question. "That would be wonderful. Thank you."

"You're welcome." He maintained strong eye contact for a few extra seconds before pulling away and grabbing his phone off the counter. "What would you like me to get?"

After coming up with a list together, Charles left just as Brittany's pickup truck pulled into the driveway. Chloe was busy this weekend, so it would just be Samantha and Brittany coming over.

But when her daughters climbed out of the truck, they were accompanied by Jenna Wakefield. Curious. They hadn't said anything about inviting her. Not that Elise minded, considering how much she loved interacting with the younger woman at the Sisterhood meetings—especially since Elise had hired her on to decorate a little over three weeks ago.

And yes, maybe she still held out some hope where Cameron was concerned. Not that either of them had given her a reason to suspect anything more between them—especially since Cameron had made it clear he didn't think of her that way. But a mom could always dream.

"Hi, girls." Elise shielded her eyes from the sun and stepped outside to greet the three women.

"Hi, Mom." Samantha closed her truck door, carefully balancing a multi-drink container from Java's Village Bean—mocha lattes, if Elise knew her daughter. "I saw Jenna at Java's just after her work shift had ended, and she looked so tired that I decided she needed a girls' night just as badly as the rest of us."

That was her kindhearted girl, always taking care of those around her. Elise smiled. "I'm so glad you did. Welcome, Jenna."

Jenna shoved her hands into the back pockets of her skinny jeans. "I told her I didn't want to intrude. I'm sorry if I am."

"Nonsense." In turn, Elise pulled each of the women into a

hug—Jenna included. "We are happy to have you. How's that sweet sister and niece of yours doing?"

"Tired, of course, but they're good. Really good."

They all headed inside the house, Jenna filling them in on Penny's progress and Gabrielle's clean bill of health.

"I'm sure you're very grateful everything worked out as it did," Elise said. Cameron had told her how distraught Jenna had been in the waiting room before Elise had arrived to drop off some brownies the day of Penny's birth.

Settling onto the leather couch and love seat in the living room, the women chatted some more about life. Samantha told them about a new children's reading program she was implementing at the bookstore in conjunction with Madison Price over at the library.

Then she turned to Jenna. "I was actually thinking of doing some remodeling in the store and was wondering if you could give me some advice. Actually, I'd love to hire you."

"Oh, you don't have to pay me. I'm happy to help. I love doing stuff like that."

"Obviously, since you're in school for it. How's that going, by the way?"

As Jenna filled them in on how much she was loving her classes, Brittany got up and headed for the kitchen. A minute later, she reemerged, the chips and salsa in her hands. "Where's all the food, Mom?"

"Oh no." Samantha's eyes widened. "We should have brought stuff! I just assumed …"

Wiping her palms on her pant legs, Jenna scrambled to her feet. "I can go get something."

"Sit, sit, all of you. I admit, I got a bit distracted with work today, so Charles went to buy some snacks for us. He'll be back soon." She chuckled. "We will have to survive until then."

"That's nice of him." After setting the chips and dip on the coffee table, Brittany plopped onto the couch, kicking her tennis shoes off to reveal her plain white ankle socks. "How do you meet a nice guy like Dad who will run errands for you after forty years together? I can't even find someone who will pay for dinner without expecting something sweet for dessert in return —if you know what I mean."

"Gross." Samantha laughed and threw a pillow at her sister. "But I kind of agree. All the single guys around here are either too young, too old, just friends, or related to us."

It was certainly true that the pickings were slimmer for those who called the Bakers cousins. Elise shook her head. "There are plenty of nice boys around town, surely."

Her gaze flicked to a red-cheeked Jenna, who now held a pillow and played with the tassels. Elise so badly wanted to ask her if she'd met any nice men in Walker Beach, but her fishing for information would be cruel if Jenna really did have feelings for Cameron. And given the horrified look on Jenna's face last month at the Barefoot renovation when she'd overheard Elise's son say he didn't want to date her, Elise's suspicions seemed likely.

"I don't know." Scooting to the edge of her seat, Samantha popped open the bag of chips and snagged a few. The salty aroma saturated the immediate air space. "Pretty sure Dad is one in a million. When did you know he was the one, Mom?"

The sound of Samantha crunching into a chip reverberated in Elise's ears. Her mouth suddenly tasted like she'd taken a trip to the Sahara.

What would her daughters think if they knew of their father's betrayal?

Elise herself still didn't know what to think, quite honestly. She'd tried to have faith that marriage counseling was doing *something*—but whenever she thought about the affair, her insides would still harden and she'd wonder if forgiveness was truly possible.

The whole process was like digging to get to the roots of a

diseased plant and then trying to move that plant from its current location to better soil, where it might actually be able to grow again. Digging, it seemed, was a necessary part of healing. But often it felt tedious, as if they'd never reach the end of it. And removing deeply entrenched roots left her raw, tender, wondering if all the irritation, all the pain, would ever be worth it.

Focus. Just answer the question they're asking. Elise inhaled. "I suppose ..." When *had* she known Charles was the one for her?

Was it upon first meeting him at the movie theater where she'd worked in Los Angeles, when he'd ordered a popcorn and she'd stupidly given him a hot dog instead ... and rather than make fun of her, he'd smiled and said a quiet thank you?

Or perhaps it was their third date, when he'd shown up to find her sick with a stomach bug ... and he'd taken care of her despite only knowing her for a few weeks?

Or was it the time he'd shared with her about his simple dreams for the future—moving back to his small hometown of Walker Beach, working at the hospital there like his father had before him, and raising a little family with a woman he loved?

No. She knew.

Her fingers touched her lips almost without thought. "It was when he kissed me. A kiss can tell you a lot, and when he kissed me at the end of our first date, I knew that I would marry him someday."

Curling into Elise's side, Samantha sighed. "Sounds magical."

Jenna stared at the ground, and if possible, her face was even more cherry colored. Maternal instinct nearly blotted out Elise's good sense, and she had to force herself to stay seated instead of going right over and hugging the girl, who was obviously uncomfortable with this conversation for some reason.

"I've kissed some guys who were really good kissers—but they turned out to be serious duds." Nose scrunched, Brittany dug a chip into the jar and pulled it back piled with salsa. "I'll probably be single forever, and I'm cool with that. Not everyone can have the fairy-tale love story you and Dad have had."

A familiar ache crept up Elise's arm. There was that word again—fairy-tale. No, she didn't want her children to know the particulars about Charles's affair. Didn't want them to feel like they needed to take sides. Didn't want to harm their relationship with their father.

But, she also didn't want to give them a false sense of what a marriage was—of what *her* marriage was. Didn't want them putting it up on a pedestal like something they could never achieve for themselves, as if fate or God had handed Elise something special that could never be replicated for them.

How did she balance telling them the truth while maintaining the respect they had for their father at the same time?

And what would happen if ...?

She sucked in a hard breath.

What if she really couldn't forgive Charles? What if they dug and dug and never got to the end of the gnarled roots? What if the roots were too damaged to ever really heal? What if they had killed the plant from the bottom up?

Nausea claimed her stomach, and the pain in her arms and chest increased. Cold sweat broke out over her whole body, and her breathing grew shallow.

"Mom?" Brittany turned in her seat then squatted in front of Elise. "You look really pale. Everything okay?"

"I ..." Elise sucked in another breath. "I'm not ..."

"Sam, call 911. I think Mom might be having a heart attack."

"What?" Her daughter's screech filled her ears.

A heart attack? No. Not possible.

But her chest felt like a clamp had fastened across it, slowly cranking down to steal her breaths. And her daughter was a firefighter paramedic. She probably knew what she was talking about.

Oh.

Oh no.

What was happening?

Was she going to die?

Somewhere in the distance, a door opened. Elise looked up, but her vision swam and she had to close her eyes against the very real possibility that she was going to faint.

A hand touched her forehead, her cheek—soft, sweet, but firm in its assessment. "It's all right, honey. Just breathe. The ambulance is on the way."

"Charles?"

"I'm here, sweetheart."

Yes, he was. And he was next to her, with her. He hadn't abandoned her, not when she really needed him.

Elise opened her eyes and focused on his face. She continued breathing, puffing in and out until the tightness finally lessened. Her heart rate slowed and the pain subsided before the ambulance even arrived.

"Oh, thank goodness." Charles took Elise's hand and kissed her palm.

"Is she going to be okay?" Sam's voice clanged like a distant bell.

"We need to take her to the hospital to get her fully checked out before we know what we're dealing with. But I think she'll be all right." He spoke to Sam, but he stared into Elise's eyes, stroking her hair, his own eyes glistening. "You're going to be all right."

Was he actually … almost … crying?

Her heart stirred and she tried for a weak smile. "Thank you for taking care of me, Charles."

"Always."

And in that moment, she felt he really meant it.

CHAPTER EIGHTEEN

JENNA

*I*f heaven existed on earth, Kiki's Antiques on Main was most definitely a stop along the golden streets.

Jenna dug around in the back corner of the store that was owned by one of Jules's older sisters. She knew from experience that this was where all the good stuff was hidden away. Oh sure, not the flashy pieces that Kiki had cleverly marked up for tourists, but the pieces that might need just a little bit of love to really shine.

Picking up a large rustic clock, Jenna ran her finger along the outer edge of the wood, which was nicked and scarred. The wood wasn't perfect, which meant it had a story to tell—just like the Barefoot B&B.

It would look perfect over the lobby mantel.

For the last month and a half since Elise had given her the job back in early September, Jenna had been hard at work making design boards and thinking about what she was going to do with the place. Of course, then Penny had come and thrown off her plans just a bit. But now that Baby Girl was nearly six weeks old and Gabrielle had mostly healed from the rather traumatic delivery, Jenna had thrown herself into the decorating process. She'd been able to make some good progress this last week while Liam had been at space camp. Not quite as much as she'd have liked, of course—school especially was still going strong.

And then there was her new relationship that had been more than a little distracting ...

Her lips curled into a smile as she stared at the clock.

"I take it you'll be getting that?" Strong arms encircled her from behind.

Setting the clock down, she twisted and snuck her arms around Cameron's neck. "How did you know?" Jenna lifted on her tiptoes and landed a kiss on his lips.

Despite having had three weeks of practice, the contact still thrilled her to her toes.

Cameron's mouth twitched. "You had the same look on your face while staring at that clock as you do whenever you look at me."

Rolling her eyes, Jenna laughed and pushed on his chest till he released her. "Don't be so sure of that. I think I like it more than I like you."

He picked up the clock. "You must really love it then, because I have it on good authority that you're crazy about me."

If only he knew how much.

"Oh man." They started weaving their way through the aisles toward the front of the store. "If I'd known kissing you would give you such a big head, maybe I'd never have done it."

False. Her pants had never felt so on fire.

After their ride on the WaveRunner, they'd returned to the rental shop, changed out of their wetsuits into their street clothes, and went on their first official date one town over—tacos and a movie. And yeah, fine, she didn't remember much about the film's storyline, not with Cameron's hand caressing hers the whole time.

A couple weeks later, after testing the waters of their new

relationship in relative secret, they'd finally gone out for dinner at the Frosted Cake. Since they'd eaten together as friends plenty of times before, townspeople hadn't seemed to think anything of it.

Not until Cameron had leaned over in the middle of dinner and kissed her, claiming she had some ketchup on the side of her mouth and he was just helping her to get rid of it.

After that, the whole place had quieted. Then people all around the café had broken out into applause.

Of course, Cameron had stood and taken a bow.

It had been humiliating—and she'd loved every second of it.

Smiling at the memory, Jenna paid for the clock using the Refuge credit card Elise had given her for expenses and left the shop with Cameron in tow. Crisp fallen leaves in brilliant shades of oranges, yellows, and reds blew from the trees on the east side of Main Street, skipping across their feet.

It was only mid-October, but the weather had already turned colder than Jenna preferred. The entire last week had consisted of days filled with rain. And if the gray clouds looming in the distance were any indication, today would have more of the same.

Together, they walked to Rise, where Jenna placed the clock in the back for safekeeping. After chatting with Cameron's cousin Rachelle, who was manning the store for the day, they headed outside and climbed into the cab of Cam's truck. He glanced at the dashboard clock. "Anything else you need to do before we go get Liam?"

"No." She wrinkled her nose. "But are you sure you don't mind driving all the way to Los Angeles with me? There are a million other ways you could be spending your Saturday off."

He bent closer and she met him halfway. Cupping her face, he flicked his thumb over her cheekbone. "There is literally nowhere else I'd rather be right now."

Then he lowered his lips to hers and she sighed, allowing

herself to get lost in his scent. Looping her arms around him, she played with the curls at the base of his neck.

Finally, she pulled back and buckled her seat belt. "We've got a long drive ahead of us. I hope you brought snacks."

"Who do you think you're dealing with here?" He thumbed toward the back. "I grabbed a bit of everything. My mom trained me well." Pulling out of his parallel parking space along the curb, he eased onto Main Street and headed out of town toward Highway 1.

Jenna twisted in her seat and pulled a plastic grocery bag onto her lap. Riffling through it, she found an assortment of chocolates, gummy candy, trail mix, and crackers. "How did her doctor's visit go yesterday, by the way?" Though she'd visited Elise a few days ago, the woman hadn't been at the Sisterhood meetings since her heart episode three weeks ago. And because she always seemed hesitant to talk about her health, Jenna didn't like to press.

"Really good, according to my dad. Her medication seems to be working to prevent any more heart attacks."

"That's wonderful." Jenna chose a bag of sour worms and tore it open with her teeth. "I know she's been a little freaked out about getting behind on work for the Refuge, but people in the community have really stepped up and helped. The renovation work is close to being finished."

"I know, it's looking good." A pause and then he flipped on some reggae music, keeping it low. "And yeah, Mom was worried, but we convinced her that her health is more important right now. She seems to be taking that to heart—no pun intended. She and Dad have started walking every day. She's trying out a new diet too, trying to get more fruits and vegetables in, fewer fried foods, that kind of thing."

At the slight wobble in Cam's tone, Jenna glanced up from the snacks and studied his profile. Even though his fingers drummed the steering wheel as if things were totally normal and all right, his face had grown a bit pale. "Hey."

His gaze flicked to her, then back to the highway. "Hey."

She placed her hand on the center console and he reached over and took it, weaving their fingers together. "You okay?"

"Yeah, of course."

"Uh huh." She let go of his hand, then traced the lines on his palm with her fingertips. "You're about as okay as Liam the year he found out the truth about Santa."

Cameron didn't speak for several minutes, so Jenna moved her eyes to the gorgeous coastline outside her window as they headed south toward LA. If she were to open her door and step out, she'd fall off a steep cliff, which gave a gorgeous but terrifying view. Even with the cloud cover, some sunlight peeked through, showing off silver-blue patches of the ocean below.

"You're right. I'm not okay." Cam huffed out a breath. "We could have lost her, you know?"

"I know." The scene had replayed in her mind on a loop for several days, and she'd woken up in a cold sweat more than once. Even though Elise wasn't her mother, sometimes Jenna's dreams had morphed—and it was like living her mom's death all over again.

Of course, she hadn't told Cameron that. Didn't want to freak him out any more than he already was.

"And the thing is … I was kind of horrible to her a few months ago."

"You? I doubt that." He didn't have a mean bone in his body —not that she'd seen, anyway.

This time around, she'd chosen well.

"No, really." Shaking his head, he choked out a caustic laugh. "I told her to stop meddling in my life. Basically, that I didn't need her anymore. And yet, she was totally right."

Jenna dug out a pink sour worm with her free hand. "What was she right about?" She popped it into her mouth.

A smile inched its way onto his lips. "You."

She coughed on the smidgens of sour sugar. "Me?"

"Yes, you. She told me that I should pay more attention to you. That you were a beautiful, funny, responsible woman who loved fiercely, and that I was basically an idiot to not be pursuing you."

"Oh." Jenna was pretty sure the tips of her ears were turning as pink as the worm in her mouth.

"Like I said—she was right." A song by Bob Marley came on the radio, filling the truck cab with a steady, punchy beat. "Deep down, I think I'd noticed all of those things. But I was just so beat up by the Mindy stuff that I couldn't admit it to myself, you know? I made up excuses, like me being your manager and you being younger—"

"It really doesn't bother you that I'm nine years younger?"

"Please, Jenna." Cameron's left hand gripped the steering wheel. "You're more mature than a lot of women my age. The way you've dealt with the tragedies in your life, the way you've used the mistakes you've made to become stronger, how confident you are, what a good mom you are—those are just a few of the things I love about you. And I still can't believe you chose me."

Yep, it was official. She was chocolate ice cream, and Cameron's words were the hot summer sun, scorching her insides with a warmth that fanned the flame she'd harbored for him for so long. And it took all her willpower not to tell him what she loved about him—and yeah, that she just plain loved him. Had for years, really.

But she wasn't a psycho, so she kept her mouth shut, allowing herself to bask in the glow of his affection for her. Which, maybe, would someday grow to match the height of her own for him.

They drove hand in hand for hours, talking about a lot of other things. Stupid, insignificant things and deeper things too.

Before she knew it, they were in Los Angeles and at the camp where Liam had just spent a week.

When they pulled into the parking lot filled with other vehicles, other parents, she got the tiniest glimpse of a future that might be.

The glimpse turned into a gaze when Liam ran to both of them, hugging Jenna and fist-bumping Cameron—and then again, during dinner at a pizza and arcade parlor, when Cameron and Liam played Skee-Ball and air hockey, calling out threats and teasing each other the whole time.

The gaze morphed into a full-blown stare as they drove back to Walker Beach in the dark, Liam asleep in the back, Cameron at the wheel, and Jenna curled up in the front passenger seat just watching the man she loved. He'd been more of a father figure to her son in one day than Brock had ever been in the kid's lifetime, simply because he'd been there. He'd made Liam feel seen and important. And it wasn't just because he wanted to impress Jenna.

What if … what if someday, this could be her life—all the time? Not just a dream, but reality?

Cameron glanced over at her, smiled, winked, and fixed his eyes back on the road.

When they were almost to the outskirts of town, Jenna's phone buzzed on the console where it was charging. She picked it up and flicked it on, momentarily blinded by the screen light, which she quickly lowered.

"Get a text?"

"No, an email." From her design professor.

Jenna opened it and started to read silently.

Jenna, I'm writing to let you know of an internship opening at my firm in San Francisco. The job actually pays quite well for an internship, and it would give you valuable corporate experience that would launch your career before you were even out of school. This is a unique opportunity that might not come around again.

We're looking for someone with a go-getter personality, high levels of creativity, and unique vision. In short, I think that someone is you.

I've taken the liberty of setting up an interview for you on Friday at two in the afternoon. If that time doesn't work for you, we can likely reschedule. But because we want the intern to begin the job within the next month (by mid-November at the latest), we don't want to wait too long.

I know you have family obligations to consider, but I want to reiterate that I have not met a student with as much potential as you in a long time. I believe in your future, and I hope you will give this job the time and consideration it deserves.

Please let me know what you think.

Regards, Renee

"Whoa." Jenna lowered the phone and bit her lip. Her heart pounded an irregular rhythm.

"What? Good news?"

"I'm … not sure." Her throat dry, she looked at Cameron. The clouds had cleared, leaving the moonlight to stream through the windshield, washing his face in a strange sort of ethereal glow.

She couldn't possibly move to San Francisco indefinitely.

Could she?

But what had her professor written? *This is a unique opportunity that might not come around again.*

With a single email, Professor Champion had upended all of Jenna's plans. Because after promising herself that she'd never again let anything—not even a man … especially not a man—hold her back from pursuing her dreams, how could she *not* try?

"Well? Don't leave me in suspense." Cameron's dry chuckle chafed Jenna's insides.

Clearing her throat, she tucked her phone away and slid her hand back into his. "Just something school related." She hesitated. "It was nothing."

Liar, liar, pants on fire …

CHAPTER NINETEEN

ELISE

*H*ow many California sunsets had she seen in her lifetime? Too many to count. And yet, just over three weeks ago, Elise hadn't been sure she'd ever see another one.

But here she stood, bare feet in the wet sand, marveling at the glorious colors emblazoning the horizon as the sun retired for the evening.

And she wasn't alone.

"It never gets old, does it?" Elise peeked at Charles, who had rolled the bottom of his khaki pants so they wouldn't get wet in the chilly surf. "To see glory painted across the sky?"

"No, it never does." Charles held his arms loosely entwined behind his back, seeming to consider the masterpiece before him in the same way he did whenever they went to a fine art museum.

This had become their new evening custom, ever since she'd recuperated from her minor "episode" during girls' night and her doctor had run tests discovering that it hadn't been her first. A major attack was in her future if things didn't change. Surprisingly, Charles hadn't thrown on the physician's hat like she'd expected, ordering her around and prescribing this and that. Instead, they'd worked together to come up with diet changes they could both enjoy.

And when he'd asked her what kind of exercise she might like doing—together—she'd remembered how they used to walk Baker Beach almost every night that he wasn't working before they'd had kids. Charles had agreed without any qualms, and he'd already turned down a travel opportunity so he could be by Elise's side as she recovered and made the necessary changes.

Had he also noticed the shift between them? From strangers living in the same house to, at the very least, friends ...

And then there were the moments when it felt like more, when his gaze seared her and she wondered if perhaps he desired her in the way he used to. She still didn't *feel* all that desirable, even though she'd quickly lost fifteen pounds in these first few weeks of exercising and eating better.

And yet ...

"Charles?"

"Hmm?" He moved his attention back to her.

Without a word of agreement, they both started walking down the long stretch of beach that made up Baker Community Park, a six-acre combo of sand, playground equipment, and ramadas on the north side of town and the future location of the Christmas on the Beach Festival. "I just wanted to say thank you for everything you've done to make this transition as smooth as possible." She scraped her hand through her hair. "For taking care of me."

"You're my wife." The frolicking waves nearly suffocated his soft words. "Of course I'll take care of you."

And yet, you didn't. You didn't take care of my heart.

But she didn't say the words warring in her mind, maybe because she didn't want to ruin this peace between them—or take a step backward or fight or feel any more pain.

Or maybe the real reason she didn't say anything? Because

she knew that forgiveness didn't merely appear one day like a gift on her doorstep, all wrapped up neatly with a pretty little bow. She had to fight for it.

She had to choose it.

And frankly, the idea of letting go of all the pain he'd caused her almost scared her more than the possibility that she and Charles might never get back the closeness they'd once had.

But she couldn't have the latter without the former.

And by not forgiving, she was making a choice of a different kind.

Elise zipped up her jean jacket. Even though the rainstorms of the last few weeks had finally receded, the weather had turned colder overall. Soon mid-October would give way to November, which would give way to December—which meant she only had six and a half weeks until the Barefoot Refuge would host its soft opening.

Elise was woefully behind, but Charles hadn't liked the idea of her doing much work while she was supposed to be resting and recovering. She'd been hesitant to bring it up to him, but perhaps now was the best time, when they were out in the open, in nature, where Charles was always happiest.

"Well, you've done a wonderful job. I feel stronger than ever." She blew into her cold hands as they progressed down the packed-smooth sand. "I feel ready to return to work."

"Elise, we've discussed this."

"I know, but the other women are having to carry far too much weight."

Thankfully, Jenna—who, in a turn of events that had thrilled Elise to no end, was now dating Cameron—had taken the reins on the redesign and didn't require much more than occasional sign-offs from Elise.

And, surprise of all surprises, Quinn had stepped in to assist with funneling through the applications for an inn manager. They'd all decided that because the women in the Refuge would ideally be filling the various positions around the hotel, they didn't want to hire temporary employees now only to displace them later when the charity got off the ground. For the soft opening, the women in the Sisterhood had volunteered to fill in wherever needed.

But they still needed a permanent manager to oversee all of the volunteer and paid employees now and in the future.

"Seems to me you were carrying too much to begin with." At Elise's attempt at a protest, Charles held up his hand. "I know you don't like hearing that, but the stress likely contributed to your episodes."

"What?" A sudden gust of wind whipped against Elise. "My work at the Refuge has been the only bright spot in my life over the last few months."

He halted, eyebrows bunched together. "I don't understand. Why does the Refuge mean so much to you?"

He was finally asking the question she'd silently begged him to ask. And now, Elise couldn't think of a coherent answer. "I suppose ... I think it's because it's somewhere I can serve. I feel ... I don't know. Needed." In a way her family didn't need her anymore.

"Hmm."

"What?" And oh, she shouldn't have used such a sharp tone, but sometimes his *hmms* felt so ... condescending.

"It's just that I've been thinking about that story you told in one of our earlier sessions with Danielle. The one about the dress your sister stole from you."

"Borrowed."

He stared at her. "Stole. And you let her. Why, Elise?" His voice wasn't accusing, but gentle.

Prodding.

Her defensiveness slid from her back like a heavy cloak, and she really allowed herself to consider what he was asking. "Because she needed it more than I did."

"Maybe." He kicked at a rock embedded in the dark shore. "It seems to me that, from a young age, you were conditioned to receive praise when you sacrificed for other people, when you put aside what you wanted and did something nice for someone else." Charles shrugged. "I hope it doesn't sound as if I'm blaming you. Anyone would do the same if that's the only sort of notice they received."

It *had* been difficult to get her father's attention as a child. He'd been so busy. And her whole world had improved anytime she could bring a smile to his face.

There was an odd sort of power in it.

Her stomach churned at the unbidden thought. "No. I like to serve to make other people happy." Not herself. That would make her completely selfish ...

"It would make sense that it became your norm to do the thing that made you feel successful, wanted." He pinned her once more with a stare. "Needed."

"I suppose."

"I do agree that you seem to come alive when working on your Refuge to-do list. But ..."

Water crashed at her feet, biting into her ankles. She sucked in a breath at the unexpected contact and moved up the coast a bit, out of the pathway of the coming water. "But what?"

"Just be careful that you're doing it because you *want* to—not out of some misguided sense of duty or some quest for your identity."

"I'm ... not." Was she?

No. She really did love the work, did believe in it, did love feeling like part of a team, working toward something good that would benefit those without a voice.

Charles reached out for her, cautiously taking her hand in his and pressing it against his chest. "Because, honey, you don't have to do something or pretend to be something you're not to be valuable—not to me."

Her lips trembled. "I want to believe you ..." So badly.

But what if he changed his mind again? What if he walked away and didn't come home this time?

"I know I've hurt you, but I see the error of my ways. I pretended that the distance between us was all your fault, when really I was the one inching away. I think, just like you, I needed to be needed. You're so fiercely independent, and that's something I've always loved about you. Until it meant that you didn't need me anymore."

"What are you talking about?" She dug her toes into the sand, seeking the warmth of being buried. "I've always needed you."

"No, you didn't. Even when the kids were babies, you handled parenthood like a champ. Probably because you had so much practice with your siblings. You never seemed overwhelmed. Meanwhile, I felt like I was drowning most of the time." He shrugged. "So I started finding reasons to stay away. At first, it was subconscious, but eventually I did it on purpose. I made up excuses to be at the office later and later. I volunteered for trips across the country. At least at work, I knew my place. At home, you had it all handled."

She stared at him, jaw slack. How could he even think that? "I'm sorry, you thought *you* were drowning? I had six babies, Charles! At the same time. Not only did my hormones and the rest of my body rebel against me after that, but I was only getting a few hours of sleep a night. I couldn't think straight half the time. For years."

"And yet, you always managed to get food on the table, keep the house spotless, and make our kids the happiest they could possibly be."

"Did we live in the same house?" She nearly chuckled at his rose-colored view of those early years of parenting. "There was always laundry piled on the couch. Someone was always fighting and getting into trouble and crying." And to cope, Elise would hide in the pantry and join in the tears while stuffing her face with chocolate-covered pretzels. "Believe me, Charles—I needed you. But you weren't there."

And she'd never blamed him for that, had she? Because he'd been doing his part. They had been partners—in it together.

Except, they hadn't been. Not really. It had only been an illusion.

If only they'd talked about their feelings then instead of holding them in. How things might have turned out differently if they'd worked as a team instead of suffering individually in silence.

It had been her fault just as much as his. She simply hadn't known how to reach out, how to ask for help. How to admit that she was failing at the one thing she'd always thought she'd be good at.

His thumb strolled along the back of her hand. "I'm sorry, Elise. For all of it." Charles inhaled sharply. "I never cheated on you before last year, but I think my heart began wandering away from yours a long time ago. I told myself that you weren't giving me what I needed—but in actuality, *I* wasn't giving you what *you* needed."

Oh, Charles. The admission sliced at her wounds, and yet, there was a healing balm in them too.

She lifted her free hand and stroked his cheek, inching a step closer. "We forgot how to talk to each other, I suppose."

"I'm glad we're talking now." Charles's gaze roamed her face, stopping on her lips for a moment before returning to her eyes.

"Me too."

And then, as if afraid of breaking a precious piece of art, Charles let go of her hand and cradled her face between both of his palms. "Elise." He breathed the word into the wind, brushing her face with the minty smell of his toothpaste. "Forgive me. For all of it. I was a fool."

I'm not ready.

But would she ever be, really? Forgiveness required a leap of faith. There was no guarantee that he wouldn't hurt her again, that allowing herself to keep loving him would end in a different result this time than last time.

Still, what was it that Danielle had said in one of their more recent sessions? *"Forgiving someone doesn't mean trust is immediate. It may never come again. Saying you forgive someone doesn't mean they hold any more power over you than before. It simply means you acknowledge what they've done, have processed how it hurt you, and have chosen not to allow it to bog down your soul any longer."*

If Elise didn't choose forgiveness, she'd never be able to move forward, because withholding forgiveness was only going to cause her own wounds to fester. Which meant not only that there would be no future for her and Charles—but no real future for her alone, either.

The walking wounded had no future.

Elise closed her eyes for a moment, then opened them again, studying this man she'd committed to loving for all her days. "Yes." And then she applied the salve she knew they both so desperately needed. "I forgive you, Charles."

He pulled her into a hug, and, smiling, she buried her face in the place where his neck met his shoulder, breathing deeply of the air once more.

CHAPTER TWENTY

JENNA

*W*hat had she been thinking?

Jenna batted back a few stray hairs that had fallen from her wide cotton headband as she stared at the tall ladder in front of her on Wednesday evening. It was about twice the height of a normal ladder—maybe three times—and leaned against the wall of the Barefoot lobby.

The entire place had been covered in plastic drop cloths, but that didn't stop her from remembering the way she'd gasped when she'd seen the transformation two days ago. New crown molding and baseboards had been measured, cut, and painted, and now waited in the wings for paint to be applied to the walls. The old wooden floors had been buffed and restored to their original majesty. Crews of volunteers had replaced the cracked windows and cleaned the ones that were fine, and the staircase now gleamed with a deep new stain that matched the re-bricked fireplace.

It had all been done according to Jenna's specifications. And now, taking in the ridiculous height of this ladder, she realized she should have paid them to paint the room too. She'd been trying to pinch pennies so she could afford an expensive set of antique coffee tables, but now ...

Well, she was pretty sure she was going to fall off that ladder while attempting to tape everything for their big painting job tomorrow. Then again, maybe that would be okay. If she got hurt, she wouldn't have to go to the interview in two days.

Ack, no. She'd been doing so well not letting herself worry about that since receiving her professor's email four days ago. But she'd be leaving for San Francisco after dropping Liam off at school Friday morning, and she still knew nothing about interviewing for a job.

"Want me to tackle the ceiling?"

"Ah!" Jenna jumped at Quinn's question.

The woman stood at Jenna's elbow, her own hand on one of the ladder's rungs. "Sorry. Didn't mean to scare you." Her blue eyes squinted at Jenna as if assessing her. "You all right?"

"She's just nervous about Friday." With a sleeping Penny strapped to her chest, Gabrielle bounce-walked toward her sister and sister-in-law.

"What's Friday?"

"Shoot." Gabrielle frowned. "I forgot it's a secret. I blame mommy brain." Her finger pointed at Jenna and moved to Quinn, lips pursed. "And don't you dare say that isn't a thing."

Quinn chuckled. "I wouldn't dare." She squatted next to the paint cans lined up against the wall and opened one. A gorgeous vintage blue winked back. "Nice choice on the color. So, what's Friday?"

Since Penny's birth, the two aunts had gotten a bit closer—as in, Jenna no longer suspected Quinn of diabolical plots aimed at hurting those Jenna loved. She'd told herself that she had every right to mistrust Quinn after she'd lied to the entire town about dating Shannon's now-boyfriend Marshall—plus the fact she'd been a total mean girl in high school—but if Jenna wanted a second chance to overcome her past, she supposed she should give others grace as well.

But to trust Quinn with this? So far the only people who knew about the interview were Tyler and Gabrielle because Jenna had asked them to get Liam from school on Friday and keep him overnight since, given the city traffic, she didn't know when she'd be home.

As for Cameron ...

Lowering herself to the couch covered in plastic, Gabrielle unsnapped the baby carrier. Must be time to feed Penny. "She's got an interview."

"Seriously, G?" Did mommy brain also cause sisterly betrayal? Jenna grunted as she snatched up a roll of painter's tape. She'd start with the doors and windows and tackle the shorter walls before climbing the behemoth ladder in front of her.

"What kind of interview?"

When Gabrielle didn't say anything else, Jenna quirked an eyebrow at her as she popped the tape onto an applicator. "You don't want to tell her?" She tried to infuse teasing into her tone, even though her feelings were a little less than friendly at the moment.

But her sister's chin trembled and her eyes got watery. "I'm sorry, Jen. I just ..." She looked up at the ceiling as Penny rooted around for her dinner. "Ugh, stupid postpartum hormones."

Great. She couldn't stay mad at Gabrielle for long. Not after all she'd been through. Sighing, Jenna marched to the couch, kissed her sister on the top of the head, then turned to Quinn and tossed her the tape. "You can start on that wall and I'll start over there."

"You got it."

Jenna grabbed another roll, attached a new applicator, and headed for the back door. After situating and climbing a short ladder, she ran the tape along the left edge of the door from top to bottom, stepping down the rungs as she went and cutting the tape using the built-in slicer. She re-climbed the ladder and did the same along the top and right side. Finally, Jenna stood back to examine her handiwork.

Yep, everything looked straight. Now for the putty knife.

She glanced back at Gabrielle and Quinn. Her sister talked softly to Penny, and Quinn had gotten on another short ladder to tape the side of a wall across the room. A somber mood had fallen over the whole place. Jenna couldn't blame them, though. It was her own attitude—her own fear, really—that had affected the vibe of the Barefoot.

Was it warm in here? Jenna slid open a window and welcomed the cool evening breeze off the Pacific.

Oh, come on. This was ridiculous. What was she so afraid of? If she wanted to know about interview tactics, there was no one better to talk with than Quinn. She'd worked in New York City. She could probably even advise Jenna on what to wear to the interview so she didn't over- or underdress.

That's not what you're really afraid of though, is it?

She cleared her throat and faced the other women once more. "The interview ..."

Quinn's head popped up. Gabrielle stayed focused on Baby Girl, but her lips curled into a soft smile.

"It's at this interior design firm in San Fran. My professor works there and they need an intern."

"That's huge. Congratulations." Quinn placed the flexible putty knife against her tape, applying downward pressure to ensure a good bond so the paint wouldn't seep underneath. "From my knowledge of the industry—albeit limited—it seems internships like that are really hard to come by. How many people are they interviewing?"

Jenna swallowed. "As far as I know, I'm the only one."

Quinn stopped halfway down the wall and looked up. "That's seriously impressive, Jenna."

Shrugging, Jenna moved to tape another wall's baseboards. "My professor is just doing me a favor."

I have not met a student with as much potential as you in a long time.

Or maybe not.

"I've told you this already, but I'm really proud of you, Sis." Gabrielle's normally commanding voice had softened. Maybe it was motherhood that had done it.

Becoming a mom had certainly changed Jenna's perspective —her everything, really.

"Thanks." The tape squeaked as it unrolled from the applicator. "There's a lot to consider. Like Liam—how would this affect him, you know? Moving away would be really hard, and I'd be taking him away from his aunt and uncle and cousin, from his friends."

"But you'd get paid more than you make at the rental shop, I'm guessing," Quinn said.

She wasn't wrong. When Jenna had called her professor to talk through some of the details on Monday, she'd nearly tripped when she'd heard the proposed starting salary. *"But of course, you should negotiate for more,"* Professor Champion had said. *"And that's just the internship salary. If you do well—and I am confident you will—then once you've earned your degree, I don't see why we wouldn't hire you on full time."*

The things she could buy for Liam, the experiences she'd be able to afford—well, he'd never need to depend on another space camp scholarship again.

"Yeah. A lot more." Jenna paused, inhaled the brackish scent of the sea whisking in through the window. "Would you mind giving me some interview tips?"

"Me?"

"Well, she's not talking to me," Gabrielle said, chuckling. "I only ever interviewed for a server position at the Bar & Grill.

Considering I've known Bud and Velma since before I can remember, well ..."

It was true. Gabrielle had dreamed of being a teacher, but instead of going to college, she'd stayed home to care for their mom and Jenna—then Jenna and Liam. And her current job at Tyler's foundation had come about when she and Tyler had started dating. Jenna had teased her about the obvious nepotism involved, but really, her sister was perfect in her role as the mentorship program director.

"Of course I'll give you tips." Quinn tapped a nail against her tape dispenser. "Want to grab a coffee when we're done here?"

Jenna crossed the room to snag more tape. "That would be great. Thank you."

"No big deal." Quinn turned back to taping, her low ponytail swinging with her motion. "It's not like I've got a raging social calendar at the moment." Despite her wry tone, there was something sad in it too, and Jenna couldn't help but wonder what was going on in that head of hers. Even after nearly three months of meeting with the Sisterhood, Quinn hadn't revealed much about herself.

But she kept coming back. Maybe that said more about her than revealing a thousand little insignificant details.

"I appreciate it all the same." Jenna returned to the back and started taping around the framing of a window. "I mean, I don't think I'll get the job, but at least this way I won't completely fall on my face in failure."

"Oh, stop," Gabrielle said as she pulled Penny off one side and settled her in for more milk on the other. "You are going to do amazing."

"You're my big sister and you have to say that."

"But I'm not," Quinn piped up. "And I agree. You're really talented, Jenna. The way you've transformed this place is nothing short of a miracle—and I've only seen the plans. I'm guessing the final product will be even better."

Had she ever heard Quinn give someone a compliment? Jenna rushed to close her flopping mouth. "Um, thank you."

"You can count on me to tell you the truth."

Jenna laughed. What? She couldn't help it. It wasn't four months ago that Quinn had lied to the whole town about a fake boyfriend.

Surprisingly, Quinn chuckled too, shaking her head as she hopped down from the ladder, her taping finished. "I know, I know. But for real. I *will* shoot straight with you, and I say you're going places, Jenna Wakefield."

Jenna's cheeks grew warm despite the breeze. She tucked a piece of hair behind her ear. But before she could say anything else, Quinn crossed the room. "The question is, where do you *want* to go? Don't take the path others have for you. It can lead to a really lonely road. Believe me."

Wow. Jenna almost wanted to tug Quinn into a hug. But the defiant tilt of the woman's chin told her in no uncertain terms that such affection wouldn't be welcome. The only person she'd ever seen Quinn hug was her sister, Shannon, and that was because Shannon could charm a rattlesnake about to strike.

So instead, she considered Quinn's question. "I'm not exactly sure where I want to end up." Jenna sat on the couch next to Gabrielle, who patted her knee. "And if I'm honest, part of me is hoping that I fail this interview."

"Why would you want that?" Gabrielle asked.

Jenna leaned over and ran her fingertips over Penny's soft toes. Time to admit what she was really afraid of.

But Quinn beat her to the punch. "Because then she doesn't have to choose. Right?"

"Yeah." She sighed. "Things are really good right now. I love school. Liam is finally breaking out of his shell. We are standing on our own. My family is close by."

"And let's not forget the handsome man you've been smooching on the side." Gabrielle winked.

"Don't say *smooch*. It makes you sound ancient." Jenna side-bumped her sister. "But yeah, things are really good with Cameron too. It's unreal, actually."

"What does *he* say about all of this?" Quinn lowered herself onto the arm of the love seat across from where Jenna and Gabrielle sat, the plastic tarp crinkling under her. "I mean, if he's the right guy for you, he'll support you and be okay with you going after your dream. So what did he say?"

"I..." Groaning, Jenna placed her head in her hands. "I haven't told him yet."

"Why?"

"Because ... I probably won't get it anyway. And then the whole thing will be moot."

"Jenna, that's the lamest thing I've ever heard," Quinn said.

Gabrielle glared at Quinn, who held up her hands. "What? It is, and I promised to shoot straight, remember?" Quinn's gaze flicked back to Jenna, her eyes somber. "That's not the real reason you haven't told him."

No, it wasn't.

Because there was a very real fear brandishing its head, one that asked a very real question Jenna didn't want to contemplate.

What if Cameron *didn't* understand? What if he *didn't* support her moving to San Francisco?

What if she'd chosen the wrong man ... again?

The fanciest building she'd ever been in before today was Walker Beach City Hall. But the skyscraper where Star & Lux Interior Design resided was a modern-day marvel.

Jenna craned her neck upward as she stood in the art deco–inspired lobby, which featured gold-accented floors, an entire wall of glazed brick, and a black marble ceiling with a sparkling chandelier that must have been at least ten feet across.

"Oomph." Jenna grunted as people poured through the revolving glass doors just behind her, shoving her aside without apology.

Many seemed to be returning from lunch, fancy black boxes of what she presumed were leftovers in hand. A few had brief-cases slung over their shoulders, perhaps on their way to meet-ings or an interview like her. The various noises inside all rose and blended together into an unfamiliar cacophony. Even when most of Walker Beach gathered at a city council meeting or some other event, it didn't sound quite so ... cold.

And yet, there was an energy here too, one that vibrated off the walls and landed back on Jenna, revving her up, encour-aging her to step into this new world—because outside of these doors, the big city awaited.

Compared with Walker Beach, a whole different way of life pulsed in the San Francisco streets. Just in walking from the BART station stop to her current location, the varied smells of garlic fries, sulfur, and fresh crab had bombarded her. The four-hour drive this morning had gone more quickly than she'd anticipated, so she'd spent time walking by the pier, listening to the clanging rumble of the city's historic streetcars and tasting a bit of sourdough at the Boudin Bakery, soaking in all that the city had to offer.

And ... she could maybe see herself here.

Going with the flow of the lobby foot traffic, Jenna arrived at the elevators just as the doors opened and people poured out. She tried smiling at them as they passed, but most had their noses glued to their phones or just lifted an eyebrow in return. Made sense though, right? They were probably going some-where important, on their way to something noteworthy.

She wasn't in Walker Beach anymore, Toto.

Jenna stepped inside an elevator and hit the button with the number twelve. As the doors shut with her and about fifteen others crammed inside, she backed into the corner, a tall man blocking her view of anything but a mole peeking out from behind his shirt collar. The space emitted an aroma as diverse as the streets, the air dense with a broad mixture of pad thai, clam chowder, and chocolate.

Jenna tugged on the bottom of her jacket, straightening it as best she could. When Quinn had insisted Jenna borrow her linen-colored Max Mara pinstripe one-button blazer and pair it with her black Gucci pants and a chunky necklace—the "perfect blend of style and professionalism"—Jenna had refused at first.

Now, after looking around, Jenna was grateful to the woman for not only equipping her with the right interview attire but also quizzing her on potential questions and the answers she should give.

The man in front of her got off on the eleventh floor. When the elevator dinged and halted on the next floor, Jenna exited with a handful of others. A large glass paneling of doors with white lettering declared she'd found her location.

Her hands gripped the strap of her purse. Biting her lip, she peered inside the brightly lit lobby boasting white walls lined with what appeared to be framed architectural plans. White leather furniture ringed the room, and potted plants brought color to the space. A receptionist sat behind the hulking desk, which seemed to tower above the mere average human.

About five young women sat in the lobby. Were they all interviewing for the internship?

Of course they were. Jenna had been a fool to think the hiring managers would chuck all their eggs into *her* basket.

One of the women, a blonde with her hair parted to the side and combed down without a single bump, had a textbook in her lap. Another was so tall that she could have been an Amazonian. Her red curls were perfectly tamed and her complexion flawless. And the boobs of every single woman were perfectly perky, meaning they had either never breastfed a baby or they could afford a much better bra than Jenna. Each one looked like she belonged here, completely comfortable in her designer clothing, in the gleaming lobby, in the city.

So unlike Jenna.

You can take the girl out of the small town, but ...

No. No, no, no. She was here, finally. And she was not going to ruin it with negative self-talk. She was going to go in there, give one fabulous interview, and basically demand they give her the job.

In a really nice way, of course.

But first, it wouldn't hurt to make sure that the chilly San Francisco wind hadn't blown her brown locks into complete chaos, or that the lipstick she'd hastily applied after eating lunch remained where it should. Scanning the hallway, Jenna located a bathroom and propelled herself into it.

"Whoa." Even the place where people did their business was fancy, from the glistening black sinks to the stalls that looked to be made from stainless steel. Compared with the tiny one-staller at Rise Beach Rentals, which also came equipped with a lovely rusty ring around the toilet, this was the Taj Mahal of bathrooms.

She pointed at herself in the mirror, lifting an eyebrow in the same way she did whenever Liam rolled his eyes at her—which, admittedly, wasn't often. "Get it together, Jenna."

Oy. Good thing she'd stopped in. Her bangs were a mess. Jenna finger-picked her way through them till they were smooth and swung to the side.

Now for a pep talk.

"You are fierce. You are a kick-butt mom who has overcome a lot to get here. Don't let anyone—yourself included—tell you that you aren't worthy."

A toilet flushed. Oh no. She hadn't bothered to check if

someone was here to overhear her monologue. Pivoting on her heel, she rushed for the door.

"I agree with your assessment."

Jenna squeezed her eyes shut. She knew that voice. Slowly she turned and peeked from behind her lashes, and there stood Professor Renee Champion in the flesh, washing her petite, well-manicured hands.

This so wasn't happening.

Oh, yes. It so was.

Renee reached for a towel, dried off her hands, and approached Jenna, hand outstretched and wearing a smile. "It's nice to finally meet you in person, Ms. Wakefield."

"You too, ma'am." Jenna shook, her lips numb. "I hope you don't think I'm a crazy person. I don't talk to myself in the mirror all the time." She paused. "Except, wait. I do. But please don't think less of me. I promise, I won't be a psycho in front of other people."

Shut up, shut up, shut up.

Thankfully, her professor laughed and waved a hand as she headed for the bathroom door. "You have nothing to worry about, Jenna. We all have our strange habits." She winked. "This is San Francisco, after all."

The band around Jenna's lungs loosened and she followed Renee into the hallway. "I'm glad to hear it. I really would like a fair shot at this job."

And, despite what she'd told Quinn and Gabrielle two days ago, she meant it.

Because if she didn't try, she'd always wonder. The question that had reverberated in her mind for the last decade would continue to plague her—what if?

Renee breezed through the glass doors of Star & Lux and Jenna tried to keep up with the woman's quick pace.

"I know I'm a bit early for the interview. Should I wait in the lobby until two?"

"No, no, come with me." She led the way past the desk, waving to the receptionist and moving herself through the tiled hallway at an alarming speed for someone in four-inch spiked heels.

As for Jenna, her feet already felt hot and blistered from the ten minutes she'd spent in Quinn's Louboutins after changing from her flats on the BART. That's what happened when a girl's feet were used to nothing more than flip-flops pretty much year-round.

Renee tapped on an office door and stuck her head inside. "Our two o'clock is here." She did the same with two other offices and then entered the conference room at the end of the hallway. The large picture window gave an astounding view of the Golden Gate Bridge in the background, shrouded in mist despite the presence of the afternoon sun.

Jenna clutched her throat. What a sight, and she'd been missing it all her life. Yes, Walker Beach had its own version of beauty, but there was something mysterious and enthralling about the city.

Renee cleared her throat behind Jenna, who turned to find two other women and one man dressed in a variety of pantsuits, sweaters, and slacks. Jenna didn't know much about designer wear—only what she'd read in fashion magazines here and there—but the smooth cut of the partners' clothing spoke of wealth and privilege. Of course, an upscale wardrobe made sense, given that the firm catered to high-end boutiques and personal clients who wanted to redo their luxury homes in Presidio Heights and other affluent areas of town.

As her professor introduced Jenna to the firm's partners, Jenna kept her chin steady and shook hands as if she did belong. And when they all sat, she made sure to keep her back straight—no slouching for her like she did at the end of a long day of renting beach equipment to tourists.

When the partners asked her question after question, she

answered honestly but in a way that told them she was confi-dent in her skills—but not so cocky that she wasn't open to learning. *Thank you, Quinn, for that tip.*

And when they gave each other surreptitious looks throughout the interview, she pretended not to notice—pretended it didn't make her heart skip a beat in joy, knowing that somehow, she, Jenna Wakefield, had one hundred percent landed this job.

"One more question, Jenna." Renee smiled at her from across the conference table. "What has been your favorite design project to date?"

So far the questions had been largely impersonal, requiring her to give the expected answers. But this … this required more of her. How could she explain what the Barefoot Refuge meant? There was so much tied up in the project. Not just in designing, but in the way the whole place made her feel.

In the fact that, were it not for the Barefoot—or the Sister-hood—Jenna wouldn't be sitting here right now.

As nice as the partners had been, she wasn't sure they'd fully understand the depth of her emotions—the way her throat closed up a bit, how her insides quivered at the joy she'd experi-enced just yesterday when she'd looked around and seen the explosion of blue on the painted walls. When she'd imagined the lobby being enjoyed by visitors, had pictured it being a place where women's lives were transformed because they'd been given a second chance at living it. At reforming it. At becoming someone new.

Jenna knew how that felt, but she didn't exactly know how to explain it. Maybe it was best to keep it simple. "The project that changed everything for me has been the redesign of the Barefoot B&B that I referenced earlier." She bit her lip, not able to hold back one more personal detail. "I look forward to seeing how the finished product is enjoyed and used in years to come."

A weight thunked in her stomach at the thought. Because

she wouldn't be there to see all of that, would she? Not if she got this job and moved to the city.

Sure, she'd get word of it from the Sisterhood, from Gabrielle, and she could see a tiny sliver of it whenever she was back for visits. Still, it wouldn't be the same. But that was the job, right? She was the designer. The decorator. She made masterpieces in other people's businesses and homes and left them to be enjoyed while she moved on to the next project.

Man, she was sure overthinking this. Pursuing a dream required sacrifice, didn't it?

Jenna noticed she was fiddling with a button on Quinn's blazer. She stopped, folded her hands on the sleek white table-top, and smiled. "Do you have any more questions for me?"

"Just one." After glancing between the other partners one last time, Renee's long earrings shook as she swung her head back to center her gaze on Jenna. "Are you free to join us for celebratory drinks in two hours?"

Celebratory? Jenna's eyebrows knit together. Did that mean...? "Um ..."

"We want you, Jenna." Once again, Professor Champion extended her hand for a shake. "Come work for us and set your dream career path for life."

CHAPTER TWENTY-ONE

ELISE

*W*alker Beach sure knew how to do autumn well.

Elise's lips puckered as she sipped her glass of chardonnay and took in the view of Heather's family vineyard. "The Barefoot Refuge is wonderful, but this place has a beauty all its own."

The sun set behind her, splashing color across an array of yellow and red hilltop trees in the distance, giving the whole landscape the look of paint splattered on a stretched canvas. In the dirt just beyond the raised back deck where Elise sat with the women in the Sisterhood, vines grew in rows, recently stripped bare at harvest by the Campbell family's workers.

"I agree." In the chair beside her, Jules crossed her legs and smiled across the lit fire pit at Heather. "Thank you for inviting us here for our meeting this week. The Barefoot still smells like paint and cleaner."

Heather grabbed an open bottle of her family's red house blend and poured herself another glass. "I love hosting. It gave me a chance to try out a new recipe on you all."

"And it was delicious." Nikki rubbed a hand in large, exaggerated circles across her slightly pooched stomach. "Maybe a little too much."

They all laughed, but Elise knew what Nikki meant. She'd tried to stick with her new diet, but the Italian bruschetta bar had been too tempting to pass up. "I still feel guilty letting you do all the cooking tonight, but it was so wonderful."

The breeze picked up and Heather tucked a strand of hair behind her ear. "I wouldn't have let you through the door with food in your hands." She winked. "We're just glad to have you back with us."

"Besides, with the soft launch in five weeks, you've got plenty of other things to do." Piper stood. "Much as I wish I could stay, I need to leave early. Our copy editor quit so I'm doing double duty as reporter and proofreader right now." She set her half-empty glass on the side table between her chair and Jenna's.

Oh, Piper. When Samantha had called her after Elise's episode, the woman had rushed to the hospital, pale. And despite her normal lack of shown emotion, she'd thrown her arms around Elise and held fast for a long time. When she'd pulled back, tears had shimmered in her eyes. *"You can't die. You're the only mom I have left."*

Elise's chest squeezed at the thought. Piper's mom didn't know what she was missing—if she was even still alive. Elise got the impression Piper didn't know one way or the other.

The rest of the women said their goodbyes to Piper, but Jenna continued to stare into the dancing flames of the round, stone fire pit. She'd been so quiet tonight. Something was most definitely on her mind.

As Piper walked around the house toward her car, the women settled back into their conversation. Jules ran a finger around the bottom edge of her wine glass and looked at Elise. "How are you doing these days?"

Her eyes radiated sympathy. She'd already expressed

concern earlier tonight that Elise was jumping back into her Refuge duties too quickly, but Elise had reassured her that Charles had given her a clean bill of health—even if he had resisted for a bit since it had only been a month since her episode.

But over the last week and a half since she'd chosen forgiveness on Baker Beach, she'd done her best to convince him that working at the Refuge wasn't stressful—that it contributed to her joy more than anything. And he'd responded well, continuing their walks, trying to better understand her. That conversation had led to others, which had started a wonderful sort of mining process that had brought all kinds of gems to the surface of their relationship.

That, in turn, had given her a different sort of joy—a hope for things to come.

The bottom of Elise's hands pressed into her thighs as she held her fingertips bent toward the warmth of the flames licking the air. "I'm well. Physically, I've never been better in the last twenty or thirty years. And you all have been so wonderful, helping out and bringing your own beauty to the Refuge."

"That's true." Heather took a drink and licked her lips. "Jenna, if I haven't told you lately, the place looks amazing."

Seemingly startled as if from a trance, Jenna glanced up, her eyes working their way around the circle. "Oh. Thanks."

"Which reminds me. My stepmom was wondering if you'd be available to help redecorate our tasting room. It could definitely use an update."

"Um—"

"Oh yeah!" Nikki interjected. "And my mom has been dying to redo our living room but didn't know what style. When she came to help out at the Barefoot on Monday, she was positively stunned into silence—and ya'll know that never happens. She said she had to hire you and wanted me to ask about your availability. I told her you were busy with school and helping

Gabrielle and finishing up the job at the Refuge, but she said when you were done she needed to be the first on your client list."

Jenna's jaw tightened and her gaze skipped over to Quinn, who arched an eyebrow at her but said nothing. What was that all about?

Shifting in her seat, Jenna tucked her arms around herself. "That's all really sweet, but I'm not sure exactly what availability I'll have."

Nikki shrugged. "Well, Mom's waited this long. Guessing she can wait another few months."

"I …" The poor girl looked positively green. Was she not feeling well? "I have some news about … well, I can't say yet. There's someone I need to talk to first. But I'll tell you at next week's meeting, all right?"

Elise resisted the urge to stand and wrap the woman up into a hug. Not wanting to overstep the boundaries as Cameron's mom, she'd held back a lot where Jenna was concerned lately. Would it be too much to ask her to go to dinner sometime? It would be nice to get to know her better outside of the Sisterhood.

The other women didn't seem to think so much about Jenna's statement, just smiled and sipped some more on their wine. Jules, wonderful leader and senser of emotions that she was, kept the conversation flowing by asking Quinn how her search for a job was going.

It had been, what? About four months since Quinn had moved back to town. But not once had she spoken about herself, her dreams, her goals, except to mention offhandedly that she had applied for multiple marketing firm positions all over the country.

Not that Elise was complaining. The woman had completely taken over interviewing for the manager job—freeing up Elise to coordinate with the women's shelters and domestic violence organizations in the surrounding big cities to gain applications for their other positions—but so far hadn't found anyone she deemed a good fit.

Quinn touched the center of her right cheek, feathering her finger along a thicker section of her scar. "I've had a few interviews."

"And?" Jules's faint smile prodded her niece to expound.

A quick glance around the group showcased Quinn's discomfort with the spotlight. "I got a job offer in Florida."

"That's incredible." Jules held up her drink in a toast. "Congratulations."

"Thanks, but I didn't take it." Quinn batted at a flyaway piece of hair that blew across her face. "It didn't pay enough for how many hours it was asking."

"Hmm."

Jules's obvious disappointment matched Elise's reaction too, though it took her a moment to puzzle out why. Maybe because in the back of her mind, she'd hoped Quinn might put herself up for the Refuge management job. But if a high salary was a requirement, then it most definitely would not be a good fit.

Hard to imagine a more efficient manager, though. Quinn had always had a rough edge to her, but it had softened over the last few months. And with her background in management and marketing, she would be a true force in helping get the inn off the ground—both as a charity and a business.

Perhaps Quinn simply couldn't see her own potential. Maybe she was stuck, thinking her future could only look one way.

Elise knew a little something about that.

"Personally, I'm glad you're staying here for now. I'd be sorry to see you go." Her soft words garnered everyone's attention, and she felt all eyes on her before she'd even fully formulated what she wanted to say. "I'd be sorry to see any of you go."

She took another sip of her wine to wash away the sudden

grit in her throat. "I'm so grateful for each one of you ladies, and Piper too, of course. You didn't have to, but you've welcomed me into your group. I know I don't say a lot, but I hope you understand ..."

Oh, bother. She blinked back a few tears. That certainly hadn't been in her plans for tonight. And yet, instead of being embarrassed, there was a freedom in revealing her emotions. "It has been a privilege to hear about each of your dreams. To sit here and soak in your hope for the future." She glanced quickly at Quinn, giving her a soft smile. "To learn from your strength."

Quinn's eyes widened ever so slightly, bright in the firelight. "There's no strength here. Just stubbornness and a desire to be different than I was—even if I have no idea how to do that."

"I call that strength, even if you don't." Elise leaned forward, eager to be heard. "Sometimes standing still takes more strength than moving toward a target. Not in a way that's complacent, of course."

Complacency had never been her problem, at least.

She inhaled a shaky breath, cognizant that all eyes were on her. "But it takes true strength, true courage, to stop and consider what we want in life when our inner voice is screaming at us to go, go, go—because we fear that if we don't, we will fall behind, be forgotten. Worse, we'll never prove our worth, to others or to ourselves."

It's why Elise had automatically forgiven Charles when he'd told her about the affair last year. Perhaps even why she'd started out working with Jules on the Refuge. "I've had trouble with my own self-image for years. Not just physically, though there is that. Emotionally too. But my health problems have given me a blessed opportunity to step back, examine, and decide what I want."

That this—right here—is where she wanted to be.

That staying with Charles and working through their problems together was what she wanted too. Not because others expected it or because she was afraid of losing her children's love if she left, but because she'd committed to him. And because she loved him despite his mistakes.

Because he loved Elise despite her own.

Given the darkening sky, it was difficult to tell the women's reactions to Elise's little speech. But maybe she was getting through just a little bit. If nothing else, she prayed they heard this next part with stunning clarity.

"Ladies, you are so much more than the image of yourself that you've concocted in your head." Elise's hand beat against her chest, spreading to feel the heart thrumming beneath. "Every one of you is beautiful and brave and strong. And I, for one, am privileged to know you."

"Thank you, Elise. I can say with certainty that each one of us feels the same way about you." From one seat over, Jules took Elise's hand, squeezing. "You, my friend, are also beautiful and brave and strong."

Elise swallowed, returned the squeeze. For the first time, her reaction was not to dismiss the compliments, but to accept them—and that was one step closer to believing they were true.

CHAPTER TWENTY-TWO

JENNA

Just rip off the Band-Aid. Isn't that what they said?

Jenna stared at Cameron's house, shadowed by a large California oak in the soft moonlight. She'd driven straight here after her Sisterhood meeting and had been waiting in the driveway for ten minutes, looking for signs of life. But the face of the small cottage remained dark.

Maybe he was already asleep. Or out with some buddies. Yeah, tomorrow would be a better day to tell him about her job offer in San Francisco—the one she'd officially accepted just yesterday, one week after her interview.

Jenna groaned. Who was she kidding? She'd already been Little Orphan Annie-ing it up with her refrains about "tomorrow" all week long. But tomorrow would turn into the next day and the next, and before she knew it, it'd be ten days from now, when she was supposed to move.

What was wrong with her? Jenna slapped her steering wheel. She had to tell him. But things were just so good between them
...

"If he's the right guy for you, he'll support you and be okay with

you going after your dream." Quinn's statement had been so matter-of-fact. And she was right.

Yes. Cameron might not be thrilled at the prospect of doing the long-distance thing, but he'd been the one to push her to apply for school in the first place. Of course he'd support her in pursuing what she knew to be the right thing for her.

Is it, though?

Ugh, there was that stupid voice of self-doubt rearing its ugly head yet again. She thought that finally making her job acceptance official would silence it for good, but its unwelcome chatter had returned tonight when Heather and Nikki had offered her work.

But starting a business was risky. And she had to admit, there was a certain prestige of taking a job in the city. Besides, it could take years to build up to the salary that she was being offered right out of the gate with this internship. That money could be used to benefit Liam now.

No more embarrassing trips to the thrift store for him. No more camp scholarships. No more being known as the kid born to a teen mom—maybe instead, for once, he would be proud of her. Proud to be her son.

And in the city, with this job, all of that could happen.

Tap, tap, tap.

Jenna jumped at the sound of knuckles against her car window. Cameron. She rolled the window down and he leaned his forearms on her door, grinning.

"To what do I owe the pleasure of your company this fine evening?"

A laugh gurgled from her tight throat as she pushed the door open against him and climbed out. "Did Samantha finally convince you to watch Jane Austen movies with her?"

His hands snaked around her waist, pulling her close. "Whatever do you mean, madam?"

"Oh, I don't know. Maybe it has something to do with your

terrible attempt at a British accent and the ridiculous way you're speaking?"

Eyebrows waggling, he brought his lips close to her ear. "Dost thou think it sexy?"

She pretended to groan even as a shiver wound up her spine. "Cameron Griffin, you are too much sometimes."

"Why, thank you." He kissed her earlobe and then found his way to her mouth. She soaked up the warmth of his kiss, allowing herself to melt into his embrace.

How could he be anything but the perfect man for her?

And that meant she owed him the courtesy of the truth.

She sighed and pulled her head back, settling against his chest momentarily before unwinding herself from his arms and closing the car door. "While I do enjoy kissing you, it's not why I came by tonight."

A hint of concern lit in his eyes, but he raked a hand through his curls and nodded. "Okay." Taking her hand, he led her up the front steps of his porch to a navy blue Adirondack chair. In one fluid motion, he sat and pulled her onto his lap, once more settling his hands around her. "What's up?"

She wove one arm around his shoulders, running her fingertips through his soft curls. How did she tell him that all of this was about to change? For a moment, she leaned her head against his, pressing her lips to the crown of his head while he tucked an arm under her knees and held her close.

"Jen?"

"Hmm?"

"You're kind of scaring me. Is everything all right?"

She nodded against him. "Yes." Then shook her head. "And no."

"Okay ..."

Oh, poor man. Being in a relationship with her was so confusing. Jenna kissed Cameron's cheek, then inhaled deeply.

"Remember how you walked in on a conversation with my professor a couple months ago?"

"Yeah. She saw how brilliant you were and wanted you to look into getting some real-world experience."

"Which, I did, thanks to you." And helping to redesign and decorate the Barefoot Refuge had turned into something Jenna could never have imagined back then. "Do you also remember how she said if I ever would consider moving to San Francisco she would be able to help me find an internship?"

"Vaguely." Was it her imagination, or had Cam's shoulders stiffened?

Her heart thumped hollowly in her chest. "Well ..." Jenna swallowed hard and nestled into Cameron's body so her head rested against his shoulder and neck. "She asked me to interview for an internship at her interior design firm."

Cameron was silent for a moment. "Wow." Another pause. "That's huge. When is the interview?" His question was quiet, restrained. She sensed a lot of emotion in it, but he wasn't letting it loose.

"Um." She shifted, and his hand holding her legs fell away just a bit. "It was last Friday."

"As in yesterday?"

"No. A week before that."

Dropping her legs to the ground with a thunk, he leaned back in his seat. "Why didn't you tell me?" He squinted, shaking his head. "And how did it go?"

"I should have told you. I know that. It's just ... I didn't know what I wanted until I was there. But then, everything was so glossy and new and different and I fell in love with the city. It has its own pace, you know? Its own aura, and while I love Walker Beach, San Francisco—which I've learned only outsiders call San Fran, by the way—has so much to explore."

And yes, she was rambling, but her nerves had gotten the better of her. If only she could make him understand, he might forgive her for not telling him sooner. "Being there made me feel alive in a way I haven't for a long time."

"Wow."

Is that all he had to say? Maybe she wasn't doing a good job of explaining. "The firm is located in a gorgeous part of the city with a fabulous view of the Golden Gate Bridge. And my professor and her partners are all really classy and friendly and smart. They wear these designer outfits and are just so ... I don't know ... chic."

Cameron's lips had hardened into a straight line. His face was like stone. What was he thinking?

She wanted to grip his shirt and shake him. Didn't he understand what an opportunity this was? She plowed on. "They took me out for drinks after they offered me the job and we went to this upscale bar with—"

"So they *did* offer it to you?"

Oh. Hadn't she said that? "Yeah."

"And you're taking it?"

"Um." She fidgeted. "Yes."

He was quiet for a few really long moments. "I guess I'm happy for you. But ..."

"But what?"

"I don't know. This job—it doesn't seem like you, Jen."

Because she was just a small-town nobody who hadn't even graduated high school? Cameron had never made her feel like that—but was it how he really saw her?

She crossed her arms over her chest. "And why not exactly?"

"It's a bunch of corporate types. You know, the kind without souls." His mouth smiled, but his eyes didn't.

Despite his body beneath hers, she suddenly felt cold. "So what you're saying is you don't think I can do this."

He groaned. "No way. That's not what I said. You can do whatever you put your mind to. But why would you want to move away from your sister, your niece ... me ... just to prove something to yourself that doesn't need to be proven?"

"It's not just about that. And who says it doesn't need to be proven? Who knows who I would be right now if I hadn't been such an idiot after my mom died? Where I might have ended up if I hadn't been a teen mom?"

His jaw went slack. "I happen to think who you are right now is pretty awesome."

"Maybe. But ... I don't know. I just feel like there's all this untapped potential, and I thought I'd never get a chance to tap it. Now, I will." She sniffed. Oh no. Nope. Jenna Wakefield would not cry because a stupid guy didn't support her dreams. Been there, done that. She straightened her shoulders. "And if you can't get on board with that, then you're not the guy I want by my side."

"Come on, Jenna. I just want what's best for you."

"I think you just want what's best for *you*. Just like ..." Jenna squeezed her eyes shut for a moment. She couldn't have been so wrong about Cameron, could she?

"Just like who, Jenna?"

She peeked out at him, bit her lip.

"Like who?" He recoiled at her silence, rubbing the back of his neck as he frowned. "Like Brock? Is that what you were going to say?"

She cringed. It did sound bad. They were nothing alike. And yet ...

"Seriously? You're comparing me to your good-for-nothing ex?"

"No, of course not." She pushed away from him and stood. "But you have to admit—it doesn't sound like you're being very supportive at the moment."

"I don't mean it that way. But I can't understand why you want to be someone you're not."

And she knew it was cliché, but she couldn't help it—Jenna

paced. Her flip-flops pounded against her heel with every step. "I don't want to become someone I'm not. I want to become my best self."

"No job is going to do that for you." Cameron stood and stuck his hands in his pockets.

"It's not just about the job. It's about being in a new place, proving to myself that I can survive without the help of my sister and everyone else who has had to hold me up. It's about exploring a new city, exploring who I really am deep down, finding out what it's like to be successful for the first time in my life. To become someone Liam can be proud of. To provide better for him than I have." Her hands trembled as she surged forward and gripped his shirt. "And I just know that I'll never be satisfied without knowing the answer to *what if*. Please, Cameron. Tell me you understand."

Yeah, she was begging, but she *loved* this man. She didn't want to leave him.

But she also couldn't stay for him. She'd always regret it. She'd always wonder.

"I can't do that, Jenna." He placed his hands on hers, swallowed hard as his thumbs made tiny circles on her fingers. "But I wish you well, and I hope you find everything you're looking for." His voice broke in time with her heart.

"Come with me." The words were out before she could think about them. But she knew they were right. Why couldn't she have the man she loved and the job she'd dreamed of too? "Cameron, come with me."

A pause. "I can't do that either."

"Why?" The word came out like a quiet, strangled cry.

"Because." A pained expression overtook his features. "You just said you didn't want to have to rely on anyone else. If I go with you, you'd always wonder if you could have done it alone. And then you'd only end up resenting me."

"That's not what I meant." And yeah, she'd practically yelled the words, but she was losing him. So Jenna did the only thing she could think to do—she pulled his head down, unleashing all of her love in a kiss.

Groaning, he kissed her back, hard, swift, and full. Her toes curled with the passion in their connection, the way his hands moved up her back, into her hair, how his lips nudged hers open, deepening the kiss. She shivered as her own hands clung to him for dear life, pulling him as close as she possibly could, desperate to keep him here, forever.

And when he finally pulled away, a glazed look in his eyes, she leaned back against the wall of the house, her head tipped up and her heart pounding.

That kiss … it had been everything. Had told her everything she needed to know.

But then, Cameron's eyes morphed, from pleasure-filled to … sad.

Why would he be sad? This was a good thing. If he loved her back—which his kiss had proven, hadn't it?—then they could work through anything.

"Cam?" Her voice, tentative, broke the silence between them.

His arms released her as he backed away, swiping his hand up and down his face, shaking his head. "I'm sorry, Jenna. I … I still can't go with you."

"But …" Her chest heaved. Had she misinterpreted the meaning of that kiss?

If he really loved me, nothing would stop him from being with me.

The truth of the thought smacked into her.

He might be willing to kiss her, to play house with her and Liam on the weekends, but when push came to shove, he wouldn't be there for her. Just like Brock hadn't been there for her or Liam. Just like Dad hadn't been there for Mom, Jenna, or Gabrielle.

As good of a guy as Cameron Griffin was, he very obviously wasn't the guy for her.

She'd chosen wrong. Again.

"Then I guess this is goodbye." Tears welled in her eyes as she turned and walked away—praying she was making the right choice.

Praying she wouldn't ask *what if* about this too for years to come.

CHAPTER TWENTY-THREE

ELISE

The last three months most definitely had not been an exercise in futility.

Quite the opposite, in fact.

Hands on her knees, Elise sat on the edge of the newly furnished couch in the Barefoot Refuge's lobby, her gaze taking in every gorgeous detail.

The wooden clock over the fireplace mantel that ticked out the time in perfect harmony with the wind chimes that tinkled from the back porch.

A handful of gorgeous chandeliers that enhanced the natural light coming through the ceiling skylight.

The pops of color all over that somehow tied together perfectly even though they were so different. Elise sure wouldn't have thought of putting them together.

Jenna had outdone herself, that was for certain.

Oh, that girl. Elise sighed heavily. She'd had such hopes of making her a daughter someday. But now, she was gone. And her poor boy ...

"Here you go, Mom." Cameron whizzed through the door from the kitchen, somehow not spilling a drop from the mugs in his hands. "Don't worry. I used coconut milk."

"Thanks, sweetie." She took one of the coffees from him as he sat next to her on the couch. A foam heart floated in the dark liquid. "I didn't know you could do latte art."

The apples of his cheeks darkened a tad. "I taught myself recently."

Ah. "Because Jenna is such a fan of coffee?"

He shrugged and took a sip, destroying whatever foam shape he'd given to himself. "I thought I could save her a little money. She was spending a ton at Java's. Guessing San Francisco coffee shops are even more expensive."

His words weren't angry or vindictive like she might have expected from someone who had broken up with the love of his life two and a half weeks ago. But they were definitely sad. "Have you spoken to her since she left?"

"Nope." He took another sip, then frowned. "I think I blew it, Mom."

"What do you mean?" She'd assumed Jenna had broken up with her son, but perhaps he'd had a part in the decision as well. Though her stomach roiled for Cameron's sake, Elise took a drink of the bitter brew—made sweeter only by the bit of frothed milk at the top.

He sighed and leaned back against the couch. "I didn't stop her from going."

"I'm not sure anything could have stopped her." When Jenna had told the Sisterhood about the job in San Francisco, Elise had sensed a restlessness. A need. An ache too.

"I could have tried, though. I just …" He closed his eyes and groaned. "I made the same mistake I did last time."

Elise patted his knee. "With Mindy?"

Cameron sat up so quickly his coffee spilled across his lap. He hissed and pressed the excess liquid into his jeans. "You knew about that?"

"I'm your mother. Of course I knew." Even though he tried

to hide behind his jokes and smiles, her youngest had never been able to conceal his emotions well. At least not from his mama.

The warmth of the mug seeped into her skin. "What mistake do you think you made?"

"I didn't put all my cards on the table. I didn't fight for her." He huffed through his nostrils as he set his mug on a coaster on the coffee table. "But she seemed so determined to go, so sure she needed to prove that she could stand on her own."

Hmm. "After relying on her sister for so long, I suppose I can understand that."

"I can too. That's the problem." Cameron raked a hand through his hair, tugging on the ends as if he could magically pull all the answers of life out of his brain. "She asked me to come with her, and Mom—I wanted to say yes more than you know. I love you guys, love living near my family, but there's nothing holding me back from picking up and moving wherever Jenna goes."

"Obviously, there's something." She spoke the words as gently as possible. "Or you would have gone."

"Yeah, there's something. Her." Waving a hand in the air, he shook his head. "If I had gone along, she wouldn't be standing on her own like she really wants to do, you know?"

"Hmm. I see." He did have a point.

"I had to give her a chance to live life on her own terms or she would always wonder if her success—or her failure—was because of me."

Despite the fact she wished he would jump in his truck and drive to the city right now to make things right with Jenna, Elise couldn't deny that perhaps Cameron had done the right thing. What did they say about loving something and letting it go? "I can see the sense in that. But that doesn't mean it stops hurting, and for that I am so very sorry, honey."

"I just have to stop overthinking it, right? I'm definitely overthinking it. And I don't do that. I don't overthink. I live in the moment. I cruise through life." His jaw relaxed. "Yeah, I'll get over it soon."

"Oh, my boy." Reaching out, Elise placed her hand on his chin and squeezed like she used to do when he was a four-year-old with a skinned knee and a trembling lower lip. "You love her. Of course you won't get over it soon."

"No. No, I don't love her." He said it with such determination, as if simply speaking the words made them true.

Now she couldn't help chuckling. "I'm your mother, remember? I've known you loved Jenna Wakefield from the moment I first saw you two together. You may think you loved Mindy, but the way you looked at her doesn't come close to the way you look at Jenna."

For a few minutes, he just sat there in stony silence, and Elise sipped her coffee until it was gone. She looked around the place, mentally noting all the things left on her to-do list before the soft launch in sixteen days.

A trip to Los Angeles in two days to meet with three different women's shelter directors.

Training volunteers.

Finalizing the breakfast menus with Heather, who had offered to cook for the first several weekends until they hired a full-time chef from the pool of Refuge applicants that would start coming in any day now.

"You ready to go?" Cameron's voice interrupted her train of thought. "I remembered something I need to do at work. Can I take you home now?"

More likely being here reminded him of Jenna—and how could it not, when evidence of her heart covered the very walls surrounding them? Before Cameron had used the kitchen's new espresso machine to make lattes, he'd been helping Elise put together a few bookcases for the lobby that had been back-ordered and hadn't arrived until after Jenna had moved. "Of course."

He drove her home without much talk. Elise checked her phone. Charles would be home soon, but she had just enough time to make him a nice dinner—perhaps roasted chicken with cauliflower mashed potatoes. She was getting quite good at those. Then they could take their nightly walk on the beach and maybe she'd get up the courage to hold his hand.

She slipped her hands over both cheeks, felt their warmth. So silly. But she couldn't help but feel like a giddy schoolgirl with a crush.

When Cameron parked in her driveway, he leaned over and gave her a kiss on the cheek. "Thanks, Mom."

"For putting you to work?" She winked.

"For what you said. You gave me some things to think about."

"I love you, sweetie. I hate to see you hurting."

"I know. But I'll be okay."

"Yes, you will." Eventually.

Elise slid from his truck and padded to the garage, where she used the keypad to open the door. After walking through the garage and closing the electronic door from the inside, she entered the house, where the scent of garlic met her nose. What in the world? Hanging her purse on the hook beside the door, she stepped deeper into the kitchen.

A set of taper candles adorned the middle of the table, where two silver chargers waited to be topped with plates. Cloth napkins had been folded in a fan shape and placed in water goblets. Soft jazz floated from the living room speakers.

"Charles?" she called.

He emerged from the pantry wearing his grilling apron, a twinkle in his eye. "You weren't due back for another fifteen minutes. The lasagna isn't quite ready."

"Lasagna?" Wasn't that full of carbs and sugar?

"It's made with zucchini instead of noodles." He drew closer and dropped a kiss on her cheek. She inhaled a sharp breath at the contact, which was unexpected—but not unwelcome. His face was smooth and he smelled of clean shampoo and after-shave. "I know I'm not as talented as you in the kitchen, but I thought you deserved a break."

He started to turn toward the stove, but her hand darted out to grab his. "Charles, this is …" A sob cluttered her throat and tears burned her eyes. She was being a ninny, but it was just so sweet.

She'd forgiven him. He didn't have to do something nice for her. Didn't have to make up for anything anymore.

And yet, here he was, making her dinner.

Just because.

He lingered in her space, his eyes studying her. Then, slowly, as if in a dance, he slid his arm around her waist, gathering her close—and she knew what was about to happen.

Something that hadn't happened in a long time.

Her eyelids fluttered closed and when his lips met hers, she welcomed them. Welcomed the sweetly familiar.

But there was something different in his kiss too.

Something … renewed.

When he pulled back, she opened her eyes, smiling. Then, on the heels of the sweet moment, an acrid smell saturated the air.

Charles's eyes lit with recognition. "The lasagna!" He turned and hoofed it to the oven, throwing it open and stepping back as a billow of dark steam rose from inside.

Elise rummaged in the drawer next to the stove and threw him the potholders, which he used to place the supposed lasagna onto the stovetop. It more resembled a bloody soup with a blackened lid of plastic sitting on top.

She couldn't help it—Elise giggled. Before she knew it, Charles was chuckling too. "I suppose there's a reason I leave the cooking to you."

Picking up his keys from the countertop, she jingled them in the air. "I think the Bar & Grill sounds excellent right about now. How about you?"

He removed the apron, plucked the keys from her hand, and snuck in a quick kiss. "I couldn't agree more. Just let me grab my phone from the living room."

Still laughing, she followed him—and stopped cold at the sight of his suitcase by the front door. "Charles?"

His gaze followed her line of sight. "Oh. Right. I was going to talk to you about that after dinner."

So dinner had been a way of buttering her up? Of telling her he was leaving again?

No, no. She wouldn't jump to conclusions. He'd been so good about canceling any business trips and sticking to his hospital schedule since they'd begun counseling, but occasional travel to other hospitals was still part of his consulting job. And just like he'd begun to support her work at the Refuge, she would support the job she knew he loved.

Clearing her throat, she peeled her eyes from the suitcase and looked at him. "When do you leave?"

"Tomorrow. The trip just came up, Elise. And if there was anyone else qualified or able to do it, I would let them go. I promise." He scratched at a place on his neck. "Thing is, it's quite a long trip. All the young guys have kids at home and couldn't do it. It means training staff, some really long days."

That wasn't ideal, but it wasn't as if he hadn't taken week-long trips before. "How long?"

"Three weeks."

She blanched. "But Thanksgiving is next week. Surely you'll be back for that?"

"I'm sorry, Elise. I'll have the actual day off, but meetings during the surrounding days. The hospital has some end-of-year goals it really needs to meet, so time is of the essence." Charles took a step forward. "I was hoping you might be able to fly out for Thanksgiving. I know it won't be the same as doing it here with all the kids, but it could be an adventure."

She frowned. Of course, she didn't like the idea, but Danielle had been talking with them about the importance of compromise. "I suppose—"

"I was actually thinking that perhaps you'd consider coming with me for the entire trip." As she began to shake her head, he placed a hand on her arm. His touch was warm and gentle and his eyes reminded her of the boy he'd once been. They were as pleading and soft as when he'd asked her to marry him. "You could spend the time shopping and reading, relaxing. There's a large bookstore that you would love."

He knew her well, but had he forgotten why it was impossible for her to go? "Charles, the soft opening of the Barefoot Refuge is in two and a half weeks. There is so much for me to do before then. I can't possibly go."

"Elise, this trip is really important for me."

"And you can go. I'm not upset." She smiled to reassure him, even though her chest felt heavier than it had a moment ago—certainly heavier than those stolen moments they'd just shared in the kitchen. "Yes, it will be difficult to be apart for Thanksgiving, but you can make it up to me some other way."

There. She'd attempted flirtation.

Silly ninny, indeed.

But there was still a furrow in Charles's brow. Why—

Then her blood ran cold. He wouldn't. "Where is this trip, exactly?"

He glanced away from her, staring at the blank television. "Boston."

She wrenched her arm back. "Boston?" And yes, her voice screeched, but how could it not when he'd just told her that not only was he resuming his business trips—not only was he going to be gone for three weeks alone—but he was going to the very city where *she* lived? "Which hospital will you be consulting at?"

He looked at her, and his gaze vibrated with guilt.

So not only the city where his former lover lived, but the hospital where she worked too. Unbelievable. Bile rose in Elise's throat.

"Elise, please. Come with me."

"I can't. The Refuge needs me. I made a commitment."

"I thought you made a commitment to our marriage too."

"Don't you dare talk to me about our marriage commitment. I'm not the one who broke it!"

"I thought you forgave me for that."

"It doesn't mean I trust you to go back to the very same place where ..." Her breathing shallowed and she slumped against the wall.

"Elise?"

"I'm fine. Just ..." Breathe in, breathe out. "Give me a moment."

And he did, although he watched her like the physician he was, about to jump into action if her body did something that concerned him.

Meanwhile, her brain somersaulted. Should she go to Boston with him?

Her stomach ached. Why was it always up to *her* to give up the thing she wanted so others could have their own way?

Elise always sacrificed.

Elise always took the higher road.

But she was tired, so very tired, of playing second fiddle to everyone else's whims and dreams and desires.

There was compromise and then there was concession—and her whole life, Elise had been conceding, convinced that she would lose the people she loved if she didn't.

But she'd been working through that fear. She and Charles had promised to be honest with each other about what they wanted. He'd promised to listen, to compromise too.

Surely he'd understand.

"Charles." Her voice trembled as she straightened. "I am not going to Boston, and I don't want you to either."

Please. Stay.

"Come on, honey. I have no choice."

"There's always a choice." If she said much more, she was going to lose all the tears damming behind her eyelids.

He stared at her for what felt like hours, then nodded. "I guess there is. And you're making it for both of us." Charles turned, grabbed his suitcase by the handle. "I think I'll see if I can get a flight out tonight instead."

Then he walked out the front door—taking with him the memory of their final kiss and the beautiful life they'd shared.

Taking with him … everything.

CHAPTER TWENTY-FOUR

JENNA

*J*enna had grown up hearing about how terrible the traffic was in the city.

But hearing about it and experiencing it were two different things entirely.

She checked the dashboard on her car for the fifth time in as many minutes, praying for the light to turn green—and fast. Otherwise, she was going to miss more than just the first half of Liam's school's Thanksgiving lunch, which had started twenty minutes ago.

"Argh! Come on!" Not like the cars in front of her could hear Jenna's shouts, but it made her feel better to do something other than sit, which was all she'd done on the BART train on her way into the office this morning.

Then she'd sat for another hour on her way out of the city four hours later.

And when she'd finally gotten to her car at the BART station near the long-stay hotel where she and Liam were still renting—yes, seventeen days in San Francisco and she had yet to find any affordable apartments that were less than an hour and a half commute from her office—there had been a traffic snarl between her and the school.

At noon!

Finally, the traffic started moving again and Jenna was able to drive the two minutes to Liam's school. She found a spot on the outskirts of the lot, jumped out, snugged her jacket around her—another note to self: buy a thicker coat for the unpredictable San Francisco weather—and raced inside the large brick building.

It hadn't been that long since she'd walked Liam to his class on his first day, but she still had to stop a few times and visualize where the lunchroom was. Her brain was already so full of the projects she'd been given back at the office, leaving little space for anything else in there.

Renee had been correct when she'd said the job would be intense but worthwhile. If only Jenna felt like she really deserved to be there. Instead, it seemed the woman had grossly overestimated Jenna's talents and abilities.

Maybe Jenna should have waited until she had more experience to dive in—or waited for a term when she wasn't still enrolled in quite so many online classes. But she'd allowed the professor's praise—and the compliments from all the people back home who had loved her work on the Refuge and wanted to hire her—to fuel her pride.

"You'll grow into it. You will."

And now she was talking to herself in the middle of an empty elementary school hallway plastered with amateur drawings of the first Thanksgiving on one side and wise sayings by philosophers on the other. A fluorescent light flickered overhead, and Jenna rubbed the corner of her left eye. What she wouldn't give for a nap right about now …

"Can I help you?"

Turning, she sighed with relief at the sight of Liam's teacher, whom she'd only met once. "Mrs. Hanniday! Hi. I'm Liam

Wakefield's mom, remember?" The older woman had kind eyes and reminded Jenna of Josephine Radcliffe back in Walker Beach.

Just like the barista at the coffee shop by the office reminded her of a younger Kiki Baker West, and the receptionist at the hotel where she was staying reminded her of Cameron's brother Spencer.

Oh, Cameron …

She pushed the homesick longings way down deep. She'd made her decision and had to see it through. Yes, it would be hard—she'd lived in Walker Beach all her life. Of course she'd miss it. Anyone would. But eventually, she'd come to make the city her new home.

How long would *eventually* take, though?

"Of course I remember you." The woman smiled. "Are you looking for the parents' lunch?"

"I am, but I seem to have lost my way."

Mrs. Hanniday chuckled and started walking. "It's easy to do. Follow me. I'm heading there myself."

"Thank you so much." Jenna tugged her purse strap up onto her shoulder, her heels—a pair of knockoff Jimmy Choos she'd found at the thrift store—clicking on the tile floor. "How is Liam doing, if you don't mind me asking? He's so quiet when he gets home from school. Not that that's unusual for him."

But sulking? Even talking back a bit? *That* was not normal for her son, and it had happened more than once. She'd assumed it was because she'd been late picking him up, or because he hated living in a studio hotel room with no privacy, or because he missed Jared and his other friends in Walker Beach.

But those things would get better in time.

They had to.

"To be honest, I haven't had much of a chance to get to know him. As you said, he's very quiet." Mrs. Hanniday made a murmuring sound in her throat. "I'm sure transitioning in the middle of the school year has been difficult for him."

Jenna's ankle twisted as they turned a corner, but she caught herself before fully stumbling. Where were her flip-flops when she needed them? "Yes, I'm afraid it couldn't be helped." Wow, listen to her. Two weeks working in a corporate office and she definitely didn't sound like the small-town girl who'd rented out beach equipment for a living.

"This job—it doesn't seem like you, Jen." Cameron's words flooded her brain for the millionth time since he'd spoken them over three weeks ago.

Much as she hated to admit it, she couldn't deny that there was some truth to it. But that didn't mean she couldn't do what it took to become that person.

Yes, being here was more difficult than she'd thought, but it was all for Liam. Being here would bring opportunities for them as a family that they wouldn't have otherwise.

Are you sure it wasn't for you?

She shoved the nagging voice of her conscience away and kept walking next to Mrs. Hanniday. They emerged into a larger hallway with higher ceilings that showed off both the bottom floor and the second story above them. That's right. The lunchroom should be just down the hall and on the right. She could hear the rumblings and chatter of a large group of students from here.

Before they entered, Mrs. Hanniday stopped to face Jenna. The wrinkles around her eyes grew more prominent as she gave an encouraging smile. "These things take time. Be patient with Liam and do your best to engage him when you're home. It's very common for children to feel a sense of loss when they move, and often they don't know how to express themselves with words."

"So what can I do to assist him with that?" Jenna had been

through therapy herself, but that didn't mean she knew how to help Liam process his own emotions.

Mrs. Hanniday placed a hand on Jenna's upper arm and squeezed. "Remind him that you are still there, that you love him, that you can be his resting place. That you aren't going anywhere."

He knew that, didn't he? Or had Jenna been so caught up in all the details of moving—finding someone to sublet her apartment, resigning from her job at Rise, putting the finishing touches on the Barefoot's lobby, and giving instructions to Jules for the final design of the guest rooms—that she'd forgotten to have a real conversation about it with her son?

And what kind of mother did that make her?

"I'm just so busy. My new job, it's overwhelming, and I didn't really think about the fact I'd be all alone up here." She'd been so used to having family nearby—had taken it for granted that she could see her sister any time she wanted. "Truthfully, Liam isn't the only one having trouble with the transition. For days, I've been counting the seconds until we get to leave to spend Thanksgiving back home."

Now, her count was down to two hours ... although maybe she could sign Liam out early after lunch and they could leave right away. Beat some of the traffic. Hmm.

"Might I make a suggestion?"

Anything! "Yes, please."

"Tell Liam that you're sad too. That you also miss your home. Doing so might help him to feel okay with telling you how he feels."

Jenna felt like slapping herself on the forehead. "That makes so much sense." Liam always had felt the need to protect Jenna, to make sure she was "okay." She'd hoped that now, here, he'd see her as finally able to take on the full role of the parent—a mom he could trust to take care of him, not vice versa. But maybe she had to help him see that by prompting him with conversation.

She straightened, restraining herself from throwing herself into Mrs. Hanniday's arms—after all, she wasn't *actually* Ms. Josephine. And though she was being kind, she was still a stranger. "Thank you so much for the insight. I will take it to heart."

"I'm sure you will, dear." With one more squeeze, the teacher headed into the lunchroom.

Jenna followed, the echoes of the tiled room with a low ceiling surrounding her. Students and parents alike filled long rows of benched tables throughout the space, which smelled salty and homey like the Frosted Cake.

Except as she passed a few tables in search of Liam, one glance at the meal adorning the plates and she knew the mashed potatoes were a cheap imitation of Ms. Josephine's—the gray gravy congealed in globs, the potatoes themselves thin and beaded instead of whipped and creamy.

A few shouts rang out across the room and someone screamed, "Fight!" What in the world?

Jenna jumped back as a group of boys about her son's age shoved past her to the far end of the cafeteria, racing with their fists pumping in the air. A whistle blew—probably a teacher trying to maintain order—and Jenna winced at the shrill blasts.

Where was Liam?

She climbed onto a bench, careful to make sure her heels didn't fall off the edge and send her tumbling, and scanned the crowd. Most people were straining from their seats for a better look at the commotion, while others had the same idea as her and stood on the benches.

Jenna located the fight in minutes. A tall boy with red hair had a dark-haired student in a headlock, but teachers were making their way through the crowd to break it up. And when they pulled the kids apart, she couldn't contain her gasp.

Liam.

She jumped to the ground, snapping the heel off one of her shoes in the process. Leaving it behind, she pushed her way through the crowd. "Move! Please!" Despite sneers and curses, she limped her way on a broken shoe.

Her hands formed into fists. A teacher might have to hold *her* back from knocking out the larger kid who had decided to use Liam as a punching bag. No one did that to her kid. No one.

Finally, she reached the inner circle where the teachers held Liam and the redhead. But instead of finding her son crying against a teacher's chest, Jenna's jaw dropped to see him lunging against the teacher's arms at the larger kid bleeding from the nose as he shouted obscenities.

"Liam James Wakefield!"

Immediately, he stilled and his eyes found hers. He blinked and his head dropped.

"Not only are you a loser, but a mama's boy too!" The other boy laughed even as the large male teacher holding him back gave him a warning.

The teachers eyed each other and nodded, then started hauling the boys toward the exit. Jenna hobbled along after them before sniffing in disgust and stopping to remove her shoes.

What in the world had happened to her sweet kid? The one who had never said a cross word in his life?

Not while in Walker Beach, anyway.

She'd done this. Her decision to move, her decision to try to be something—for Liam—had turned him into a kid who fought.

Maybe Jenna had to face the facts.

And the fact was, no matter how many pairs of high heels she wore or how many dollars she made or how many hours she worked, Jenna Wakefield would remain exactly what she'd always known she was.

THE INN AT WALKER BEACH

A screwup.

Someone who ruined the lives of those she loved.

Yep. The fact was, there was something very wrong with her —and there was nothing she could do to ever fix it.

~

If Jenna wasn't careful, she was going to chop off her finger with this knife.

And a trip to the emergency room on Thanksgiving Day wouldn't exactly improve her stellar mood.

On the other side of the kitchen, Gabrielle sang off-key to "Jingle Bells"—apparently she'd been listening to Christmas music since the beginning of November—and worked on peeling what had to be her twentieth potato. They'd be bringing their mom's cornbread dressing and a pile of mashed potatoes with them to Tyler's family gathering, and since there were a ton of Bakers, there needed to be a literal ton of potatoes.

"'Oh, what fun it is to ride in a one horse open sleigh—hey!'" Gabrielle warbled.

Jenna whacked at the onions on her cutting board, trying to drown out the happy sound. Despite being back in Walker Beach for the holiday weekend, there was nothing happy about today. Liam hadn't spoken a word to her since his fight yesterday, which had made for an oh-so-pleasant four-hour car ride home.

No, not home.

Home now was San Francisco, not Walker Beach.

Then why didn't it feel that way?

And why, yesterday evening, when Gabrielle had asked Jenna how her job was going, had Jenna burst into tears like a little child? Thankfully her sister hadn't questioned Jenna. She'd merely held her and then curled up with her to watch *White*

Christmas, their mom's favorite movie—which had only served to press an even deeper ache into Jenna.

Thwop, thwop, thwop. She blinked back tears. Stupid onion.

"You done murdering that vegetable yet?" Her sister glanced over Jenna's shoulder.

"You shouldn't tease a woman with a large knife." Maybe if she pretended to be her sassy self, Gabrielle would take a hint and not do her big-sister thing, just for today.

"Hey, so …"

No such luck.

Lifting the cutting board, Jenna used the knife to scrape the onions into the bowl with the chopped celery. "I told you, I'm fine." She flicked on the stove burner and set a skillet with a large dollop of butter on to melt.

"Of course. Because it's completely normal to burst into tears when someone asks you how your dream job is going."

"Please, G. Just drop it." Jenna kept her back to Gabrielle as she dumped the onions and celery into the pan. The familiar aroma of melted butter and frying onions—the one she'd smelled every Thanksgiving morning growing up—filled the air and she tried to relax her shoulders. "Let's just enjoy our day."

"How can I enjoy it if I know you're upset? I'm just worried about you."

"I know." But Gabrielle wouldn't understand. She'd never disappointed anyone a day in her life. Even now, she was rocking the wife and mom thing, and she'd surely rock the working mom thing when she started back at her job part-time in a few weeks.

Jenna stirred the celery and onions, allowing her mind to wander to the to-do list her boss had left for her to complete this weekend "when you have a moment."

She supposed that was the cost of—

"Do you want some help with that?" Gabrielle asked.

"Help with what?" Jenna glanced down at the pan and pulled

it off the burner quickly at the sight of blackened onions. Seriously? She couldn't even cook the one dish her mom had made without fail every year? The one Gabrielle had continued to make perfectly after Mom had died?

What a metaphor for her life.

She grabbed the pan, stalked to the sink, and hammered the skillet with scalding hot water, washing away the offending mixture. Hot tears poked at the back of her eyes. "I can't do anything right."

Approaching, Gabrielle touched her elbow. "It's okay, Jen. You probably just didn't put in enough butter. You have to keep adding it so they don't dry out and stick."

Of course. Any idiot would know that. "I'm sorry, G." A tear finally pushed past her eyelids and emerged onto her cheek. Look at her, crying over burnt vegetables.

Except it was much more than that.

"It's not a big deal. We have more onions and celery." Her sister's soothing tone belied her worry—the same worry she'd had to carry for years because her younger sister was such a screwup.

Jenna shook her head. "You should do it. I'll go far away from here where I can't mess anything else up." Turning to leave, she stopped when Gabrielle put an arm on her shoulder and pivoted her back.

Her warm blue eyes crinkled in concern. "Sis, what's going on? Why are you so upset? It's just food."

"No, it's not!" And man, she hadn't meant to yell, but didn't Gabrielle see? "Everything I touch, everything I do ... I ruin it all. First, Mom had to quit pursuing her dreams because I made stupid choices. Then I did the same thing to you when I got pregnant. And then I was depressed for so long and you didn't feel like you could leave your pathetic sister alone because your nephew needed you and I couldn't handle being his mom on my own." Her lips trembled and she slumped with her arms over her chest, the counter digging into her back. "Well, maybe it wasn't the depression. Maybe it was just me."

"Jen, what are you talking about?"

"Liam got into a fight at school yesterday."

"Seriously? What happened?"

"I have no idea. He won't talk to me. All I know is that he's been sullen and apparently angry and it's coming out in ways I never dreamed. And all because I took a job to make his life better." She swiped at the tears—what right did she have to cry? She'd brought this on herself, on all of them. "Except maybe I really did it for myself and I'm so screwed up I can't tell the difference."

Her sister slid an arm around Jenna's shoulder and hugged her. It was so tempting to sink into her embrace, to allow Gabrielle to speak words of comfort, but that wouldn't solve the central issue.

The problem was that Jenna didn't know what would.

"Gabrielle, what should I do?"

Gabrielle's fingers stroked the hair at Jenna's scalp, the motion as steady and constant as her love had always been. "I know you think you screwed up my life by having Liam, but don't you know how much fuller our lives are because of that kid?"

Stiffening, Jenna pulled away, eyes wide. "I didn't mean that. I can't imagine life without him."

"Neither can I."

"I just meant that I wish my stupid decisions hadn't kept you here. After Mom died, you could have gone to school. Could have joined Tyler in Florida. Instead, you had to stay here and help out your dumb teenage sister. There's no way I could have survived without you and you knew that and were too good to leave me behind to fend for myself, even though that's what I deserved."

Gabrielle took a deep breath, her mouth in a firm line. "I

never would have left you here by yourself, Liam or no Liam." Then she gripped Jenna's upper arms and looked her square in the eyes. "And you were not pathetic. You were struggling with a mental illness. That was not your fault."

"I know."

"You say that, but do you really know it? Do you believe it?"

"I want to." So desperately. But she also didn't want to let herself off the hook. "But what if ... what if I *did* cause it?"

"You didn't. Sure, it may have been triggered by the weight of everything you were dealing with, but come on. It wasn't a divine punishment or a curse or something you did wrong. It's a disease, and it can affect anyone—anyone."

Jenna's eyes burned. She could admit that part was true. When she'd attended a support group last year, she'd met a lawyer, a deacon at the local church, a high school student, and a stay-at-home mom who'd just had a baby. All of them had also been struggling with depression, most of them in silence.

Still ... "Others just seem to deal with it so much better than I did. It took me years to finally seek help. I wasted so much time."

"Everyone is different, yes, but I'm willing to bet that what you see in others' lives and wellness journey is probably not the full story. Maybe they feel just as lost and overwhelmed as you." Gabrielle squeezed. "All that matters is that you *did* seek help, you are working toward complete health, and, most importantly, you aren't alone."

Jenna considered the possibility that what Gabrielle said was true. One thing was definitely certain. "You're right. You've made sure that I was never alone, and I can't thank you enough for that."

Gabrielle pulled her in for another hug, then released her. Turning, she walked into the pantry and emerged with another onion, which she tossed to Jenna. "Then hear me on this. I don't regret for a moment how everything turned out. Those years apart changed Tyler and me for the better. We emerged different people—people who were better able to love and commit to each other. And so much of the change in me was because I had the privilege of caring for you and Liam. I wouldn't change one second of our story, except to have Mom here with us, of course."

Jenna peeled the onion and started to chop again. This time, she let the tears flow. What point was there in holding them back? "I miss her so much."

"I do too." Gabrielle sidled up next to her with another cutting board, where she placed a few celery stalks and made quick work of chopping them. "She would be so proud of you, Jen."

"I'm not sure about that." Jenna put her cut onion into the bowl and Gabrielle's celery joined it.

"I am." Gabrielle handed Jenna another skillet and stick of butter, which she placed on the burner once more. The butter sizzled and popped, spreading out as it melted. "And I know you said Mom quit her dream to stay with you after the marijuana incident, but I don't think she saw it that way."

"How could she not?" In went the vegetables. This time, Jenna kept a careful eye on the mixture while she stirred.

"One day I was sitting with Mom during a chemo treatment and she told me she was so thankful she quit school."

"What?" For a moment, Jenna lifted her gaze from the skillet and looked at her sister, whose eyes were very serious. Frowning, she then reached for the butter and sliced off another large chunk for the skillet. "Why?"

"Because she got to spend the last few years of her life with her daughters instead of pursuing what she thought was her dream. Because while she did love the idea of being a nurse—and there was nothing wrong with going after that dream—the thing that mattered most in her life was her family. Her kids. Us, Jen. The thing that was most important to her was spending time with us, watching us grow, helping us to become the women she hoped we'd be."

Steam hit Jenna's face as she stirred the onions and celery with a spatula. "Did Mom really say all of that?" She could hardly breathe past the lump in her throat. "You'd better not be lying to me to make me feel better."

"You know me better than that, Sis."

Yeah, she did. Could it be true? Maybe her mom really hadn't resented Jenna. Maybe all of Jenna's mistakes had somehow worked together for ... good.

"And here's another truth you need to hear. You've been so busy trying to make a better life for Liam because you feel inadequate, but does your son think that? No! He adores you! He doesn't see a screwup. He just sees his mom."

"I ..." Jenna bit her lip, looked away.

"Sis, you were created with a purpose, and that purpose is to bring beauty into this world." Her sister smiled softly. "It doesn't matter how you do it—working at a fancy job in San Fran or decorating a beachside inn or renting beach equipment to tourists looking for a fun time. The *how* doesn't define you. It doesn't determine your worth or value. It just matters that you do what you were created to do. And do you know what your most beautiful creation has been?"

There was no question about that. "Liam."

"You got it." Gabrielle hip-bumped her out of the way. "I'll take over here. Go find your kid and talk to him. It'll make you feel better."

Shaking her head, Jenna choked out a laugh and pushed away her tears. "You're so bossy."

"It comes with the big sister territory."

"Thanks, G. I love you."

"I love you too. Now go."

"All right, all right." Taking in another deep breath, Jenna left the kitchen, following the sounds of the television out into the den where Liam and Tyler silently watched the Thanksgiving Day parade.

The two of them glanced up as Jenna entered the room. Liam crossed his arms over his chest, hunkering down into his sweatshirt hood like a caterpillar in a cocoon.

Tyler stood. "I'm going to see if Gabrielle needs anything before Penny wakes up from her nap."

Jenna nodded at him as he passed, then walked to the couch and grabbed the remote to mute the TV. "Hey."

Liam stayed silent, scowling.

"Talk to me, Liam. What's going on with you?"

More silence.

Okay then. Maybe instead of listening, he needed *her* to talk —to be honest. Isn't that what Mrs. Hanniday had said yesterday?

Even though there remained an entire couch cushion between them, Jenna shifted in her seat so she faced him. "I know you don't like San Francisco, Liam."

More scowling.

"To be honest, I'm not sure I like it either. Not in the way I thought I would."

He was still silent, but now ... now he was at least looking at her. That was enough to encourage her to continue. "I miss everything about Walker Beach. I miss being near our family and our friends. I miss my meetings at the Barefoot. And ..." An ache tore through her middle. "I miss Cameron. But do you know what I miss most of all?"

"What?" His voice was rough around the edges, like a little boy trying to be a man.

"I miss you, Liam. I miss who you were here."

His jaw tightened.

"I miss seeing you smile and laugh. I miss you talking to me. I miss us just hanging out." She rubbed her fingers over the bumps on the remote still in her hand. "And I know I've been a bad excuse for a mother in so many ways. I've worked too many hours, left you with friends and family too often, allowed myself to be sad and stay in bed too many times, dragged you up to a city where you knew no one, and then got so busy I forgot to ask you how you felt about all of it."

Wow, okay. She definitely hadn't meant to spew all of *that* out. Was there such a thing as being too honest with a ten-year-old? Probably.

She rushed on. "I know that's a lot to process, buddy. And—"

"Mom?" Liam pushed back his hood, removing the shadow from his face.

"Yes, baby?"

He sat up straighter and looked at his hands in his lap. "I've never thought you were a bad mom. You're a great mom. You do more with me than a lot of my friends who have two parents. And you work hard to make sure I have the stuff I need."

"I'm not perfect."

"Me either." Liam tugged at the strings attached to his hoodie. "I'm sorry I got into that fight. I just ..." His shoulders sank and his lip trembled.

Jenna dropped the remote, hauled herself over a cushion, and wrapped him in her arms. But instead of talking, this time she listened.

After a few moments of quiet, Liam continued. "I tried really hard to like living in the city. I know it's your dream job there. And I know that if you didn't have me, you would have gotten there a long time ago. You never would have been depressed in the first place."

Oh no. No, no, no.

What a cruel irony—that she'd spent years believing there was something wrong with her, that if she hadn't been born, her father would never have left their family, that if she wasn't there, her mother would have been able to pursue her own dreams.

And now her son had believed the same thing about himself.

"Because while she did love the idea of being a nurse—and there was nothing wrong with going after that dream—the thing that mattered most in her life was her family. Her kids. Us."

Oh man. Gabrielle had been right. She had to be. Because if Jenna's mom felt even an ounce of the love for her daughters that was cascading through Jenna's veins right now, then of course she wouldn't have seen Jenna as an inconvenience—as a mistake.

Jenna pulled back and took hold of her precious son's shoulders. "Look at me. Please, baby."

With a frown, he did.

"You need to know something, Liam. I love you with every breath in my body. Every single breath. Despite all the bad choices I've made in my life, having you was never one of them."

He didn't speak for a few very long seconds. "Really?"

"Absolutely." She tugged him to her again in a fierce embrace and tears plopped from her cheeks onto his dark head. "And I'm sorry that I've never told you that before."

"It's okay." His words were muffled against her. "Mom?"

"Yeah?"

"You're kind of making it hard to breathe."

She laughed and let go of him. "Sorry, kid. Mom just loves you."

That soft smile of his that she loved emerged. "I know."

Then she flipped the sound back on to the TV and they sat there, shoulder to shoulder, watching the parade. Together.

And even though she didn't know what the future held, for now, being here—with him—was enough.

CHAPTER TWENTY-FIVE

ELISE

"*I* can't believe we really did it." Jules pulled her legs underneath her as she settled into the wicker chair on the back porch of the Barefoot, where the solitary beach stretched to meet the ocean.

Her hair looked a brighter red than normal against the freshly painted white wood of the railing and porch posts. Twinkle lights above them had just started to glow with the beginning of the sunset. Seagulls ducked into the water, on the hunt for their dinner.

"It's not hard to believe. I hear the owner is wonderfully determined." Elise handed Jules a mug of chamomile tea, her own latest drink of choice to settle her nerves each evening. The house had been too quiet since Charles had left two weeks ago. Not that Elise had been there much. Every moment awake had been spent readying the Barefoot for the soft launch this weekend.

And somehow, they'd finished a day early. Probably had a lot to do with the fact Jules had finally offered Quinn the manager's position—and the woman had actually accepted. Tomorrow, friends and family would arrive to stay at the inn for the soft launch. It would be a hectic day, but right now, they were going to enjoy the well-earned peace and quiet.

Jules blew into the mug, creating ripples across the surface of the liquid. "The owner would have gotten nowhere without her trusty sidekick." She looked at Elise. "Without her friend. And as a friend, I couldn't help but notice that you haven't quite been yourself recently. What's going on?"

"Oh. Nothing."

Nothing except pain eating her from the inside out. A shudder shook Elise's hands as she leaned toward the small table where the teakettle sat.

"You don't expect me to believe that, do you?"

"I suppose not." Taking the smooth handle of the teakettle in hand, she poured water into a mug empty of all but a tea bag.

If she couldn't talk to Jules—who at this point she saw more as her friend than Charles's cousin—who *could* she talk with? Certainly not her children. And not the rest of the Sisterhood. As lovely as they were, Piper's close friendship with Samantha complicated things. "Charles left a few weeks ago for a business trip."

"So you're missing him?"

"Yes." The water in her mug started to turn sunshine yellow. Elise frowned. Perhaps a plain black tea would have better suited her mood. "But that's not the whole of it."

And as the sweet herbal infusion of her tea came full body, she recounted the story of her fight with Charles. "Maybe I should have gone with him. But I'd committed to the Refuge and wanted to see that through."

"I'm so sorry he left." Jules sipped her tea, a thoughtful crease on her brow. "Have you spoken with him since that day?"

"No." Multiple times, she'd picked up her phone to call him —and multiple times, she'd put the phone down. Once, she'd even gone online, chosen a flight to Boston, filled in all the information, and chickened out at the payment window.

Because what if he had decided he was done?

What if even now he was in *her* bed?

Elise looked out across the horizon, from the fluffy clouds covering the sky to the undulating waves below. "I thought ..." Raising the tea to her nose, she breathed in the sweet aroma, the warmth and comfort it offered. But it wasn't enough. "I thought we'd grown stronger, closer, to the point where we could be honest with each other. But the moment I asked for something I truly wanted—something that went against what he wanted—I lost him. It's as if I'm forced to choose between being happy and being truly known and loved for who I am."

"Oh, Elise."

Both of them remained silent for a few minutes, drinking their tea tinged with apple notes, watching the waves—one moment calm, the next foaming and wild. Life was like that too, wasn't it? Elise was so tired of never knowing if she could relax or needed to fight in order to merely stay afloat.

"A relationship is a give and take." Jules's singsong voice lilted through the air, twining with the lyrical melody of the ocean. "One person shouldn't always be giving and the other taking. It should be a gentle ebb and flow, like the ocean."

"I don't want to make it sound like Charles is some tyrant. In general, he's been very accommodating. Going with me to counseling, spending time with me every evening, things like that." Elise rubbed her thumb over the mug's slightly raised Barefoot Refuge logo that Heather's sister had designed for them. "But other than counseling, this is the only thing I've really asked of him."

"I'm not trying to defend his actions. But to be fair, he *did* ask you to go."

"I wouldn't have been able to finish my work with the Refuge. I'd have missed the soft opening." Although perhaps she could have done some of the work from afar. Maybe she could have come back in time for the opening. "It wasn't a fair thing to ask."

"But he did ask. My ex was a narcissist who didn't truly value me, who saw me as a thing to be controlled. He never asked. He only told. And took." Jules kept her focus on the sea, her mug carefully balanced in her hands. She inhaled deeply, as if in a meditative pose. "It wasn't until I decided that I'd rather be alone than be controlled that I truly broke free. I realized that it wasn't just okay but necessary for me to take care of my personal needs, that it wasn't selfish to care for myself first so I could better care for others."

Yes, lately Elise had seen evidence of that in her own life as well. When she'd finally taken time for her own health, for her marriage, her work with the Refuge had ceased being something she did for acceptance, to gain value, and became something she did because she wanted to. Which meant that, for the first time, she could truly serve others without ulterior motives.

But she sensed Jules had more to say. "Is that when you moved back to Walker Beach and Chrissy befriended you?"

"Yes." Jules set her mug on the porch railing and twisted in her chair to face Elise, her eyes two large orbs filled with depth, with understanding. "She ministered to my wounded heart and gave me a home while I got back on my feet. She was excellent at accepting and loving people right where they were."

"I think you got along well for a reason then." Elise reached across and patted Jules's arm.

"Thank you for that." Tears appeared at the corners of Jules's eyes. "Anyway, while I waited and recovered, I started painting again. I'd quit because Timothy had told me it was a waste of time, that I'd never amount to anything. I quit because I believed him."

"But you're so talented." Elise could never hope to be as talented as that at anything.

Jules's gentle smile thanked her. "The world is a more beautiful place when each one of us brings our talents to it, when we pursue our passions. When we let others tell us we can't or shouldn't—when we listen to them because we fear rejection—the world becomes darker."

With trembling hands, Elise set down her mug for fear she'd spill the entire thing.

"You should do the things that bring you joy because that is going to make the world a better place. Ideally, your husband will understand that."

Elise sighed. "I actually think he does." After all, he'd joined Elise at the Refuge, engaging her with questions about it, contributing financially toward the effort. She couldn't forget those little and big ways he'd supported her. "Maybe I overreacted. But when I heard him say he was going back to Boston, and for three whole weeks, all of the shame and fear over losing him that I've felt over the past year returned full force. I think, subconsciously, I wanted to make him choose. Me ... or his job."

"You wanted veritable proof that he valued you and your life together."

"Yes, and perhaps without realizing it, I was trying to punish him for the past. I've lived with this pain, with the fear that he will leave me, for so long. Do you think it's possible that I pushed him away so I could stop fearing what I saw as inevitable?"

"That's definitely possible." Her friend squeezed Elise's hand. "Talk to him, Elise. My cousin is a good man, despite his mistakes. But whatever happens, I'll be here to support you. So will the entire Sisterhood. I'm guessing your kids will as well. The people who love you want you to be happy. You don't have to choose one or the other. But I do think that happiness requires being truthful with ourselves and others about what we really want and who we really are."

"And I haven't been truthful?" Her lips parched, Elise choked out the question. "I lost Charles because I told him what I wanted."

"Were you really honest with him?" Jules paused. "And have you actually lost him?"

"I …" Elise's lips parted, but she found herself bereft of words.

Because Jules was right. Elise had never really told Charles about her fears. Not completely.

She'd never divulged how unwanted she felt. How his affair had cut her to her core because she was sure she'd driven him away with her extra weight. How she was at the same time torn by the breaking up of her family and relieved when he'd finally walked away, instead of living every single day afraid of the inevitable.

In front of Elise, between her and the ocean, a breeze stirred a cluster of sea oats that stood out in the open. No shadows had blocked the daily dose of sunlight from the plant, allowing it to reach its full growth.

But no wall or obstruction also meant no protection from the wind, which blew against the wispy branches, hurtling them in all directions at the breeze's invisible will.

Still … as Elise studied the plant closely, she noticed something both mundane—expected—and also extraordinary.

The plant held up. It didn't break with the wind's friction.

In fact, it always ended back upright no matter how many times the breeze knocked it sideways. Why? Because it was rooted in the ground, just like Elise was rooted in a truth deeper than herself.

Which meant perhaps it was time to see exactly what Elise Griffin was made of.

~

The house was quiet as she entered it, her heart still sore from the gentle beating Jules had given it an hour ago. Elise flipped on the living room lights and sat in Charles's recliner, running her hands over the soft leather. Bending over, she inhaled, hoping to catch a whiff of his cologne, his shampoo—anything.

But it simply smelled like leather.

She knew what she needed to do. And it could either happen now, before she chickened out, or not until sometime after the soft opening this weekend. It would be difficult to find time even next week, when she and the team of volunteers Quinn had assembled would be working to improve anything that didn't go well for the soft opening before out-of-town guests started arriving for the Christmas on the Beach Festival.

Elise fished inside her large purse for her phone. She stared at the screen for several minutes. It would be nearing eleven o'clock in Boston. What was Charles doing at this moment? It wasn't unusual for him to be out late wining and dining his clients.

If he was at his hotel, she only prayed he was alone.

"Stop being ridiculous." Her attempt to talk bravely to herself only made her giggle. Oh goodness, what was happening to her? Perhaps she was losing her ever-loving mind.

Finally, with nausea bubbling up in her throat, Elise unlocked her phone and dialed Charles's number. It rang and rang—and went to voicemail.

Should she say something?

No. What she had to say required a response.

Elise hung up and sat there while her feet grew numb. Sighing, she stood and cringed at the sudden pain as she walked to her bedroom. She changed into her nightgown, washed her face, brushed her teeth, and took her nightly medications.

But something stirred inside of her, like the wind on the beach. She'd never sleep tonight if she didn't get all of this off her chest.

Her relationship with Charles was not going to end on her watch, because of *her* decisions. Elise wasn't going to let fear take her—or her marriage—down.

Not anymore.

Stalking back to the living room, she grabbed her phone, dialed, and waited. This time, if the voicemail beeped, she would leave a message.

No answer.

Charles's standard voicemail recording.

Beep.

Closing her eyes, she spoke. "Hello, Charles. I'm sorry it has taken me so long to call you. There was a lot to process. And to be honest, I was clinging to anger. You were right. I said I forgave you, but at the first test, I withheld that forgiveness again." Elise walked to the mantel, her eyes focused on a family picture from when the sextuplets were about eight or nine. "The truth is I've been so afraid you didn't love me anymore. *I* didn't even love me anymore—that much was evidenced by the way I ate to hide my emotions, to keep myself from thinking too hard about why you cheated on me. And I'm still afraid, Charles. I am afraid that you don't want me for me. Maybe you only want who I used to be. Maybe you only want the mother of your children."

She sank down on the edge of the couch. Her voice was hoarse now from all the tears clogging her throat. "Do you know that it's been three years since we've made love, Charles? Three years. I just … I don't know what to do with that. I know we are not twenty-year-old lovebirds anymore, but I want my husband to want me. Is that so wrong?"

The phone beeped again, a warning that the voicemail was getting too long and she'd soon be cut off.

"Anyway, I don't even know exactly why I'm leaving this message, except to say I'm sorry for anything I've done to push you away. I shouldn't have asked you to choose between me and your job, just like I wouldn't want you to ask me to choose between you and the thing that makes *me* come alive."

Elise exhaled again, her breath finally coming steady, strong. "I know it's early for me, but I'd better go to bed. Tomorrow is a big day."

She pictured her husband when he would receive this message. It was likely going to be a lot for him to handle. Maybe too much.

But all she could be was honest.

"Feel free to call me, and I'll do my best to answer."

The voicemail cut off before she could say anything else. Goosebumps covered her skin, but a peace settled there too.

Elise headed once again to her bedroom. Then, pulling back the covers, she got into bed and allowed the darkness to envelop her.

The next morning, she rose with the sun, made coffee, showered, and dressed in a pair of soft slacks and low-heeled wedges that Chloe had bought for her. Padding out to the living room, she grabbed her purse and phone, looked at the screen—and blinked.

Charles had tried calling her.

Several times, in fact.

Glancing at the time, she considered returning his calls, but she would be late to the Barefoot if she did. And this conversation might run lengthy.

Perhaps she'd text him back and arrange a time to call. Yes, that could work.

Elise headed for the front door, opened it—and nearly dropped her bag. Because there, on the stoop, keys in hand and lifted to the lock, stood Charles.

His face was haggard, and he clearly hadn't shaved in at least forty-eight hours. Shirt and pants rumpled, he looked as if he'd slept in his clothing. And his eyes—they were bloodshot. If she didn't know any better, she'd think he was drunk, but he hadn't touched alcohol in years. Said he'd seen the ill effects of it and wanted no part in drinking it.

He simply stood there, staring at her, a frown plastered across his face, his leather laptop bag slung over one shoulder.

"Charles? Are you all right?"

Her husband pushed a hand through his hair, which was slightly greasy and stood on end just behind his ears. "No. I'm not all right, Elise."

He sounded angry.

She sighed. She didn't have time for his temper right now, though she did owe him a conversation. "I'm sorry about that voicemail. I know it was likely … awkward to listen to. Can we talk about it when I get home tonight?"

"No, we can't." He pushed his way inside, flinging the door back so hard it hit the wall and rattled the framed photos hanging there.

Elise stepped back. She'd never seen him like this before. Charles was always the epitome of control and propriety. But his eyes at the moment, the way he stood his ground, made him appear wild. Fierce.

Passionate.

She swallowed hard. "What are you doing here, Charles?"

"I took a red-eye as soon as I got your message."

Mercy. "You didn't have to come home. We could have—"

But she stopped talking when he moved toward her, swooped his hand around her waist like some sort of Casanova, dipped her back, and kissed her like she hadn't been kissed in … oh goodness.

Quite a long time.

Finally, he straightened them upright and looked into her eyes. His gaze had softened now, and he stroked her cheek. "I still want you, Elise. How could I not want such a wonderful, loving woman?"

Her heart pounded triple time. Was it possible to have a

heart attack from joy? "I wasn't so wonderful when I refused to go with you to Boston."

"I understand why you didn't. And I'm sorry I left. I was angry, confused ..." He shook his head. "It doesn't matter. All you need to know is that I will spend every minute until I die proving to you how much I love you. Whatever it takes."

She settled her head against his chest. "This is a good start."

He put his hand into his pocket and pulled out a piece of paper. "Remember Robert Jeffries? He used to work here in Walker Beach." At her nod, he continued. "I stayed with him in Boston, not in a hotel. I asked him to keep me company every night. The days were taken up with work. I promise you, Elise, I didn't even see Tracy. You can call Robert. He will vouch for me."

She took the paper from him, chewing the inside of her cheek as she looked at Robert's number. Charles had understood her fears—and hadn't thought her ridiculous.

Yes, he wasn't perfect, but neither was she. And it would take both of them to fix the broken things.

"Happiness requires being truthful with ourselves and others about what we really want and who we really are." Could she lean into the things she wanted without fear, accept who she was—and love that person, regardless of how others might treat her?

"I don't think that's necessary." With a gentle smile, Elise ripped the slip of paper in two and looped her arms around Charles's neck. "And I love you too, Charles." She kissed him again, this time slow and soft. "Now, about that whole proving you love me stuff?"

"Yes?"

"When exactly did you plan to start that?"

He lifted an eyebrow. "I don't want to make you late."

"It's all right." Quinn and Jules had things handled. Besides, this was much more important at the moment. "Make me late."

And with a wicked grin that she had oh-so-missed, he did.

CHAPTER TWENTY-SIX

JENNA

*S*he'd never imagined quitting her dream job.

But the moment she'd handed Renee her notice, Jenna had also never felt so sure of anything. Because as much as she'd relished the idea of the city—of being "more" than she was—now she knew the truth of the matter.

She'd been chasing a fantasy all while living a real-life fairy tale.

No, there weren't pots of gold at the end of a rainbow, but there was a handsome prince—and maybe, just maybe, Jenna could win him back.

But first, she had a festival to attend.

She turned to Liam. "What do you want to do next? The line at Santa Claus is getting kind of long." She pointed toward Bud Travis, all dressed up in a puffy red suit. Walker Beach's new mayor sat with a child on his knee in a large sleigh that someone in town had constructed and placed on the sand just for today's Christmas on the Beach Festival, which was in full swing at Baker Community Park.

"I'm a little old for that, Mom."

Placing a hand over her heart, Jenna dramatically angled her

THE INN AT WALKER BEACH

chin toward the crystal blue sky. "Say it isn't so! I swear you were just in diapers yesterday."

Liam rolled his eyes and smiled. "Could we get some food?"

"Sure. The question is, what kind of food?" There were countless vendors here today. She'd already hugged Ms. Josephine, who had snuck her a piece of pie, and said hi to Heather Campbell and her daughter, Mia, who sat at the booth for Campbell Wines.

The event organizers had set up a stage near the rocks at the south end of the park, which divided it from Baker Beach and the downtown area. Even from her position near the food tents, Jenna could see and hear Nikki strumming her ukulele and crooning "Mele Kalikimaka."

Before all of this had begun, Jenna had stopped by the Barefoot this morning—she'd gotten in too late last night—to see the finished fruits of her labor. Quinn, the new manager, had informed her that the soft opening last weekend had gone really well, that she'd received several rave reviews regarding Jenna's design and décor, and that the inn was booked through New Year's.

Which meant they desperately needed to hire some full-time employees. Sounded like they had a stack of applicants—women who wanted to be part of the Refuge's program, now that it had officially been awarded charity status—with more applications rolling in every day.

"Can we get some pizza?" Liam's question dragged Jenna back to the present.

"Absolutely." She steered them past the booth where Samantha Griffin and Dottie Wildman were helping a group of kids with some Christmas wreath crafts toward the Froggies booth. After ordering a few slices, she and Liam walked nearly to the edge of the water and, after a few minutes of navigating the crowd, found a spot to sit and eat.

"How do you feel about moving back?" Jenna had agreed to

continue working at her internship through Christmas Eve, so she and Liam wouldn't officially return until then. Thankfully, Gabrielle and Tyler didn't mind them moving in until the sublease on Jenna's apartment was up in a few months.

"I'm happy." Liam attacked his pizza with a flourish, wiping some sauce off his mouth with the back of his hand. "But where are you going to work?"

"I've told you not to worry about that." She'd toyed with a few ideas, actually. Had even called up Jules to ask her if she had any openings at the gallery, but she hadn't heard back yet. Returning to work with Cameron didn't seem like a good idea. After all, she'd hurt him with her leaving. She knew that.

And as soon as she could, she was going to make it right—much as that was possible, anyway.

Polishing off his slice, Liam toed the sand. "Uncle Tyler said he'd be playing at the volleyball tournament at one. Can we go see?"

She checked the time on her phone. Oh wow. The day had flown by already. "Sure." They stood, threw out their trash, and headed toward the volleyball pits. But before they made it, someone touched Jenna's elbow.

When she turned, Jules and Elise both pulled her into quick hugs.

"So good to see you ladies." She turned back to Liam. "Look. Aunt G and Penny are over there in the stands. Why don't you snag us some seats and I'll be right over?"

"Okay." He lunged away from her as she tried to ruffle his hair, laughing as he went—and her heart soared to see him so happy again.

And not because she'd achieved anything great. Just because they were together.

And they were home.

Jenna faced Jules and Elise again. "I'm surprised to see you ladies here. I figured you'd be bogged down at the Barefoot."

Tossing her hair over her shoulder, Jules waved her hand in the air. "Oh no, Quinn is managing that thing like a well-oiled machine already."

"I don't doubt it." Jenna snuck a shy smile at Elise. Not having had a moment alone with the woman since she'd broken up with Cameron, she hadn't been sure how she'd be received now—but Elise's eyes were as welcoming and genuine as ever. In fact, with her bright cheeks and a healthy glow to her skin, she'd never looked more at peace. "I got a chance to stop in this morning. The place looks amazing. And Quinn told me you're full up!"

"It does look amazing." Jules pressed her lips together, as if trying not to laugh at how Jenna had basically complimented herself.

"That's not what I meant." Jenna could feel her cheeks growing warm. "I love how the community worked together toward something that is going to help a lot of people. Quinn said the soft launch went well?"

"Yes, wonderfully smooth," Elise said. "There were only a few snags, but that was to be expected. And so far, we've only heard rave reviews from the current guests."

"Speaking of guests"—Jules interjected—"I've had more than one ask for the information of the interior decorator who made the place feel both modern and timeless." She winked. "So my answer to your question about whether I have a job available for you is yes. Just not at the gallery."

"What do you mean?"

Jules placed a hand on her shoulder. "I want to be the first investor in your interior design and decorator business here in Walker Beach. The interest is there. You can work while you attend school, if that's still something you want to do."

She'd considered whether she wanted to keep going to school. "I think I would still like to get my degree. Not because I need to, but because I want the knowledge and connections it will bring." Jenna paused. "Are you sure about investing in me? I'd hate to let you down."

"I've never been surer." Jules touched the side of her nose. "I've had a feeling about you from the start, Jenna."

"Thank you so much." Stepping forward, she hugged Jules, breathed in her lavender perfume. "For everything."

"So you're staying?" Elise asked.

Jenna had been so caught up in Jules's kind words, but Elise's question reminded Jenna that Cameron's mom was still there. "Yes." She shoved her hands into the back pockets of her jeans. "How do you think he'll feel about that?"

Elise's lips pulled into a thoughtful smile. "That's something you'll have to ask him. All I know is I haven't seen him this mopey since the day he lost his favorite Ninja Turtle toy when he was six."

What exactly did *that* mean?

Elise must have rightly interpreted the confused look on Jenna's face, because she laughed. "Jenna, at the time, he *loved* that toy more than anything in the world."

Oh. Whew. So his mom thought he loved Jenna.

Jenna had thought so too. Then, she'd believed that because he hadn't come with her to San Fran, he didn't love her.

But for the last several weeks, she'd been mulling over Cameron's professed reason for not moving with her. *"You just said you didn't want to have to rely on anyone else. If I go with you, you'd always wonder if you could have done it alone. And then you'd only end up resenting me."*

And she hadn't wanted to admit it—but he'd been right.

So maybe she hadn't misinterpreted his parting kiss after all.

Maybe he really *did* love her.

Hope sailed, then crashed, burned. Because even if he loved her, he might not forgive her for leaving the way she had.

But whatever he felt, she needed to apologize. A second

chance was probably out of the question. But maybe someday they could be friends again.

Jenna inhaled a shaky breath. "I've been keeping an eye out for him all morning. Do you know where—"

"The last I heard, he was working today."

Really? Many of the other shops in Walker Beach had closed for the festival. So why was Cameron hiding out in the shop when the entire town was here? "Thank you."

Elise winked—winked! "You're welcome, dear."

After another round of hugs, Jenna stopped by Gabrielle and Liam to let them know she was running a quick errand. The volleyball game was in full swing, with Tyler and his cousin Ben facing off against Derek Campbell—Heather's brother—and Shannon's boyfriend, Marshall.

Her sister, whose baby was snuggled against her chest, narrowed her eyes at Jenna's proclamation. "What kind of errand?" When Jenna didn't answer, Gabrielle's eyes lit. "Oh. That kind." Then she smiled. "Good. Go get your man back."

"I don't think it's going to be that simple."

"When are you going to learn that your big sister is always right?" Gabrielle kissed the top of Penny's head, her eyes twinkling. Then she sobered. "Whatever happens, I'm here for you, okay? Have I mentioned I'm glad you're moving back?"

"Only about a million times." Jenna grinned as she walked away, maneuvering through the crowds until she reached Main Street, which was surprisingly empty for a Saturday afternoon. But with most of the actual stores closed and shop owners participating in booths at the festival, that made sense.

She paused at the door of Rise Beach Rentals, her heart jumping like a kid playing hopscotch. What would Cam say when he saw her?

Only one way to find out.

Jenna pushed her way inside. Nothing looked all that different, and the place still smelled like citrus, yet it at once felt familiar and foreign.

Or maybe it was simply Jenna who had changed.

At her entry, Cameron looked up from his spot behind the front counter—and stiffened. He didn't say a word as she approached.

Come on, Cam. Crack a joke. Yell at me. Something.

But he just remained frozen, staring at her with those eyes that made her want to dive in for a swim.

"Hey." The word emerged froggy from her throat.

Still he didn't respond, though his lips did part slightly.

Oh, she couldn't stand this. There had to be some way to break the ice, right?

Jenna rounded the counter and hopped up onto it so she sat right next to where Cameron stood. *Please don't walk away.* "So."

His eyebrow quirked at her, as if he was trying to figure her out. Maybe he was.

"I'm in need of a rental."

"What kind of rental?" Cam's posture loosened a tad, and he leaned an elbow against the counter. He was only a foot away.

Oh, how she'd missed him.

She assumed a casual position, pushing her bangs out of her eyes and pretending to consider his question. "A surfboard."

"A surfboard." Now the poor man just looked bewildered.

"Yes, a surfboard." She longed to run her fingers through the curls that he'd let grow out longer than usual. "You see, I had this amazing surfboard. But I lost it, because I was really stupid."

He straightened and took a step closer. His pineapple scent filled the space between them. "Why? What did you do?"

"Well." She swallowed at his nearness, at the way his hand bumped against her thigh. "I was afraid that it was holding me back from my true surfing potential and I tried surfing without it. And for a while, body surfing was exhilarating. I got a high from riding the waves all alone." She bit her lip. "But then I realized that I really do need it. That I didn't like the feeling of drifting with no anchor. That it's not weakness to surf with a board, because a board makes surfing so much more fun."

"That's a lot of stuff to realize."

"Tell me about it."

"So what happened to this board?" He inched closer, his expression deadpan.

"Well, when I got back to the beach, it was gone. And now I'm afraid I'll never see it again—all because I didn't realize what I had before it was too late."

Cameron turned his body so he now stood directly in front of her. "So let me get this straight. You had a board. You lost that board. And now you want to rent a new board?"

Shoot. Her metaphor had gone awry. "No. I want my old board back." A pause. "There is no other board for me out there."

"Why? What was so special about that board?" And while he'd used a teasing tone, the flicker in his eyes told her that he really wanted to know. That her leaving had undone all of her work to convince him that she'd chosen him—that, unlike Mindy, she wanted him.

Only him. No one else.

Oh, Cameron. "That board supported me better than I deserved. It kept me afloat when I desperately needed it, and it brought me so much joy. I ... I'm not sure I can surf without it. I'm not sure I can *live* without it."

He was quiet for several long seconds. Then he leaned in, a grin curving his lips. "That sounds like a pretty sexy board."

Jenna full-on belly laughed. Leave it to him ... "Sexy, huh? I didn't know a board could be sexy."

"Maybe not normally. But I'm just calling it like I see it."

"Fine." Slowly, praying he didn't pull away, she looped her arms around his neck. "It's a very, very sexy board."

"I can see why you like it."

Here went nothing. "I don't just like it." She blew out a quick breath. "You see, I actually love that surfboard."

After a few heart-rending moments of silence, he lifted his hand and traced her bottom lip with his thumb. "That surfboard has been adrift at sea without you, because it loves you too." Cameron placed a gentle kiss against her mouth. "And in case it wasn't clear"—he whispered, his lips a hairbreadth from her own—"I'm the surfboard."

She giggled. "I think that was pretty clear."

"Just wanted to be sure we were on the same page." He wrapped his arms around her waist and pulled her against him. "And just so you don't complain in the future that I never actually told you this except in some weird metaphor, I love you, Jenna Wakefield."

And then his lips were on hers again, his kiss like fire and ice, like plunging under the sea but without the drowning part. It was equal parts elation and trembling—the way he held her like she was precious but at the same time kissed her with a ferocity and passion that promised years of pure bliss ahead.

He set his forehead against hers. "So you know I'm totally moving to San Fran now, right? I can't stand to be apart from you a minute longer. And I don't want to hear about how you don't want some grand gesture, because that's just what a guy does when he loves a woman."

"Hey, now. Guys aren't the only ones who can perform grand gestures." She curled his hair around her fingers. "Besides, I quit the internship and am moving back here."

His forehead wrinkled. "Not for me, I hope?"

"No." She kissed away every crease in his brow. "For me."

Because everything she wanted was right here in Walker Beach—right here in her arms.

EPILOGUE

JULES

Somehow, they'd done it—taken a broken-down inn and transformed it.

Of course, it represented so much more than that.

From her spot on the Barefoot's private beach, Jules Baker craned her neck upward to peer at the place that would soon welcome women to their new home at the Refuge. A place where they could start over, could find hope again.

Just like Jules had all those years ago.

Even from here, a mile or so away, she could hear the calls of the festival crowd. She'd return in a little while for the fireworks show—but first, she wanted to check on Quinn, another woman who needed hope in her life, though she might not even realize it.

Jules walked to the back patio and opened the door. A few guests lingered in the lobby, chatting, drinking lemonade on the couches, playing board games at one of the small tables by the back door. Twin twelve-foot Christmas trees flanked the fireplace, their lights twinkling in the room that grew dimmer with the setting of the sun just beyond the beach.

Rounding the corner into the front foyer, Jules found Quinn

sitting behind the reception desk. A plate of cookies sat on the upper edge of the desk, and Quinn held a ginger snap absently in her fingers as she studied a stack of papers in front of her.

"How's it going? Do any applicants stand out to you?" Jules hoped to offer a few women spots in the program before the end of the year—if they found the right ones.

"I don't know." Quinn nibbled at the cookie in her hand, her nose scrunched as she kept her attention on the papers. "They all seem equally in need of what the Refuge has to offer. How are we supposed to narrow it down?"

"Mind if I take a look?"

"Be my guest." Quinn handed over the applications and stood, stretching.

Jules scanned a few applications before glancing up at her niece, who yawned. "How long have you been here? Have you even been out to the festival yet?"

"This is my job, Aunt Jules."

"So that would be a no."

Lifting a shoulder, Quinn avoided eye contact. "It's fine. Shannon is glued to Marshall's side this weekend since he's in town—and of course I don't blame her for that—and my parents are busy at the Froggies booth and volunteering elsewhere. Tyler and Gabrielle are doing their own thing too." Her lips pursed. "I don't exactly have a lot of other friends in town, so I don't mind being here today, tucked away from it all."

"Hmm." Jules continued to flip through the applications, the paper rigid beneath the tips of her fingers. "Don't you get along with the other women in the Sisterhood?"

"Um." Quinn paused. "They're all really nice, don't get me wrong. I just don't know that we really click, you know?"

"Aha!" Jules held up an application. "This is it. Our first member of the Refuge."

Snatching the paper from her aunt, Quinn read it over. "Holly Smith. Says here she's from Los Angeles, has been staying at a shelter with her young son for three months, and is looking for a fresh start." Quinn glanced up. "I don't get it. Why her? There's nothing that really stands out about her application. They all read like this."

"I just have a feeling about her." And no, she couldn't explain it. It was just some internal tingling that she'd learned to listen to over the years. So far, it hadn't led her astray.

After all, it had led her here, to the Barefoot.

"Aunt Jules, I don't think I'll ever understand you."

"Why is that?"

"You make decisions with your heart. Sometimes ones that make no sense—like inviting me into the Sisterhood in the first place, then giving me a job. After the things I've done, the way I've treated our family ..." Quinn shrugged. "I just don't understand you."

"Oh, niece of mine. You just wait." Jules threw her arm around Quinn's shoulder, nearly laughing at how stiff it was—like a soldier going into battle. Her niece had been like that even as a girl, ever since her accident, anyway. Determined to hold everyone at arm's length. To hurt instead of being hurt.

But Jules knew something that apparently Quinn didn't.

People could change.

She'd see soon enough.

Jules could just sense it.

I'm so grateful to you for reading *The Inn at Walker Beach*! I hope, like me, you enjoyed your time in this charming little town that's grown close to my heart. If so, join me, Quinn, Holly, and the rest of the Sisterhood in Book 2 of The Barefoot Sisterhood series, *A Refuge by the Sea*, coming in 2022.

CONNECT WITH LINDSAY

If you enjoyed *The Inn at Walker Beach* (or any of my books, for that matter!), would you do me a favor and leave a review on Goodreads, Bookbub, or your favorite retail site?

Also...I'd love to connect with you. Sign up for my newsletter at www.lindsayharrel.com/subscribe and I'll send you a FREE story as a thank you!

Want more of Walker Beach? Check out my Walker Beach Romance series, starting with Tyler and Gabrielle's story in *All At Once*.

BOOKS BY LINDSAY HARREL

The Barefoot Sisterhood Series

The Inn at Walker Beach

A Refuge by the Sea

Walker Beach Romance Series

All At Once

All of You, Always

All Because of You

All I've Waited For

All You Need Is Love

Port Willis Series

The Secrets of Paper and Ink

Like a Winter Snow

Like a Christmas Dream

Like a Silver Bell

Standalones

The Joy of Falling

The Heart Between Us

One More Song to Sing

A book is only as good as all the people who help put it together. And in the case of this one, I had so many wonderful helpers—so I hope that has translated for you, amazing reader!

First, I want to thank my sweet husband and kids, who may have felt a bit ignored while I was head down writing this book. I love and appreciate each one of you. I hope you know that I can only write about happily ever afters because you have been mine.

Also, thank you to my seriously awesome editors. Becky Philpott, this story would not have been what it is without your insights. You helped me take it deeper, and for that, I am so grateful. Barbara Curtis and Charity Chimni, thank you for your eagle eyes and attention to detail.

Thanks to Dr. Allan Sawyer for help making the hospital and medical scenes more realistic. All the women and babies you have served over the years (including me and mine!) have been so blessed to have you and your expertise in their corner. Any mistakes in the text are my own.

Lisa Davis, once again I have to thank you for your help with getting the mental health and counseling-related content right.

Thank you for lending your expertise! Any mistakes are my own.

Kristi Kappes and Sara Carrington, thank you so much for being my sensitivity readers. I so value your feedback and experience.

Randy and Nancy Harrel, this book would not have been written without you. Thank you for watching my boys every week so I had extra time to work! I am so lucky to call you my in-laws.

To my writing peeps—Gabrielle, Melissa, Alena, Liz, Jennifer, Sara, Sarah, Erin, Tari, Ruth, and Rhia—thank you for your support and love. Just being around you makes me a better writer!

To Rachelle Gardner, agent extraordinaire, thank you for your continued support and guidance on this writing journey.

My dear readers, thank you for all of the wonderful reviews and notes. I couldn't do this without you.

And to God, the one who gives my life purpose, thank you for allowing me to create beauty through story. It is such a privilege and I give you all the glory for each and every creation.

ABOUT THE AUTHOR

Lindsay Harrel is a lifelong book nerd who lives in Arizona with her young family and two golden retrievers in serious need of training. When she's not writing or chasing after her children, Lindsay enjoys making a fool of herself at Zumba, curling up with anything by Jane Austen, and savoring sour candy one piece at a time. Visit her at www.lindsayharrel.com.

facebook.com/lindsayharrel
instagram.com/lindsayharrelauthor

The Barefoot Sisterhood Series

Book 1: The Inn at Walker Beach

Published by Blue Aster Press

Cover: Hillary Manton Lodge Design

Editing: Becky Philpott

CPSIA information can be obtained
at www.ICGtesting.com
Printed in the USA
LVHW020034280921
698854LV00006B/452